From *Myra*

to *Laura*

From *Myra* to *Laura*

Shirley Proctor Twiss

To order additional copies of this book, contact:
Xlibris LLC
1-888-795-4274
www.Xlibris.com
Orders@Xlibris.com
620602

In Memory of
Elizabeth Medlock Proctor
A grandmother I never knew
but is a part of me

Louis S. Proctor
My Father
Who gave me the love of justice, baseball,
Uncle Remus and Margaret Mitchell

Inez McIntyre Proctor
My Mother
I wish you had been with me longer

Special Thanks To

Readers who enjoyed Myra's story and were not ready to give her up. Your encouragement inspired *From Myra to Laura*.

Carolyn Helms and Janet Musco, my good friends and playmates, who willingly became proofreaders for the second time.

My daughter, Erin Ryan, who was always available when Mama messed up the computer.

Melvie Stephens, my muse, for all your wonderful tales.

To Swainsboro, GA for giving me a childhood worthy of remembering.

To Ann, Annette, Yvonne, Frances—the girls of '53—just because we have been friends since first grade.

Author's Note

Again I caution you that as a born and bred daughter of the South, I have the liberty of writing dialogue in the dialect of the speaker. Readers of *Cotton in Augusta* and *Joy in the Morning*, I hope you are now familiar with verbs missing final g's, words not found in Websters, ain't not frowned upon, dinner at noon, movies were picture shows and y'all know what all else I'm talkin' 'bout.

Throughout the first two books, African Americans were referred to as colored which was the most acceptable word to use. In *From Myra to Laura* the most acceptable word had become black. Today we use more correct terms, but in Myra's time this was unknown. I am sure she would like this much better.

Writing *From Myra to Laura* has been a catharsis for me. The news events described in the book are factual. Readers will see these tumultuous times through Myra's perceptive.

Cover Photograph courtesy of Brian Brown/
Vanishing Coastal Georgia
www.vanishingcoastalgeorgia.com

Contents

Chapter I

1955

The porch swing moved slowly back and forth with creaks and squeaks to the rhythm of Myra's body motion. A sweater across her shoulders felt good in the cool air of early morning. The quarter moon hung in the sky like a sentry waiting for dawn while the whole world seemed to be sleeping. Soon the night sky would be filled with the brilliant colors of orange, pink, and sometimes red. She had seen the sunrise almost every day of her life and cherished this peaceful time before starting the work that lay ahead. When she was a child, this meant going to the field as soon as dawn broke to start a day of planting, chopping, or picking cotton. Later, it meant cooking meals, cleaning, washing, and all the other necessary chores of raising a houseful of children.

James would have been by her side sipping coffee as the swing motion set the pace of early morning. *He'd done oiled these chains. Nothing bothered him more than somethin' squeakin'. I best ask Stephen to oil 'em.* Her beloved husband was gone now, dead for nearly a year. Gone—but not to her. She could still feel the memory of the warmth of his body and smell the special odor of a fresh starched and ironed shirt, cigarettes, and Old Spice aftershave. When unpleasant memories tried to creep into her thoughts, she closed that door.

James went to Jesus—at least that's where she prayed that he went—and left Myra in a place she never expected to be. She thought James would always be by her side, even if sometimes he did aggravate her to death. Thinking back on that day when the sheriff came to their house in Campbell and told her James had been found in his car by the side of the road and was already dead seemed like yesterday. She hurt so bad that she thought it would kill her; even her bones ached, but she didn't die. There were still times when that old hurting deep inside of her came back just the same as when her papa, mama, angel baby, and her brother, Jesse, died. She was well acquainted with wearing the yoke of sadness that pulled your shoulders down so that you couldn't lift them.

Time helped ease the pain after losing the others, but this time it would be with her for the rest of her days. She couldn't say she didn't have times when she was happy, but even in the middle of a good time, the feeling would overcome her, and tears would fill her eyes. She'd never been one to do a lot of crying. Working and keeping busy used to be her deliverance. Now the tears wouldn't stop. Late evenings and nights were the worst. Dreams about being lost and trying to find James haunted her. When she awoke in the early morning, the feeling of anxiety made her afraid to face the new day. She wanted to pull the quilt over her head and stay hidden from the challenge of another day of being alone.

Every night, her pillow absorbed many tears. She still slept on her side of the bed and did not roll over onto the empty space where James's warm body had been. His soft snoring used to keep her awake, and she would poke him with her elbow. Now the silence kept her eyes wide open. The dark of night let her know that he was gone, but mornings gave her hope after she reminded herself that the Lord had not forsaken her. Sometimes she seemed to catch a glimpse of James sitting in the swing or coming up the steps onto the porch wearing his smirk of a smile. She dared not mention this to anyone, for they would think that she had lost her mind.

Right after James died, her son, Stephen, talked her into moving close to him in Fitzgerald. He owned a little house that was almost in his backyard. She knew it was for the best, but it was just another step away from her life with James. When she brought up memories of him, it was always in their last home in Campbell.

Stephen and Arliss, his wife, had done everything they could to take care of her and give her pleasure. He moved as much of her furniture into the little house as it would hold, hung a porch swing, and planted quick-growing trees for shade. Stephen kept a big garden all year long, and she could pick whatever she wanted. It was nice to have the vegetables for her table without doing any of the work. Still, she couldn't keep from pulling weeds that sprouted. It felt good to work in the dirt.

Gardening and canning fruits and vegetable to save for the winter had been a big part of her life. Now she had learned to keep many foods in the freezer the children had given her for Christmas a few years back. This was easier, and the foods did taste fresher, but she had saved her jars. There were still some things like tomatoes and berries that were better from a jar.

Moving to be near her oldest son seemed best to all the family, but the hurt came with her. She and James had started their married life in Glencoe where he had lived all his life. They had a comfortable home, and all their children were born in Glencoe. When the Depression started, James couldn't find any work, and times got hard. Then their house burned down, and they had to move to Armity, a settlement outside of Glencoe, and finally to a farm even farther out in the country. After a few years, they returned to Glencoe to live in the family home with James's sisters. When James's sister, Olieta, died, the home was left to his youngest sister, Grace. This suited Myra fine, for they were able to buy a home in Campbell, a nearby town. The years in Campbell had been some of their best times. James had quit drinking and stayed home with her.

I have to be honest and admit that he did that most of the time. James just had a need to be places where folks were drinking and cuttin' the fool.

It was hard to leave Campbell and her home. She especially missed her friend, Annie. They had been friends since they were girls together in Sullivan's Corner. When she moved to

Campbell from Glencoe, she was surprised to find that Annie had lived there for years.

Campbell was close enough to go to the cemetery in Glencoe. James had always taken her there at least once a week to tend to the graves of her angel baby that had only lived a few weeks, her mama, her papa, and her brother, Jesse, who was killed at Pearl Harbor. Now James was sleeping beside them. She tried not to think of their graves being untended.

`As the sun was rising in the sky, Myra always said her prayers. *Dear Lord, thank you for this new day. I know ya've always been beside me and helped me through the hard times. I was mad at ya when you took my James away, and I'm 'shamed of that. I ask forgiveness for the time I turned away from you. I hope you did forgive James, and he's there with ya. He did have some bad ways, but he was a good man—lovin' and kind and always tried to help folks that needed help. If he's with ya, I know you're enjoyin' his company. Everybody always did. He had a way of makin' folks laugh and feel better.*

Help my daughter, Idella, any way that you can now that LeGrand's not doin' well. I hope ya see fit for him to get better so he can help her raise their little girl. The rest of the young'uns seem to be doing fine, and I thank you for that. Wallace would shore like to have a baby, and I hope you'll see fit to send her one. She and Grady would give it a good home. Help me to keep myself from sayin' spiteful and hurtful words. I am gettin' better about that. Now, Lord, I'll start my day and do the best that I can. Amen, Myra.

She ended her prayer as the first rays of sun lightened the sky. There was joy in the morning.

"Miz MacTavish, Miz MacTavish, you're up and out mighty early. Mind if I sit with you for a bit? I got up feelin' kinda lonesome."

This was Mrs. Donovan. She lived in one of the apartments across the road that everyone called the Projects. The government had built the Projects to provide a home for old people who didn't have a place of their own. Myra thought this was a mighty fine thing for the government to do. She'd never been inside any of the apartments, but from the outside, they looked nice enough. She and Mrs. Donovan had met at the little store down the street and struck up a friendship. From what Myra could tell, she was a good woman but had a hard time making ends meet.

"Come on the porch and sit with me. I was just startin' to think about cookin' me a little breakfast. If you ain't et yet, come and eat with me. I can't seem to learn to cook for just one."

"I shouldn't do that. I eat with you too much, but I do enjoy it. Yore cookin' is the best I have ever et."

Myra expected her to accept when invited. She had seen the meager groceries her neighbor bought at the little store. Myra knew these meals helped her friend, but it was also good to have someone join her at the table.

"We'll eat and then watch *The Breakfast Club* and *Queen for a Day* on the television." Myra had watched television with Stephen and Arliss but never desired to own one. After she moved to Fitzgerald, Ruth and Woody gave her the set, and Grady put up a tall antenna so she could see the pictures well. She found it gave a lot of pleasure and helped pass the time.

Mrs. Donovan followed her into the kitchen as she started coffee perking, a pot of grits bubbling, biscuits in the oven, sausage frying, and eggs ready to pop in the grease as soon as the sausage was done. She still loved homemade biscuits, but now she could buy them in a can, turn on the electric stove, and bake in no time. She'd seen many changes that made life a lot easier, but her homemade biscuits *were* better. If James had seen her getting biscuits from a can, he would have said, "Ole gal, you're gettin' plum lazy." She'd never put such on the table for James, but now she took the easy way. Maybe she was getting plum lazy in her old age.

After finishing their breakfast, the two ladies took their second cups of coffee into the living room to watch television. After *Queen for a Day* came another good program and then another and another. Before she knew it, the morning was gone, and she hadn't done one thing—but again, what did she have to do?

It was like the programs she watched every afternoon that Stephen called soap operas. *These are the days of our lives.*

Chapter II

1955

In the late afternoons when Myra heard Stephen's truck pull into his yard, she knew her son would be with her soon. He always came to sit on the porch and talk with her for a bit during her loneliest time of the day. Before the death of James, she had always sat in the swing and waited for him to drive up and park his car under the pecan tree. Supper would be cooked and keeping warm on the stove while they sat together and shared their day. Now the close of each day brought the fresh acceptance that her beloved husband would never be coming home. Stephen had always been close to his mama and did his best to be with her in the late afternoon.

His first words were always "Mama, how's your day been?" On this day before Myra could answer, he said, "I hope you haven't started supper. I brought home a big mess of fish that one of the fellas caught from the pond. Arliss has already started frying them. She said for you to come on over 'cause there's more than aplenty for all of us."

"You don't need to feed me so much. Y'all just eat 'em and enjoy. I got plenty here to warm up."

"You mean you're turning down fried catfish, corn dodgers, and that slaw you like so much? I want us all to sit together for supper. Bonnie Ruth and Andy love for you to eat with us."

"Now you done said the magic words—Bonnie Ruth and Andy. Let me take off my apron and smooth down my hair, and I'll come on up."

She didn't want to be a nuisance and spend too much time with her children, but it did feel good to sit at the table with family. Stephen and Arliss were doing a good job raising their son and daughter. Both were well behaved and showed their grandma a lot of love.

After eating the tasty fish dinner, Myra tried to help Arliss clean the kitchen, but there was never much to do. Arliss cleaned as she cooked and kept a pan of hot, soapy water ready for the dishes. Myra was proud to see the clean and neat house her daughter-in-law kept and how good she and Stephen got along. She had never heard a cross word between them. She couldn't say that about her and James. Her children had heard plenty of cross words and worse between their mama and papa. Now those fusses seemed to be of no matter to her.

After supper, Andy walked her home. Before leaving, he turned on the lights and got her settled into her chair. He hung around and seemed to want to talk. After chatting a bit, he said what was on his mind.

"Grandma, Daddy told me that my grandpa always said one of his young'uns would be the governor of Georgia."

Myra laughed and said, "Yeah, he named yore Aunt Wallace for a governor and thought she might be the one." (James had selected the name before the governor turned out to be a baby girl.)

"Do you reckon he'd like it if I got to be the governor?"

"Andy, he'd be mighty proud of you. That's why he always called you Andrew instead of Andy. That sounded like a better name for a governor."

"I'm gonna try to make him proud."

"You do that, Andy. This state needs a smart man like you're gonna be."

Another day had passed. She didn't have anything to show for the day, but somehow she did have a good feeling about it. Her life changed the day she met James MacTavish, and it changed the day he died, but . . . maybe it hadn't changed. When she bowed her head at the table to hear her grandson say grace, she could feel her husband's presence. *James, I hope you were listening when Andy talked about being the governor someday.*

Chapter III

1955

Without James, the days seem to never end, but the weeks and months passed like lightning. It was December 2, nearly a year since she had seen him or felt his touch. She had found that one way to set her mind on the new day and forget the loneliness of night was to turn on the television. With her old blue chenille robe wrapped around her and still wearing her night socks, she moved across the cold brittle linoleum floor to turn on the little gas heater. When she turned a knob, the flame flicked up, and soon the room was toasty. She had lost her first home to fire and chose arising in a cold house rather than leaving the heaters on while she slept.

James always listened to the news on the radio, but she could never keep up with what was being reported. When the station came on in the morning, news was the first program. She waited

for it to end to enjoy the next program, *Good Morning Macon!* On
that program, someone usually talked about cooking, sewing,
or gardening, which held her interest.

This morning, the news was still on long after the time it
should have ended. Macon was the only channel her antenna
would bring in, so she had no other choice. A mass of people
and confusion filled the screen with lots of policemen and loud
talking. She noticed a colored woman in the middle of this
ruckus.

What is she doing there? Myra thought. The woman was neatly
dressed in a coat and hat with the strap of her pocketbook over
her arm. Myra couldn't stop looking at her and thought she
looked familiar. *You better hold on tight to yore pocketbook in that
crowd.*

Finally, she was able to make out some words from the
reporter. "Arrested—wouldn't give up her seat on bus to white
man—against the law." They said a name, "Rosa Parks."

Myra was shaken to the core. She had ridden the Greyhound
a few times and knew it was the custom for colored to sit in the
back and whites in the front. That was just the way it had always
been. Maybe this woman came from somewhere up north and
didn't know the custom, but arresting her seemed a harsh thing
to do. This had happened the day before, but it was news to
Myra. She kept the television on all day and became even more
confused. They showed the woman being led into the jail. Her
pocketbook was gone, and that troubled Myra. *It probably had all
her money in it.* She finally heard this was happening in Alabama.
Although she looked familiar, Rosa Parks wasn't anyone Myra

would have ever known. Still, she felt concern for her and hoped her pocketbook hadn't been taken by the wrong person.

Mrs. Donovan made her usual morning visit and walked in while the television was showing the events in Montgomery, Alabama. "Ya watchin' that messin' goin' on in Alabama, Miz Mac? I heard 'em talkin' 'bout it in the store. She oughta be horsewhipped fer tryin' to stir up trouble."

Myra did not say a word. Nor did she ask Mrs. Donovan to come in and sit with her. After looking at the screen and standing awkwardly for a few minutes, she said, "Well, I'll get on home. Looks like ya busy."

Myra still did not say a word but felt as offended by Mrs. Donovan's words as though she had been talking about a friend. When Mrs. Donovan walked out the door, Myra scurried to the bathroom to throw up but only heaved because there wasn't a thing in her stomach. It was nearly time for dinner, and she hadn't eaten a bite since waking. She knew no food would go down her throat.

That afternoon, Stephen brought the newspaper with him. "Mama, have you been watching the television?"

"I've watched all day. I can't understand what's happenin', but I'm shore worried about that colored woman."

"You don't need to worry, Mama. Somehow, it will all get worked out. They won't harm her."

"Well, they done stole her pocketbook."

"They'll give it back. The police won't take her money. I brought the paper so I can read you what has happened

"On December 1, 1955, Rosa Parks, a forty-two-year-old colored woman who worked as a seamstress, boarded a

Montgomery city bus to go home from work. She sat in the middle just behind ten seats reserved for whites. Soon all the seats in the bus were filled. A white man entered the bus, and the driver insisted that all four colored sitting behind the white section give up their seats. Rosa Parks refused. She was arrested for violating the laws of segregation."

Tears rolled down Myra's cheeks. "If she's been hunched over sewin' all day, I know what that's like. Her back ached, her eyes were burnin', her legs were crampin'. She was too tired to get up. I know that's the way the law's always been, but that don't make it right to treat anyone like that."

"I know how you feel, Mama. Somehow, this will all work out. You just can't take it to heart so."

"Let me see her picture in the paper. She shore looked familiar to me."

Stephen handed it over and said, "I want you to understand that this happened in Montgomery, Alabama, and not around here. There's no way you could know her."

Myra stared at the same woman she had seen all day on television. The woman looked stern but not frightened.

"Let me keep her picture, Stephen. I got some prayin' to do tonight."

Stephen started to leave but turned around and said, "Mama, listen to me now. Just be quiet about this stuff. It has nothing to do with us."

"It's been on television all day."

"I know, but some folks are gonna have strong feelings, and it's just best that we don't get mixed up in it."

Myra was more confused than ever. Stephen had always been fair and treated everyone, colored and white, fairly, but he also respected the law and did not like commotions. She looked at the picture of Rosa Parks for a bit, and then she knew the only place to turn.

Lord, I am shore mixed up on this. I don't know why I'm so worried about that colored woman when I don't even know her. Maybe it's 'cause her name is Rosa, like my colored friend in Glencoe. I know what the law says, but I can't see where she broke the law. She sat in the colored place like she should've. Can the law tell her to sit there, and then tell her she has to get up and give her seat to a white man? I'll do what Stephen said and keep my mouth shut, but somehow, that makes me feel even worse. I got that feelin' like I get when a hearse passes even if I don't know who's inside it. The colored pray to you and shore do like to sing yore praises. You must care fer them too. If ya could help me figure this out, I'd be most thankful. Now I'll leave it with you. Amen, Myra.

Myra continued to watch the news just like James had listened to the radio news all during the war. Seeing the folks on television right in her living room made her feel involved. She did what Stephen told her and said nothing when she heard others talking about the events. No matter what bad things she heard, she could not erase the image of Rosa Parks standing so dignified, holding onto her pocketbook. The news continued to run the pictures and tell what was happening with the colored in Montgomery, Alabama. She wasn't taking sides, and she was keeping her mouth out of it.

In a few days, other events were the news of the day. Myra was relieved to learn that Rosa Parks was released from jail after paying a fifty-dollar fine. When the news mentioned that she was fired from her job, Myra wondered how she could make her living. Then Montgomery was back on the top news. The colored had started a boycott of the buses. Myra had to ask Bonnie Ruth the meaning of that word, and she told her grandmother it meant the colored people would not ride on the buses until this was settled.

A young, colored preacher started appearing on the news every evening. His name was Martin Luther King Jr. Some of the things he said made sense to Myra. She heard lots of bad talk about him and the boycott wherever she went, but she continued to follow what Stephen had advised her and didn't join in the talk.

Chapter IV

1956

Prayers were all that Myra could do for her eldest daughter. Idella had not taken her mother's advice in many years, and Myra had accepted that her daughter would follow her own path. This had been hard for both of her parents who only wanted what was best for their daughter. Of course, Idella thought she knew what was best for her. *Maybe she was right.* Her girl had always had a haughty way that made Myra think of her sister-in-law, Olieta, who thought that being a MacTavish gave her the right to look down on folks that weren't as high standing. This scorn included Myra, and until Olieta's death, she tried to make life difficult for the wife of her precious brother. Myra learned to ignore her sister-in-law's cutting remarks after realizing that being a MacTavish was the only thing the old lady had, since she had never known the love of a husband or had children.

James adored Idella and encouraged her to feel that she was special. Myra was proud of her oldest daughter too, but they seldom agreed on anything. When the hard times of the Depression came, Idella couldn't adapt to the changes like the other children. She got away from their meager new lifestyle as soon as she found a way. That way was to marry LeGrand Porter. He was a good man and could give Idella the life she wanted. He was just so much older and different from the young fellows her age. James could not accept his daughter marrying a man older than her papa.

The Porters had a high standing in their community and owned a big family home in Swainsboro. Even during the Depression, LeGrand was able to remain prosperous by putting on sales in stores around the area. (Merchants at that time would hire someone to direct a weeklong sale in their store. The sale promoter received a percent of the profits which was very lucrative, especially during the Depression.)

Idella and LeGrand had a little girl Laura Jean, a fine home, and a good living. This was the life her daughter had desired. After the Depression ended and times were better, LeGrand's income diminished. Then he started having trouble with his heart and couldn't work steadily.

Fortunately, Idella had taken a business course and could use those skills to find work. This enabled them to keep the new house they had built (with a twenty-year mortgage) and keep up with their living expenses. Idella was much too vane to reveal her problems to anyone. Myra could tell her girl was worried by the lines appearing in her pretty smooth skin and the short temper she easily lost.

The family, especially James, were concerned about her. Before he died, James would often say, "I knew it would come to this. Look how well the young fellas that Idella turned down are faring now."

Idella had not seemed a part of the family since she married. LeGrand was older than James, and his heart trouble kept him from being active or taking much interest in their young daughter, Laura Jean. That seemed to affect the child, and she was always quiet and kept to herself. She seemed afraid that she would upset her mama or her papa. That wasn't a natural life for a young child. Myra and James had quarreled loud enough to rattle the rafters, but their children had paid it no mind and ran, hollered, laughed, and played like young ones should.

Myra had been married long enough to recognize trouble between a husband and wife. Because of his age and bad health, she knew he was unable to be much of a husband in many ways. It was never talked about, but the family knew that Idella's life was a disappointment to her.

The family tried to find ways to assist their sister without making her feel that they thought she was in need. Idella was very sensitive about receiving help, and this made it difficult. Myra's sewing provided Laura Jean with plenty of nice clothes, and for as long as James lived, he kept the little girl in spending money. Carlton made sure Idella's home was in good repair and her car running well. Since he and Laura James grew most of their food on the farm, they shared fresh vegetables, eggs, and often chicken, beef, and pork with her.

This did ease Myra's concerns for her daughter, for she believed if you had a home and enough to eat, you could get by without other things. She was not prepared for what came next.

Arliss came to her mother-in-law's house in the middle of the afternoon which was not the time she usually visited.

"Miz Mac, Carlton just called with some terrible news. I hate to be the one to have to tell you. I called Stephen, and he said to let you know and tell you to get your things ready to go to Swainsboro. He's coming to get us as soon as he can get here from the farm."

"Why are we goin' to Swainsboro this late in the evenin'? I don't know if I got anything I can pack. How long are we gonna stay?"

"Forgive me, Miz Mac. I'm so upset that I didn't even tell you the reason. LeGrand had another bad heart attack this morning and died about twelve o'clock."

"Oh my Lord, I got to get to Idella. She's left with that little girl to raise and that house to pay for all by herself. We need to get there to help make the arrangements. I hope I got something fittin' for a funeral." As Myra talked, she pulled out her suitcase and started picking out clothes to pack.

"I have to get the young'uns from school, and Stephen should be here by the time I get back" Arliss said as she headed to her car.

Everyone was ready and waiting when Stephen arrived. It was a sad trip and quiet until Myra thought to ask Stephen a few questions.

"Has the word got to the rest of the family?"

"Yes, Mama, the first one I called was BJ, and he took over from there and called Ruth and Wallace. He called back and said Wallace and Grady were on their way already, and Ruth will come tomorrow. Woody had to make arrangements to be away from the restaurant."

"Where we all gonna stay? Idella don't have room for all of us, and there might be some of LeGrand's folks stayin' there. I wonder if she let his grown young'uns know. They hadn't ever had anything to do with their papa after he and Idella married, but they need to be told. They might not care about comin', but at least they should get the news."

"Well, telling his son and older daughter is up to Idella. You or one of the girls need to stay with her. Some can stay with Laura James. BJ said not to worry about that. He will get as many motel rooms as we need."

"We can't let him pay for all those rooms"

"Mama, he wouldn't have offered if he couldn't afford it. You forget he's not a struggling young lawyer anymore. He's a partner in one of the biggest and best law firms in the state."

Myra didn't say any more after that. She put her mind on thinking about what she could say to comfort her daughter. She knew how it had been with her when folks attempted to express their sympathy. Some of the things they said hurt more than helped. Of course they meant well. She did believe the ones who helped most just sat quietly with her. She knew she wasn't the best one to talk to Idella. Ruth would be better.

Cars were parked up and down the street when they reached Idella's house. Laura Jean met them at the door and led them to a back bedroom where her mother was sitting on the bed.

Wallace was beside her. She and Grady had just arrived also. Everyone hugged Idella and tried to find words of comfort. She was quietly sobbing but hugged every one of them close. When it was Myra's turn, she put her head on her mama's shoulder and sobbed even harder.

"Mama, what will I do without him? I don't know how we can live. I can't go on without him."

"Honey, I know your heart is breaking in a million pieces. I wish I could tell you somethin' to make it hurt less, but there ain't nothin' that will. Just be thankful that you had him to love and give you a little girl. You know your family will always be beside you to help any way we can."

"I need you to go to the funeral home with me tomorrow. I don't know a thing about handling funeral arrangements— never thought I would need to know."

This surprised and relieved Myra. At least there was some way she could be of help.

Stephen spoke up for the first time. "Make the plans and don't you worry about the bills. We will take care of that."

"Thank y'all. I am thankful to have my family. Stephen, I hadn't even thought about expenses, but I guess I have to start now."

Sleeping arrangements were worked out and divided between Laura James's house and the motel. Ruth and Myra spent the night with Idella. The doctor had given her a sleeping pill, so she slept through the night. Myra and Ruth lay awake for several hours, as they discussed all the hardships that were ahead for Idella.

The next morning when Myra, Stephen, BJ, and LeGrand's sister went to the funeral home with Idella, they received a welcome surprise. As they looked through the caskets and other requirements, Idella started asking about costs.

"Don't you even think about that, Mrs. Porter. A long time back, LeGrand came in and arranged for his funeral and paid for it in full," the funeral director said.

One weight had been lifted from Idella's shoulders. Stephen was willing to help, but her pride would have been crushed if her family knew LeGrand didn't leave enough money to pay for his own funeral.

When they returned to the house, Ruth, Woody, and their seven-year-old son, Jess, had arrived. Immediately, Ruth became the one who could comfort her sister. Myra hadn't seen Jess in several months and was glad to see him even if it was such a sad occasion. She had a special love for him because Ruth had named him for her uncle Jesse who was killed in the war. He was the spitting image of Woody, and both were so proud to finally have a son.

During the day, Myra had not seen Laura Jean; and with so much happening, she had not even asked about her. She learned that her granddaughter had gone to the farm with Carlton and Laura James the evening before. Carlton had to feed the animals, and Laura James thought it would be good for her niece to spend the night in the peace of the farm. Wallace and Grady spent the night there also, and Laura Jean returned with them the next morning. Now she was at home but avoiding the folks who came to call. LeGrand's body would be brought to the house in the early afternoon and remain there until the funeral. Myra knew the hardest time for Idella would be seeing the casket closed and LeGrand leaving the house for the last time.

The next morning shortly before leaving for the funeral, Myra was curious when she saw a man in an army uniform and a nice-looking woman arrive at the house. A neighbor went into Idella's room and told her that LeGrand's older children were there. At first, Idella refused to talk with them, but Myra and Stephen insisted that she should. She finally joined them as they looked at their papa in his casket. *It was too late to be visiting their papa. Were they up to something, or did they just want to make it look like they cared?* That was Myra's thoughts but hoped she was wrong and they were asking forgiveness for the way they had turned against their father.

The church was overflowing with mourners when the family arrived. Stephen escorted Idella down the aisle behind the casket. The funeral director lined them up with LeGrand's older son and daughter walking behind Idella. Next came his sister and her husband and finally all the MacTavish family. Laura Jean was left out except for being with her mother's family. Ruth put her arm around her niece and broke into the line ahead of the older children. That was the proper place for LeGrand's youngest child.

After the long service, where several men spoke about how valued LeGrand had been in Swainsboro, the long procession followed the hearse headed to the cemetery. Instead of heading straight to the cemetery, the procession circled the courthouse square. This was a sight to behold. The streets were lined with townsfolk. Everyone came out of the stores, and men took off their hats, and everyone bowed their head and placed their hand over their heart as the hearse slowly drove around the square. Myra had never seen this before but was told it was a Swainsboro tradition to honor a respected member of the community. Myra felt regret that she had only known LeGrand as Idella's husband and never got to know him as his townsfolk knew him. She was proud of the way her daughter held up through the service and showed respect for her husband. LeGrand was laid to rest in the city cemetery with his mother, father, and beside his first wife. No one tarried at the grave site on this cold, windy February day. After taking a flower from the casket spray for both her and Laura Jean, Idella took Stephen's arm and returned to the car.

Everyone except Ruth headed home after the service. Ruth would stay a week and then ride back to Jacksonville on the Greyhound Bus. All agreed that Ruth was the best one to help Idella get through the things she had to face immediately.

The family had gathered with Idella to say good-bye when there was knocking at the front door. Laura James went to the door and was surprised to see LeGrand's son and older daughter. They asked to talk with Idella. Laura James asked them to wait until she told her sister. Idella refused to see them, but again, Myra and Stephen convinced her that it was the right thing to do. Possibly they had come to apologize for all the heartache they had caused their father and maybe say a few words to their little sister for the first time.

BJ stiffened and told Ruth to go into the room with them. They had not come to comfort but rather to ask about the will and suggest a lawyer to help them.

Ruth immediately said, "She already has a lawyer." Then she opened the door and called BJ into the room. The talk went on for a while before the two older children walked out without saying a word to anyone. Laura Jean watched, but they did not acknowledge their little sister. Myra couldn't understand how anyone could ignore their flesh and blood. No matter what anger they held against their papa, the little girl was not a part of it.

They were anxious to hear from BJ about the talk in the bedroom. He had stood up for his sister when they tried to convince her of their legal rights. There was no will, but the house had always been in Idella's name. The only inheritance left to divide were unpaid bills and a fifteen-year-old Packard. He made them all laugh when he described how their mouths had dropped open.

On the drive home, Myra shared with Stephen her concern that Idella would not have enough money to live on and keep up the payments on the house.

"Mama, you don't need to worry about that. BJ and I went to the bank before the funeral and paid off the loan. It was only sixteen hundred dollars. They'd been paying on it for a long time."

"That is a relief and a mighty fine thing for you to do. I still have money that James left me, and I can pitch in my share."

"No need—no need. We can both handle that amount and want to do it for our sister."

"Did you tell her?"

"No, we left it for her to find out when she receives the paid mortgage papers."

"You need to tell her so she can give you credit and thank you. She might give LeGrand the credit."

"That's what we want, Mama. This way, she can keep her pride and feel like he had provided them with a home."

"James MacTavish shore raised some fine boys."

"Don't give him the credit, Mama. The goodness we learned in our life came from you," Stephen declared. "It was always you, Mama."

Myra started to defend James but decided that her son spoke the truth.

Now Idella was a widow just like her mama. Myra wished she could share some of the upsetting times she had experienced and help her daughter to get through the hard days. Ruth could help, but there are some things that only another widow can share. Myra was willing, but she was not the one. Stephen made a telephone call to his sister every week. Myra always went on the line and talked, but their conversations were never meaningful. Myra always ended the talk with "If you need me, just call, and I'll be there." Idella never needed her mother.

Chapter V

1957

At eleven o'clock each day except Sunday, Myra took time out from whatever she was doing to sit by the front window and watch for the postman. It fascinated her that he walked up to her door and put mail in the box hanging by her door. He was always there about the same time. What surprised her most was that she received mail almost every day. This was a new experience for her because James had always kept a box at the post office and picked up the mail on his way home. Of course, seldom was there any mail for her. *Sometimes she wondered if he received mail that he did not want her to see or question.*

She did not welcome envelopes with little windows because these were bills. There was a light bill, water bill, and in the winter time, a bill for gas for the little heaters that kept her house as warm as toast. James must have received bills and paid them without mentioning it to her. Now she saved the bills for Stephen to write out the checks, and she just signed her name, *Myra S. MacTavish.* She had practiced until she could write her name legible enough for others to read.

Two checks also arrived every month. One came from money James had paid into an account set up for his retirement. After his death, BJ arranged for her to receive money from it every month. The second was interest on money made from sale of the house and other properties that Stephen had put into a savings account. It was hard for her to believe that banks sent her money just for keeping her savings. One of the checks was adequate for her to live well, so she continued to save the interest on money from the property. She didn't understand how all this worked, but Stephen said the money would come for the rest of her life.

James had always been close-mouthed about his finances, and she never suspected he was buying property or putting money into a retirement fund. When she had nagged at him about throwing his money away, he was actually saving it for their old age. It didn't seem right to spend money unless it was necessary, so Myra was as thrifty as she had always been. The children fussed at her for not spending more on herself, but there didn't seem to be any need in buying new things for the house, clothes, or anything except necessary groceries.

Today, the postman left a picture postcard from Ruth, an envelope of pictures of BJ's new house, and a letter that she would have to wait for someone to read to her. *Who would be writing a letter to me?*

Later, she saw Bonnie Ruth walking home from school and called to her, "Come here, honey, I've got a letter that I need you to read to me."

Bonnie Ruth enjoyed being with her grandma and was always ready to help. She ran over and sat by Myra in the swing.

"First, I want ya to tell me about yore day at school. Did ya learn a lot?" Myra put learning ahead of anything.

"It was good. We had a geography test, and I think I made a hundred. It was mainly about maps, and I'm good at that."

"Learn all ya can. I know you'll make somethin' out of yoreself. Girls get to do a lot more now than they did when I was yore age. Of course, I had to work in the fields and didn't get to go to school much. That's why I'm so backwards."

"Grandma, you're not backwards. You're one of the smartest people I know, and nobody can make pretty dresses like you. My friends always think I order my clothes from *Seventeen Magazine*. You might not have gone to school much, but you know almost everything."

Myra had to laugh at that. She had always felt ashamed of her lack of education, but she had made out all right—at least according to Bonnie Ruth. She handed over the letter for her granddaughter to read.

"I can't think of who this letter might be from. I shore hope it ain't bad news."

"It's from Dolly Stuart, 1790 Walton Street Apartment 14-F, New York City, New York. Do you know who that is, Grandma?"

"It's from my baby sister, Dolly. I ain't heard from her in so long. Read it to me."

Dear Myra,

When I talked to you after James's funeral, I told you I would keep in touch, but I haven't been good about it. I am just so busy at work, and when I come home, I have to cook dinner and help Anthony with his school work.

I have good news. Anthony and I want to come to see you. Arno insists that I take some time off. I decided that I do need a rest. Most of all, I want to see my sister. You haven't seen Anthony since he was a baby, and I want him to know his Aunt Myra.

It will be a good experience for him since he has never been anywhere except New York City. We will drive down in one of Arno's rental cars. Let me know if this suits you and tell me a convenient time that we can come. Don't you go to any trouble for us. I just want to be with you, eat some Southern food, and show off my boy.

I love you, Dolly

Myra took the letter from Bonnie Ruth's hand and cradled it like a baby. Then she even kissed it. "My baby sister, Dolly—I never thought I'd see her again. When she and my brother, Arno, called me after yore grandpa died, I didn't even know their voices. Dolly said she was comin' to see me, but I never expected that to happen.

"Bonnie Ruth, take a piece of paper out of yore notebook and write down what I tell you. You make it sound right and turn it into a letter."

"Okay, let's go, Grandma. You tell me, and I'll write. Mama can check over the spelling and address the envelope."

"Start it out with dear Dolly. Now write this down. I'm so happy that you and Anthony are comin'. I hate for you to take that long trip by yoreself, but I want to see ya so bad that I won't think about that. You come whenever ya can. I'm always at home ready for company. Seein' you is the best medicine to make me feel better. Tell Arno that I wish he could come too. I'll shore cook you some old-time Southern food. Come as soon as you can. Love from yore sister, Myra. After you finish, put a stamp on it and tell yore papa to take it to the post office tonight. The sooner it gets to her, the sooner she'll be here."

A week later, a letter came back to say that they would leave on Thursday before Holy Week and stay until the Monday after Easter. Anthony would be out of school during that time. The trip would take two days, and they planned to stop halfway to spend the night.

For once, Myra did not think about the cost to her sister or even about her driving by herself for that long distance. All she cared was that she would see her baby sister and her nephew for the first time since Jesse's burying, and that was at least fifteen or sixteen years ago. Now they would be with her in two weeks. She was happy that it would be such a pretty time of year and that they would be with her for Easter.

Stephen was excited that Dolly and Anthony were coming and spread the news to the family. Everyone was eager to see their aunt. Stephen started sprucing up Myra's house. The outside had siding that didn't need painting, but he sent a man to wash it clean and touch up the inside. Myra bought new sheets and a spread for the guest bedroom and wondered where she could put Anthony to sleep. She was sure he had never slept on a pallet. Stephen solved that when he brought in a cot from his cabin by the pond. Now all she had to think about was cooking.

A few days before their arrival, Myra thought of another problem. "Stephen, how will she know how to get to Fitzgerald? She ain't never been here."

"I'm way ahead of you on that, Mama. She'll have maps that will get her from New York to Fitzgerald, and I drew a map to my house and sent it right after we heard she was comin'. She's been drivin' in New York City, so I'm sure she can make it with no trouble."

"What about a flat tire or car trouble along the way?"

"She's worked for Uncle Arno in that garage all these years, so I'm sure she can change a tire. Believe me, she'll know how to handle any car trouble."

"You're always ahead of me. I'm glad to know all that."

Even though she was busy, the days couldn't pass fast enough for Myra. At last, Stephen received a call from Dolly that they were spending the night in Florence, South Carolina, and would be in Fitzgerald in time for supper on Friday night.

"If you'd let me put in a phone for you like I wanted, she could have called you direct. Now I'm gonna get a phone put in tomorrow, no matter what you say. You need to be able to call folks yourself. Now don't tell me that's just another bill. I'm putting it in my name."

What to cook, what to cook? Dolly had been up north for so long, and Myra knew her sister was used to eating different foods—but she did say she wanted some Southern cooking. Everything had to be ready and warming in the oven when they arrived because she knew they would be hungry. She thought back to the things her sister might remember and miss from her childhood. Of course, that meant chicken and dumplings and fried chicken. Fresh snap beans, new potatoes, squash, and green onions were already bearing in Stephen's garden. That would be a good meal for anyone—Yankees or Southern. She would make tea cakes and a big pound cake to have plenty of snacks for the boy. After the first meal, she would take it one day at a time and find out what they liked to eat, especially Anthony, since he might find he didn't like Southern food.

The next morning, Arliss took her to the beauty shop to have her hair done. After the time she got so mad at James and declared that she was a person and not just his wife, she started changing herself and wearing her hair short, getting perms, and having a shampoo and set every week. She found this a pleasure and liked feeling fixed up.

At the grocery store, Myra stocked up on everything she might need. She took Arliss's suggestion to buy cereal, chocolate milk, and ice cream. Anthony was about the same age as Bonnie Ruth, so they should like the same things. She wanted to give the boy food he would enjoy but would need suggestions.

Everything was set. Supper was on the stove waiting to be served. House was clean and shinning. Myra was looking her best when a fine black car stopped in front of the house. Myra ran to meet her baby sister as she stepped out of the car. They hugged and hugged and both shed tears of joy.

"Let me look at you. I was scared I would never see you again, and here you are just as pretty as you've ever been. I'm old and haggard and know I must look a sight to you."

"Myra, you will always be the prettiest sight I could ever see. Anthony, come and hug your aunt."

The boy was nice-looking with black curly hair, dark eyes, and olive skin. He was tall and lanky, so he must take all this from his papa. Since his aunt was a stranger to him, Myra expected him to be shy.

She gathered him into her arms and said, "My, you're a fine-lookin' boy. We gonna have a fun time while you're here. The first thing is to feed ya, and I got a good meal awaiting. Tomorrow, yore cousin, Stephen, and his young'uns will come over and talk about some of the things y'all can do to have a good time. Have you ever been fishin'?"

Anthony only gave a shy smile and tried to take in this new place and new aunt.

Dolly had changed a lot. She looked older, but she was still as pretty as her name. Her hair was shoulder-length and styled like Myra had seen in magazines. She was wearing a simple skirt and blouse that looked expensive. Her speech was more northern sounding and very proper.

"Oh, Myra, I am so thankful to be here. I hated that I couldn't come when James died, but you know how much my heart was with you. I loved him like a brother. I will always remember how much he helped me. The smells coming from your kitchen tell me I'm home at last."

"Then let's eat. I hope I have something Anthony will like."

"He loves fried chicken and biscuits. I tried to make dumplings but never could make them as good as you."

Myra was glad to see the boy had a good appetite. He answered questions but didn't make conversation. Myra would win him over. Dolly had so much to tell about her life in New York, Arno, Ava, and their business, and she seemed content with her life.

After finishing his supper and two pieces of pound cake, Anthony went to watch television. She only received one channel and knew he was used to more. Luckily, the Macon channel was showing a program that he liked.

The best place to talk was sitting around the table after the meal, and that is what they did for several hours.

"Myra, tell me how you are really getting along. I know you'll always miss James, and it was hard to give up your home."

"Folks always ask me that, and I can't honestly say. Sometimes I look at myself and think how blessed I am to have this little house close to Stephen and the other young'uns coming around often. James left me plenty to live on, and the days seem to go by . . . but sometimes I get so lonesome for him that I don't want to go on livin'. I shouldn't worry you with that, but I don't let on to the young'uns about the bad times."

"You can always talk with me about anything. I'm glad you have a telephone now. Sometimes I ache to talk with you. Out of our big family, no one is left but you, me, and Arno. We need each other."

"I feel better knowing that my baby sister is here to listen. I will use that telephone when I need someone to talk with, but I don't want to make a nuisance of myself."

Dolly put her hand under Myra's chin and held it up, so they were looking eye to eye.

"Dear sweet sister, you will never be a bother to me. I owe you so much for all that you have done for me during my entire life. Except for Anthony, I love you more than anyone in the world."

Myra had one thing that she had to ask, and now was the time. "I see you are still using the name Stuart. Does that mean Anthony's papa's not around?"

With a weak smile, Dolly waited a minute and then started to talk in a low voice. "That's a long story and not a good one. No, we have never married as he promised. He is still with his wife and family. There has always been some reason that he can't leave her. The main one is that he is Catholic and can't be forgiven and take communion if he is divorced. That means so much to him. He is good to us and loves Anthony but doesn't see him as much as when he was small."

"Why is that?" Myra didn't want to pry, but she did want to understand.

"He's busy with his business and his family. Also, he moved out on Long Island, so it's a long trip for him to come into the city."

"You said with his family—does that mean he still lives with his wife?"

"He never left her because of the children. They have six now."

"You said *now* like they have had more young'uns together since Anthony was born."

"Well, you know Catholics have large families. They've had two more since Anthony was born."

"I don't know nothing about such as that. Well . . . the way I look at it is . . . he should do right by Anthony even if he stays with his wife and children."

"I know you don't understand, but I just have to accept things the way they are. He is good to us."

Myra shook her head at that. "I hope being good means he supports his son and pays for the things a young'un needs."

"He does now because the court forced him to pay child support. When you sent me the two thousand dollars from Jesse's insurance, you saved my life. Alberto was trying to break up with me and coming to visit less and less. He had almost stopped giving me any money. Arno's business hadn't gotten as successful as it is now, so he couldn't pay me much. I used that money to pay a lawyer to take Mr. Alberto Mundo to court. We had to prove that he was the boy's father, but when you look at him, there's no question about that. It turned out Mr. Mundo was much better off than he had told me. The judge didn't have any sympathy for him having a wife and other children to support. He set an adequate monthly child support, and he has to pay for all his son's medical, dental, and education expenses. Believe you me, his son goes to an excellent private school and will go to an expensive college.

"So thanks to you and dear Jesse with the salary I'm making now, and the security of knowing I will receive child support, we are doing just fine. I also didn't mention that Arno and Ava helped me so much. We stayed with them until I could get on my feet."

"That is a long story, honey. You said it wasn't good, but it is a good story. You have that beautiful son who will be a blessing to you forever.

"You shore do have a fine-looking car, and it looks brand-new and like it cost a lot." Myra had never heard of a rental can and had assumed her sister owned the car.

"Oh, Myra, Myra, I don't own a car. I couldn't afford any kind of car, and besides, it's not practical to own a car in the city. We can ride the subway or bus anywhere we need to go. The car belongs to the business. Arno has twelve that he rents out. He insisted that I drive down."

Myra had never heard of such and just shook her head. Her little brother was as smart as ever to figure how to make money renting cars.

Chapter VI

1957

The next morning after devouring two servings of pancakes and sausage, Anthony went outside to roam around Stephen's big backyard. Being alone in so much open space was amazing to the boy. The sisters remained at the table and resumed their talk about the past and their loved ones. Dolly didn't remember anything about her early years and begged Myra for tales of their parents. She wanted to know everything and questioned when Myra left out some of the unpleasant facts. She seemed to understand their mother and her mental problems much better than Myra ever could. Dolly called it depression and said that happened to lots of folks, and some could cope with it better than others. This helped Myra to feel less resentment about her mother's neglect of the family when they needed her most.

"I have an idea, Myra. If it suits you, we'll take a little trip the first of the week."

"You mean just for a day? Where will we go?"

"We'll go back to our old homes and visit everyone that you want. Arno asked me to stop by Mama and Papa's graves and see if there is anything that needs improving or repairing. He gave me money to do whatever you think is needed."

"I'm glad to hear that he still thinks of them. There is somethin' that I've wanted to get done. Before I moved here, I always went to the graves of our family about once a week. Me and James pulled the weeds sproutin' up around the plot. Now that I can't go often, I know the weeds are takin' over. I've seen some grave plots that have a coverin' of little white rock. That looks nice and keeps down the weeds. I don't know how much it would cost, but I could chip in too."

"We'll certainly see about that. Arno will pay whatever it costs. I think this makes him feel better about being so far away and unable to be of help."

"He's helped more than he knows. I'll never forget him sending me fifty dollars after the house burned. That shore was a big help, and then he gave you a chance to have a better life.

"If there's time, I'd like to stop to see Annie. I don't know if Rosa is still livin', but I'd love to see her." Myra's voice was bubbling with excitement.

"How about we leave Monday and not come back until Wednesday. We could spend one night with Idella and one night with Laura James. I would love to see their homes, Idella's daughter and get to know Laura James's husband, Carlton."

"Am I dreamin'? What a good time we'll have. I'll pack a big lunch to eat along the way. Dolly, use my telephone and make a call to both of them. Tell 'em not to go to any trouble about fixin' supper. I'll help when we get there."

On Saturday afternoon Stephen took everyone to his farm for the weekend. There was a big pond and a cabin for all to sleep. Anthony entered a new world. He stood holding his fishing pole and gazing at the pond with total confusion. Weeping willows surrounded the water with low limbs dipping into the surface. Ducks were swimming around, and the water rippled from the gentle breeze. The only sounds were from the birds—quite a sight for a boy from the streets of New York. He had a fishing pole but did not know what to do next.

Stephen's son, Andy, came to the rescue and showed him how to bait the hook, which took a few tries. He was leery about sticking the hook through the worm and held the fishing pole awkwardly. With Andy's help he soon got the knack of both. The boys found their own private spot to sit on the ground and wait for the fish to bite.

Dolly watched her son's every move and beamed when he began to fish like it was the natural thing for him to do. "I love seeing him doing things that I did as a child. I remember well the first time James took me to the creek and taught me to fish. He sure could make anything fun."

"He did that." Myra agreed.

After an hour of fishing, the boys came to the cabin with a string of three large and several small bream. Stephen said, "You fellas, clean 'em, and we'll fry 'em for supper." Anthony's eyes shined to hear that. (Stephen had an additional supply of fish to thaw from the freezer to ensure a good mess for all.)

Myra wondered how the boy would take to gutting and scaling the little fish, but he followed Andy's instructions and cleaned a few.

Stephen's cabin was actually an old farmhouse that he had fixed up with modern conveniences. There was room for all to sleep in the two bedrooms and cots for the children to sleep on the big screened porch. Myra had always loved to go there because it seemed like olden days. It had never been painted, and the outside looked just like it did when it was a farmhouse.

"Stephen, this is going to be so much fun. It gives me some memories of where we lived before Papa died." Dolly exclaimed.

"Well, Dolly, if you really want to relive those times, you can start by using the outhouse. I didn't tear it down. I even left the wasp nest that was always there. Believe it or not, it gets used sometimes when a crowd is here."

"You mean the wasp nest gets used, Stephen? How is that used?"

"Ah, you silly ole Yankee gal, you know I mean the toilet. So make use of it."

"I will still pass on that, Country Boy."

It made Myra's heart smile to hear them joking and picking at each other like they did when both of them lived in her home.

Stephen and Andy were in charge of supper and fried the fish, potatoes and corn dodgers in an outdoor fryer. Arliss made her special slaw and bought a big coconut cake to add along with endless glasses of sweet iced tea. Stephen reached into the pile of fried fish and placed three large bream on Anthony's plate.

"Son, you caught these three and cleaned 'em, now you eat 'em." The boy gave a satisfied grin and picked up his knife and fork to eat his catch.

"Fingers, fingers, Anthony, that's the way to eat fish." Stephen proceeded to show him how to pull the flesh away from the bones and pop it into his mouth. Soon, the boy was relishing the crispy fish dipped in tartar sauce and licking his fingers like the rest of the folks at the table.

The next morning, Myra fixed a light breakfast of cinnamon rolls that she had made and frozen earlier in the week. She wanted to save their appetite for the big Sunday dinner she had planned. Stephen and his family went into town to attend Palm Sunday services at their church.

Myra put a beef roast in the oven with potatoes, carrots, and onions. A pot of green beans, rice to top with the good gravy from the roast, and a blackberry cobbler made from the berries in her freezer would round out the meal. She could sit on the porch and relax while the food cooked. Anthony tried his luck at fishing again and learned that fish do not always bite, but he enjoyed the time anyway. Dolly went to the garden to see what was bearing and came back with a big mess of mustard greens and lots of green onions.

"Myra, would it be too much trouble to cook this mustard? I haven't had greens since I left Glencoe."

"Nah, all I have to do is wash 'em and put in the pot. Greens will wilt down in no time and be ready to eat."

Stephan and his family had just returned and brought a gallon of ice cream to eat with the cobbler. Arliss was anxious to help her mother-in-law. "Let me do that, Miz Mac. The washing takes longer than the cooking. You sit here on the porch with Dolly."

Just as dinner was being put on the table, Wallace and Grady drove up.

"Mama, I hope you don't mind us coming today. I couldn't wait to see Dolly, and I want to have as much time with her as I can."

Dolly loved the surprise. Myra was glad she had added the greens to the meal because Grady was the biggest eater in the family. It was a pleasure to see him enjoy his food.

Dolly and Wallace insisted on taking over the cleanup after the big dinner since they had not done any of the cooking. Then they joined Stephen at the pond. He was casting for one of the big trouts that he knew were in the pond. (The large fish were bass, but at that time, all Georgia fishermen call these trout.) The girls mainly paddled around the pond in the rowboat. Andy took Anthony exploring through the woods and hoped to see deer. Bonnie Ruth had brought a friend from church, and the two girls spent the afternoon playing board games that were kept in the cabin. Arliss and Myra had time to rest on the porch.

On the drive home, everyone declared they were not hungry after the heavy dinner, so they made no plans for supper. Stephen stopped at the Dairy Queen when they reached Fitzgerald, and ice cream cones were one last treat. All were ready for an early bedtime. Myra had one last thing to do.

Dear Jesus, I thank you for yesterday and today. I've been as happy as I have been in a long time. Seeing my baby sister and her son enjoying being with the family makes me know how much you love us. I gotta try to think back to this day when I get those times of feelin' sorry for myself.

Forgive me for not always rememberin' how good you are to ole Myra.
Now I'm mighty sleepy. Amen and good night, Myra.

When Myra promised to make a lunch to take on the trip, she didn't realize that leaving early Monday morning would not give her time to cook. Dolly told her not to worry; they would enjoy finding some little cafes along the way.

The next morning after an early breakfast, Myra, Dolly, and Anthony drove straight to Tennille. It was amazing to Myra that Dolly could find the way so easily just by using a map. Tennille had not changed or grown much in the years since they left.

Myra shook her head and said, "My, my, when I came here as a young'un, I thought it was a big city. It's hardly bigger than Norristown, but it was the biggest place I'd ever been."

"I don't remember a thing about the town because I always got left at home with Ma. Did y'all bring home candy for me?" Dolly was taking in the sight of the town.

"We shore did and snuff for Ma."

After parking, they walked down the main street for Myra to point out the store that had been Aunt Mary's. She was their papa's sister that Myra did not get to know until after he died. The bank was the same as the day she, her sister Annie Lou, and her brothers had met with the banker to receive payment for their share of the cotton crop they had finished growing and picking after their papa died. She wondered if anyone would remember her uncle John Early, who had once been the sheriff of the county.

Dolly didn't wonder—she went right in and asked a teller. He smiled and said, "Just a minute." Then he walked into an office and came back with a young woman.

"Did you know my grandfather? I am Rebecca Stuart Smith."

"Lordy mercy, honey, he was my uncle. This is my sister Dolly Stuart and her son."

A real family reunion took place right in the bank. Rebecca invited them into her office and caught them up on her part of the family. She was curious to learn about her grandfather's brother. She had never known of him. Myra explained that her papa had been dead for a long time, and there had been a falling out in the family. She didn't explain more.

Myra had no trouble locating the way to the farm where they had lived, but she was surprised to find that it was much closer to town than she had remembered. They found Miz Sara's house empty and falling down. It had once been a fine home. She told Dolly and Anthony how Miz Sara taught her to can foods in jars. Their tenant house was completely gone, and the beginning of a new cotton crop covered up any remnants. She pointed out the exact spot where Papa had the spell in the field and died before the doctor could get there.

Seeing the young cotton plants filled her with reminiscences— the way the ground in the cotton patch felt under her bare feet—eating fried side meat in a biscuit at noon, drinking water from a syrup jug that was so warm it didn't satisfy her thirst on a hot day; and as a twelve-year-old walking home in the evening so tired, she was ready to drop. Those were not sad times, for she was walking beside her papa and knew he would soon say, "You done a good day's work, little girl."

"Goodness, Myra, I never realized how hard life had been for all of you. By the time I could remember much, we were living in Glencoe. I don't know how you and the boys could have kept us surviving after Papa died." Dolly had heard the tales, but seeing the desolate place made it real.

"Well," said Myra, "I can tell you how we did it—by working ourselves nearly to death and eatin' mostly flour-water gravy and biscuits. Yore brothers made a crop as good as any man.

They found a little café in Tennille, and Dolly suggested getting lunch. That brought up another story for Myra to share about the time she and her brothers came to town to sell their cotton crop and bought cheese, crackers, pickles, and soda pop to eat while sitting in the wagon.

Anthony got all excited and said, "Let's do that, Mom, ple-e-e-e-ze."

They laughed; both said no and went into the café. The smell of food whetted their appetites, and they ordered hamburgers, fries, and Cokes.

The trip from the farm to Sullivan's Corner in the heavily laden wagon pulled by a mule had taken almost two days. This time they reached it in a little over two hours. The little town looked just like Myra had last seen it, except some of the stores were vacant. Annie's parents' store was open, but it now sold what Dolly called antiques and Myra called junk. Dolly had a great time looking around but didn't buy anything.

The house where they had lived with Nannie, Uncle Bunk, and Izzy had burned to the ground. It looked even more like a remnant of the Civil War with two chimneys standing over the burned timbers. Myra pulled back the kudzu vine and found boards from her brother Will Rob's chicken pen. She told Dolly more about their Aunt Nannie and their life in Sullivan's Corner. Standing on the spot and hearing about Nannie brought some remembrance to Dolly. She said she remembered crying for Nannie after they moved to Glencoe.

"She loved you and took good care of you. She was really the first one that seemed like a mother to you. I'm glad you have some memories of her."

They decided to skip Donovan, the saw mill town where they lived just before moving to Glencoe, and head right to Swainsboro.

Idella had taken the afternoon off from her work at the newspaper and was sitting on the porch when they arrived. She ran to the car to greet Dolly. Myra had not seen her daughter this happy in a long time. Dolly was her aunt, but they were close in age and had been like sisters during the years Dolly lived with them.

Myra planned to give them time alone and hoped that Idella would open up and talk with Dolly. Myra knew her daughter was still grieving over her husband, but there seemed to be more troubling her that was causing a barrier between herself and the family.

"Dinner is ready. We can sit down to eat as soon as Laura Jean gets home. I told her to be here when you arrived, but she does as she pleases. Anthony, I bet you never go off and not tell your mama where you're going."

Anthony blushed and didn't know what to say, so Dolly spoke up. "Oh, Idella, that is just how teenagers are. Besides, she doesn't even know us, so she might be shy. I do have to say that Anthony always lets me know where he is going and comes home on time. It has to be that way in a big city like New York."

Idella didn't say more, but Myra knew she felt put down that Dolly lived in the largest city in the country. Idella had always wanted to be the one who did the most and had the most.

"She might not know Dolly and Anthony, but she shore knows me. It ain't often that I get to come to see y'all, and I'd thought she'd be wantin' to see me. She used to come runnin' to the car." *Now why did I go and say that? I only made matters worse. No wonder Idella don't want to talk with me.*

That talk ended when Laura Jean came walking down the sidewalk. "Laura Jean, we've been waiting on you. Say hello to your Aunt Dolly and Anthony. They've come all the way from *New York City.* You go quick and change out of those shorts into a dress and comb your hair before we have dinner." Idella didn't give anyone a chance to say more.

When Laura Jean came to the table, she did look pretty and said, "I'm sorry to be late. I am happy to meet you."

Idella served a nice meal of ham, macaroni and cheese, garden peas, and rolls. There was ice cream for dessert. Sitting around the table made everyone relax, talk, and laugh a lot. Most of the conversation between Idella and Dolly started with "Do you remember when . . ." Hearing about their mothers when they were young girls and courting kept Anthony and Laura Jean giggling.

Laura Jean invited Anthony to play a card game on the back porch. It was a hot night, so Idella plugged in the oscillating fan for the ladies to sit on the front porch. Myra decided this was a good time for her to say good night and give the younger women time together. Dolly didn't come to bed until very late, so she knew they had a long talk. Maybe Idella could talk freely because Dolly also had unhappy times to share. Myra hoped her sister would give her some insight about Idella's feelings, but she wouldn't ask.

When they drove into Campbell the next day, Myra was so filled with emotions that she could hardly breathe. She seemed to see James on every corner. The first stop was at their former home which looked about the same, except the new owners weren't keeping up the yard and garden like she had always done. She quickly asked Dolly to drive on, for she couldn't bear to be there any longer.

Next stop was to visit Annie at her husband's store. They had a reunion just like Idella and Dolly, and every sentence began with "Do you remember . . ." Their memories went all the way back to when they were girls in Sullivan's Corner. Dolly had been a baby then. Annie's mother had helped Myra make a little dress for Dolly, and that was the first dress she had ever made. It was hard to leave, but both promised to see each other again soon. Of course, that probably wouldn't happen.

In Glencoe, they drove to the lot where their first home had burned. The Old Folks Home that was nearby had expanded, and there was a two-story brick building on the place where their home had stood. Myra wasn't surprised to see the vine her sister-in-law Olla had planted was still growing and covering everything in its path. (Now we know this is kudzu, the vine that is trying to eat the South.)

"Dolly, park the car. We'll have to walk through the branch (bushes and vines surrounding a small creek) to get to Rosa's place. It's not far."

Anthony looked doubtful and made no attempt to leave the car.

"You come on here, boy. If I can make it, I know you can. I'd be scared to walk where you live with all them people, but here, there ain't nothin' but a squirrel or maybe a rabbit."

Anthony had already developed a strong attachment to his aunt and was willing to attempt anything to please her. He jumped out of the car and ran ahead of them to show his bravery.

Rosa's little house was empty and rotting down. The front porch was gone. Probably, the boards had been used for firewood.

"I hope she ain't dead. She's lived here forever and always had a bunch of her young'uns and their young'uns living with her," Myra said as she pushed back the tall weeds.

Rosa and Myra had become friends when Myra and James were first married, and they had remained close and shared many good and bad times. Myra loved her black friend like a sister. She was very disturbed that her friend's home was deserted.

"Pore ole' Rosa. She was always proud of that little house. She wouldn't have left it unless she was made to move. I guess she could've died."

"I'm sorry, Myra. Let's head on out to the cemetery. I want to see what you mean about those little white rocks around the graves."

On the road to the cemetery, they passed a row of small concrete block apartments like the ones in Fitzgerald across the road from Myra. "Stop, Dolly, stop! There she is sitting on the steps," Myra yelled with joy.

She hurried from the car, calling, "Rosa, Rosa, is that you?"

"The good Lord has sent my angel. Come here, Miz Myra."

After a long hug and flowing tears, Myra told her about how upset she had been when she didn't find her at the old house.

"I left there last summer. The government set up these 'partments, and my girl Gloria saw about it in the paper. She worked hard and filled out a lot of papers and went to talk to a lot of folks. Finally, they say I qualify to get one. I guess that means I's pore enough." She laughed.

"Well, I'm happy for ya. I know this must be a lot better than the old place. How do you pay for it?"

"That's another good thing. The government or president or somebody sends me a little check every month. The rent is taken out before it's sent to me. I can still get them commodities like we got in the Depression. Lord, I ain't never lived so good or even been warm in the winter time. Gloria helped set it up. She's mighty smart and works cleanin' the school."

Myra was as thankful as her friend. Time was getting short, so Dolly suggested that Rosa ride with them to the cemetery to have more time to visit. They talked as fast as they could, and again, every sentence started with "Do you remember . . ."

At the graves, Myra sat on the ground between James and the baby girl and talked in a low voice. It could have been prayers or just talking to them. Rosa and Dolly stood by quietly until Rosa went over and helped her up.

"Come on, Miz Myra, they sleepin' in the arms of the good Lord now. We gonna see them all again."

"I want to think that, Rosa, but you know James wasn't always as good a man as he should've been."

"What you talkin' 'bout?" she said huffily. "Mr. Mac was as good a man as God ever made. He might not've been a churchgoin' man, but he shore seen when folks needed help. Me and my young'uns would've starved many a time if it hadn't been fer him. Other folks might not know that, but the Lord knows it, and that's what counts."

"You'll be right there with them, Rosa, just from the way you've always stood by me. You were right there anytime I needed you. Think about the good time we'll all have together in heaven." Myra's mood lifted, and she felt thankful rather than sorrowful.

Dolly looked around the cemetery at lots that had the white rocks, and she agreed. "Myra, we must find out how to get that done, and I also want to have coping put around the lot."

"I betcha Carlton will know about that. He's not too far from here and could take care of it. I hadn't thought about the coping, but that does look nice. I can chip in on the money."

"After we talk with Carlton, I'll call Arno and see what he thinks. He gave me a cashier's check and said he would send more if needed."

After dropping Rosa off and looking through her nice little apartment, they headed to Norristown. Before leaving, both Myra and Dolly put a little money in Rosa's pocket and told her to buy something she wanted for her new place. On the drive, they passed the church graveyard just out of Soperton where Aunt Mary was buried. They didn't get out but stopped by the side of the road to pay their respects.

Myra was enjoying the ride in Dolly's comfortable big car. She pointed out places all along the way. As they drove through Norristown, Anthony was amazed to see a town with only three stores, a church, and a post office.

"Just you wait, Anthony. You'll see the real country in a few minutes. I remember the first time yore Uncle Stephen and I came to see Laura James and Carlton. I didn't know how we would find their house when there was nothing but pine trees all around. Carlton had whitewashed an X on a tree at the—I won't call it a road it was more like a trail—where we turned to get to their house. Then they lived in a little log house, but they have a nice big house now." Myra enjoyed sharing this memory with her nephew.

"Honestly, a real log house. I wish I could see that. Sounds like pictures in my history books."

"You can see it. People are still livin' in it. There's a lot more for you to see. Carlton has about every kind of animal you can think of, and he'll probably let you ride a horse."

"Can I, Mom, can I? Take my picture on the horse."

Dolly beamed at her son's excitement. "First, let's see how you like sitting on the horse. They are a lot taller than you think."

"I won't be scared."

Myra had no trouble locating the road to turn into. It was much wider than years ago, but it was still dirt.

When they went around a big curve in the road, Myra called out, "There it is, Anthony, see the little log house. Ain't that a nice home?"

"It sure is. It looks like the pioneer cabins in the history books. Can I walk down here and get a better look and take a picture?"

"Sure, you can. Get Carlton to tell you about how his grandpa built it for him and Carlton's grandma to live in right after they married."

Laura James and Carlton now owned a large acreage of land covered with pine trees. Carlton had been very successful selling turpentine during the war. Now he grew the trees for pulpwood that was used to make paper. He also grew crops and raised livestock to sell. They lived in the large house that had belonged to his grandparents. It was an old house, but they had put in all modern conveniences, added some rooms, and painted. A wide porch wrapped around from the front to the side. To Myra's delight, there were swings on both ends. All her family owned nice homes, but to Myra, this country place was the finest.

Laura James and Carlton were sitting on the front porch with a big pitcher of lemonade on a table between them. Both jumped off the porch and ran to greet their company.

"Dolly, I can't believe you're here and look at this handsome young man. I've longed to see him." Laura James had always looked up to her aunt. She and Carlton had not been able to have children, so Myra knew how much she would love Anthony. Carlton had never known Dolly, but he was as happy to see her as Laura James. Anything that made his wife happy made him happy.

"Honey, you look wonderful, and this home is a paradise. I know you're happy and proud. Now tell me all about what you've done since that last day I saw you in Glencoe. You had just taken my job working for the dentist, Dr. Sasser, and we were all surprised and tickled that he picked you instead of Idella to be his assistant."

Myra had to chime in on that one. "That was shore a comedown for Idella. She always figured she'd be picked first in anything."

Laura James shook her head and said, "I never wanted to hurt her—but I shore did want that job."

"She was more embarrassed than hurt. She didn't really want the job anyway—but she did get upset when Dolly said that you were the one Dr. Sasser picked. I do sometimes wonder how her life would have turned out if she had never started working in that store and met LeGrand."

"Mama, don't talk that way. Things do turn out the way they should. She got the life she always wanted, and without LeGrand, we wouldn't have our precious Laura Jean. I am just so sorry her daddy couldn't have lived to see his daughter grown." Laura James always saw the best in anything.

"Come on, Anthony, let's get away from this 'women talk.' I need to feed up, and I can always use some help. How 'bout I call you Tony? That sounds more like somebody who is fixin' to slop the hogs!"

Anthony grinned and said, "All my friends call me Tony. I like that better, but Mama and Nona Mundo always call me Anthony."

Carlton didn't know much about the father and didn't want to mix in their business, but he asked, "Nona, some of your folks up there in New York?"

"Yes, she is my grandmother. Once a week, I ride the subway to see her in the Bronx."

"Good that you can go to see her. I don't know nothin' about riding that subway, but how would you like to ride a horse?"

"I've always wanted to ride a horse. Can I do it now?"

"Yep, let's get through with this feeding, and I'll saddle up Cornbread and Biscuit, and we'll ride through the woods and then back to the house."

"I am so happy. You are the best uncle in the world! Is that their names? It doesn't sound like horse names." The boy had entered a world he had only known in books and movies.

Carlton saddled the horses quickly before explaining the names. "I give names that I like, and there ain't nothin' I like better to eat than cornbread and biscuits. That little mare in the stall belongs to Laura James. Her name's Sweet Tea."

They rode a trail through the woods that ended up back at the house. After getting over his nervousness, Anthony—or better Tony—took right to riding. The ladies were surprised when they rode up on the horses. Dolly pulled out her camera.

"I'm ready to put supper on the table, so y'all hurry up and get them back in their stalls. I bet Anthony is ready to eat after all the work Carlton had him do."

The boy just grinned and followed his uncle to the barn. Even though he had never seen Carlton until that day, he immediately found a hero in this uncle. (They were all actually cousins, but since he was so much younger, they settled on calling them aunts and uncles.)

Laura Jane set out a spread of steak and gravy, rice, corn on the cob, little white acre peas, and potato salad. A big pitcher of iced tea kept their glasses filled. After finishing, they went back to the porch for Carlton to churn ice cream to eat with Laura James's buttery pound cake.

"Mom, can we stay here forever?" It had been quite a day for a boy who had only seen nature in a park.

After supper, Dolly brought up the improvements she wanted to make to the cemetery lot of her parents. Carlton knew exactly what was needed and who could do the job.

"There's a man in Soperton who can take care of all of that. If you can stay long enough in the morning, I'll follow you there, and we'll talk with him. He's taken care of a lot of the graves in our church graveyard. The little white rocks will help to keep down the weeds. You can take right off from there and head back to Fitzgerald."

"Mama, we like to ride around on Sunday afternoons, so we'll just start driving to Glencoe every now and then and check on how things look. We can pull up weeds. I never knew my grandparents, but I remember when you used Uncle Jesse's insurance to move them from where they had been buried and put them together in the Glencoe graveyard. I've visited Papa's grave and put flowers on it and Uncle Jesse's. I'll start putting flowers on all their graves."

"Well, if you have enough flowers, don't forget yore baby sister. She's only got a tiny marker."

"Oh, I won't, Mama. All through the spring and summer, I have plenty of flowers."

"I'll rest easier knowing that you're doing that," Myra said. She did not bring it up, but making the same improvements to the lot where James, her angel baby, and Jessie were buried was already in her thoughts. She'd talk with Stephen about that.

"Arno will rest easier too. He has talked about their graves so much," Dolly said.

All was accomplished the next day, and the expense was completely covered by Arno's check with a little left over. The time passed too quickly after returning to Fitzgerald. All the family gathered on Easter Sunday for a big picnic and egg hunt where all participated by either hiding or hunting. Ruth stole the show when she brought out a tape recorder she had recently bought and had everyone tell a memory of Myra.

Anthony surprised them when he said, "I was scared to come on this trip. I had heard all kinda stories about the South, but as soon as Aunt Myra hugged me, I knew that I was meant to be a Southerner. I'm coming back real soon."

All too soon, Myra was standing on the porch waving good-bye as the big black car pulled out into the road. Dolly had promised that they would come again, but Myra had the old feeling of sadness to see loved ones leave when you didn't know if you would ever see them again. She had faced this many times. There was a feeling of comfort in knowing that Dolly was managing her life well and raising a fine son.

After Dolly's visit, Myra enjoyed rethinking their time together. Dolly had changed a lot, and it wasn't just the way she talked and dressed. Sometimes she was still her sweet little sister, and other times she seemed to be as hard as nails, especially when Myra tried to bring up Anthony's papa. It wasn't any wonder that she had grown a tough skin.

Her little sister had gone through many changes since the day she was born. She never knew her mama or papa. She lived with her oldest sister, Annie Lou, until she was grown. Horace, Annie Lou's husband, had tried to have his way with her, and she stood up to him. When she told Myra about this, James insisted that she come to live with them. They gave her the best home that they could, but with their large family, there was never enough of anything. She didn't even have her own bed. She lost the little that she did have when their house burned. Arno asking her to come and live with him in New York was the best chance she ever had. Then she got messed up with Anthony's papa, and he kept telling her he would marry her when he could get a divorce—but he never did.

Sweet Jesus, the way has been rocky for my baby sister, but you musta been with her 'cause she's made it through and come out with that fine son. Keep on watchin' over her if you can, and if there's a good man out there who would love and take care of her and Anthony, I pray he comes her way. Now I have to ask for my own girl. Idella's life ain't easy either, but then easy ain't what you always give us. All I can do is keep on praying and loving 'em. Amen, Myra.

Chapter VII

1957

With August came the *dog days* near the end of summer. Searing heat, no rain, gardens drying up, cotton open and ready for picking were harsh memories of her childhood that haunted Myra during these days. Her life had not been affected in many years; still the end of summer brought her a feeling of melancholy. Her early life was dominated by cotton—planting, chopping, picking, and most of all, praying for a crop that would give them enough money to keep away hunger through the winter. That seldom happened, but her papa always managed somehow to keep a roof over their head, shoes on their feet, and food in their bellies. Her children had never gone through such times, and she was thankful for that. True, there had been hard times during the Depression, especially after the loss of their home from fire. Throughout those times, she was always able to keep her pledge that her children would never have to work in a cotton field. She knew the truth of the matter was the good Lord answered that prayer in one way or another.

Myra could not keep Idella off of her mind since she and Dolly had visited her oldest daughter. *Something was just not right.* Idella looked as pretty as ever with her hair in a good style, dressed nice and face made up, but her eyes looked so tired and sad. She was showing some wrinkles and crow's feet, which seemed to be coming much too early. There wasn't anything her mama could do because Idella had never been willing to talk about her problems. She did have a good job at the paper, and that was her whole life, except for Laura Jean.

The other children seemed fine. Stephen worked too hard, but Myra knew that was his nature. BJ probably did too, but she wasn't around to see that. She didn't know for sure, but she got a feeling that BJ's Charlotte depended on him for everything. His wife talked mainly about the clubs and parties she attended. Myra didn't know anything about that kind of life, so maybe that's what a lawyer's wife does to help her husband. Ruth, Laura James, and Wallace had good, hardworking husbands, but all three pitched in and carried their share of the work.

"James, I have to say we raised some good young'uns. You always thought I was too hard on 'em, and I thought you were too easy. Maybe that's why the Lord put us together to balance each other out. Now I'm sittin' here in the swing catchin' the cool breeze of the evenin', and my heart plumb aches to put my head on yore shoulder. I better stop that, or I'll be bawlin' when Stephen stops by."

"Mama, what you doing sitting out here in the heat when you've got that good oscillating fan inside. This heat's not good for you."

Myra jerked her head up and couldn't tell if she had been dreaming or talking with James. "Heat don't bother me. At least I ain't pulling a cotton sack."

This gave Stephen a chuckle. "You won't ever forget those days, will you?"

"Don't want to. Those were the only days I had with my papa."

"Well, you go on in the house and dream in front of the breeze from that fan. I need to get home, but call if you need me."

This was the way her days started and the way her days ended. She had to say it was an easy life, but she had learned long ago not to trust the good times to last. Maybe this was the time in her life when she should feel secure. After losing James, there wasn't anything worse that could happen. There might be ups and downs, but she had been through the worst, so what lay ahead shouldn't be a bother.

Dear Lord, I'm plumb ashamed of myself. Here, I got it so easy and nothin' to worry 'bout but seems like I just feel restless—seems like there's somethin' I oughta be doin'—I can't figure out what that oughta be. I like goin' to Stephen and Arliss's church. The folks are real friendly to me, and I'm proud to see the young'uns all dressed up, Arliss singin' in the choir, and Stephen takin' up the offerin'. Maybe there's still somethin' out there for me to do. If you'd show it to me, I'd shore appreciate it. I'm gonna try to listen better in church, and maybe I'll learn somethin' from that. Amen, Myra.

She knew one thing that was bothering her. Not as often, but Rosa Parks was still on the television. Every time they showed the picture of Rosa holding her pocketbook, it gave Myra a feeling in her stomach like she'd been kicked. The poor soul hadn't done nothing but want to sit when she was tired. The races had never been allowed to mix in ways like sitting together, but there was a lot of mixing going on in other ways. Trying to sit together did stir up a heap of trouble, and this was disturbing. Her head hurt when she tried to think about which way was right. Maybe the law said the races shouldn't mix, but she and her Rosa had done more than mix. It was her friend, Rosa, who took her dead angel baby from her arms. You can't mix any closer than that.

Television still gave her much pleasure but also troubled her mind. Not long after Bonnie Ruth and Andy started back to school, the evening news showed nine black students trying to go to a white high school somewhere in Arkansas. *The colored young'uns did look nice with their starched school dresses and shirts. They oughta know trouble would come from that.*

There was a picture of the black girls and boys walking into the school through a mob of folks hollering and spitting on them. They looked scared, but they walked right into the school. *A bunch of grown folks hollering and spittin' at young'uns don't seem like the way to act no matter what the law said about race mixing.*

Most of the folks she heard talking were real upset and saying what the Arkansas governor and the president should do. Their talk sounded as if they didn't care how bad the black students were treated. That filled Myra's heart with pain, but she kept quiet like Stephen had told her. He was real closemouthed bout it and didn't show how he felt. She knew he cared about all folks and had always treated everyone who worked for him more than fair. It was a puzzlement, and she didn't know which way to think or feel. Later, they reported that President Eisenhower had sent in the Arkansas National Guard to keep the black children safe. She felt relief at that and declared President Eisenhower to be a good man.

Myra had kept the newspaper picture of Rosa Parks, and she often looked at it and thought about how Rosa had stood up to all those angry people. Stephen had read her all about it from the newspaper. When she looked at Rosa, she wished she could read it for herself. Funny that she had never thought about reading before; now she wished she had gone to school long enough to learn.

I probably couldn't have learned anyway. I know how to work, but I'm dumb as a post about everything else. It would shore seem good to read the Bible for myself.

She had already put on her gown and was heading to bed when the telephone rang. As always, when the phone rang at night, she hesitated to pick it up. It had to be bad news. This call brought a surprise.

"Hello, Grandma, this is Laura Jean."

"Hey, honey. What you doin' callin' so late. Is everything all right?"

"Mama's mad with me and says she's tired of me asking her to buy me things all the time. Grandma, she don't understand that I just ask for what I need."

"Well, you don't be too hard on her. She has a struggle to keep y'all goin'. What is it ya need?"

"I'm going to the District Meet in Statesboro on the debate team, and I really need a new dress. I found just what I want in *Seventeen Magazine,* but Mama is too stingy to let me order it. I was the only freshman picked for the debate team, and I can't wear my grammar school clothes."

"Don't talk like that about yore mama. I don't know what debate team is, but I'm proud you was picked. What's this dress like?"

"I can send you the picture from the magazine."

"Send the picture and tell me the color and trim you want, and I can make it. Get yore mama to measure ya 'cause you might have growed since last time I made you a dress."

"You are the best grandma in the whole world. I'll run over to Mrs Ostine's and get her to measure me. Mama's in her room with the door closed, and I know better than to bother her. I'll mail it tomorrow."

"I'll make it for you. Don't you worry yore mama no more about it."

"Don't tell her I called you. I'll just say you sent me a present."

"All right, I'll get it done as soon as I can."

Myra didn't mention that Idella would see the call on her telephone bill. She never made a call to her mama. The only way they heard from her was when Stephen made the call.

Now here I was worrying about Rosa Parks, a black woman I ain't never seen. I can't do nothin' for her, but I can help my grandbaby. I just wish I could help Idella. She seems so troubled and is never happy, but she won't turn to any of her family, least ways not me.

Making the dress was the easy part. Keeping her daughter from thinking she was interfering would be hard.

After the phone call, Myra had trouble sleeping. When she finally dropped off, she had a dream about Rosa Parks wanting a dress made to wear to jail. Then in her dream, somebody handed her some papers to sign, and Myra couldn't read a word on the papers. As day was breaking, she got up and went to the swing. Her mind was filled with things she did not understand.

Chapter VIII

1957

"Good mornin', Miz Mac. I ain't seen ya at the store lately. What's been goin' on with ya?" Mrs. Donavan greeted Myra as she walked into the little corner store.

"Oh, I been tryin' to stay outta the store as much as I can. I spend too much money here." This was true. Myra had found the items in the supermarket where she shopped with Arliss every week to be priced much lower. The real reason for avoiding the corner store was that she didn't like to hear the gossip that circulated there. Their talk was mostly about the blacks trying to mix. She could sense their exasperation when she never joined into this talk, but that didn't bother her one bit.

"What have you been up to, Miz Donovan? You haven't been over to watch the stories in a long time. A lot has happened since you watched them last."

"I didn't think you were watchin' the stories anymore since you always had the news on when I came to see you."

Mrs. Donovan was trying to draw some comments out of her and find out which side she was supporting, but Myra was too sharp for that.

"Oh, I still keep up with the stories, but I also like to watch the news. Since I can't read the newspaper, it's good to hear it on television. It ain't always to my liken, but I don't make it—I just watch it."

That left Mrs. Donovan even more puzzled about Myra's position.

A lady that Myra had never met walked over and said, "Excuse me for interruptin', Miz MacTavish, but I couldn't help overhearin' that you can't read the newspaper. You kinda sounded like you wished you could. I couldn't read either, but I started goin' in the afternoons to a program at the Presbyterian Church that teaches readin'. I'm gettin' where I can read a little bit. We've never met, but I've seen you in the store a few times. I'm Hazel Martin, and I live in the Projects. It's not too far to walk to the church. I'd be glad to have you walk there with me if you want to look into it."

Myra couldn't believe what she had heard. *Did the woman really say they had taught her to read? She's probably smarter than me. I ain't goin' there and let them laugh at my dumb country ways.*

"I 'preciate yore offer, Miz Martin, but I don't think I have time for that. My housework and sewin' keeps me busy."

"I thought the same thing, but now I wouldn't take nothin' for startin' the class. You think more about it and let me know. I live on the first row in the Projects. The number is fourteen."

Myra quickly gathered up her purchases, paid, and hurried from the store. Her mind was already troubled enough. She didn't need to take on another aggravation. *It's no business of that Miz Martin whether I can read or not. I've got by this long without readin', so why should I bother with it now?*

The next morning, Arliss invited Myra to ride to the drugstore with her. There was always a few things she needed, so she went along. She browsed around and finally picked up a bottle of aspirin. While she waited for Arliss at the counter, she spied a rack of newspapers by the door. It was the *Atlanta Journal*, and that was the best paper to report the news. She didn't walk over to the rack, but she could see pictures of some young black folks and several policemen. Before she realized what she was doing, she had picked up the paper and paid for it along with her bottle of aspirin.

"If it ain't too much trouble, ma'am, would you give me a sack big enough for my paper? It looks like rain, and I want to keep it dry."

The clerk didn't reply but transferred the little bottle of aspirin into a larger bag. There wasn't a cloud in the sky so not much chance of rain, but the clerk didn't mention that to Myra.

Myra folded the paper and stuffed it into the bag. She didn't want Arliss to tell Stephen and have him ask her why she bought a paper. She only wanted to look at the pictures—not just the picture of the black folks—she enjoyed looking at all the pictures. She convinced herself of this.

I'll just take a walk by that church and see if it's too far a walk. I don't want to get mixed up with that Miz Martin and her tellin' me that

I should come. I shore don't want to tell any of the young'uns that I'm even havin' such thoughts.

Myra sat in the swing, holding the newspaper and trying hard to discourage any more thoughts of reading. *Besides that, I ain't got time for such with the days turning cooler and needing to do some more sewin' for Laura Jean. I want to make a few dresses for Bonnie Ruth too—even though she don't need nothin', I don't want her to feel left out.*

A few days later, Myra had finished her chores by dinner time, and all that was left for her to do was watch the stories— she decided to take a walk. She had overheard one of the ladies at the store saying she had to be at the church at one o'clock for the reading class. She allowed enough time for all to be inside the church so no one would see her and think she was coming to the class. She started walking toward the church.

The woman I saw in the store bought a notebook and pencils. I guess that means you have to write. I can't write nothin' but my name, so they probably wouldn't take me in the class. I believe I could print out the letters and learn them. Bonnie Ruth could help me. I wouldn't want her mama and papa to know. Shaw, I couldn't go this time of day anyway—I'd miss the stories.

She was ready to turn around and hurry home to catch the last of the stories when she reached the small brick church with a steeple and cross. It was in a pretty setting surrounded by shrubs and shaded by big trees with the leaves just beginning to turn. Myra had never been to any church except Baptist or whatever kind was held in the tent revivals. She had never even known any Presbyterians and wondered how they were different from the Baptists. Something about the small church looked welcoming to her. She stood in front and observed for a few minutes and got a nervous feeling. This wasn't for her, so she hurried to get home in time to see *As the World Turns. Why would she need to read when she could see everything on television?*

The next morning, she decided she needed a carton of Cokes and a bag of the Cheese Doodles that she had grown to love. She drank a Coke every afternoon, and it always made her feel good remembering when James was courting her, and he bought her the first Coke she had ever seen. Of course, that was before Coke was put in bottles, and he bought it from the fountain at the drugstore. Now she kept Cokes in her refrigerator all the time. Between stories, she would run to the refrigerator to open a Coke and get the bag of Cheese Doodles. She was ashamed to say it, but sometimes she ate the whole bag. Since she was out of both, she headed to the little neighborhood store.

She took the carton of empty bottles; if you did not return the empties, a deposit was charged on the new bottles. She was always careful not to break a bottle. Everybody loved Cokes. When she had company, she put the Cheese Doodles in a little bowl. That looked nicer, and also they wouldn't eat as many as they would from the open bag.

The Cheese Doodles and carton of Cokes were as much as she could easily carry. Today, she had to juggle her purchases because she had also bought a notebook and three pencils.

Now that was a plum waste of good money. I ain't got the time or the sense to go to that school. I'll just put this writing stuff in the bureau and give it to one of the young'uns. I betcha that Miz Martin is exaggerating about how good she can read.

She kept convincing herself to forget about learning to read—but that did not stop her from watching the ladies from the Projects walking together headed to the church. She started buying her Cokes and Cheese Doodles from the Jitney Jungle once a week. That saved her from having to listen to the gossip at the corner store and let it upset her—or hear more about the reading class.

The rest of the year passed without her giving more thought to reading. Sewing, gardening, and several visits to her children filled her time. *Shucks, even if I did learn, when would I have time to sit down and read?* However, she continued to watch the ladies going to and from the reading class at the church.

Chapter IX

1958

Raking leaves and picking up pecans were pleasant fall activities for Myra. A large oak tree in the corner of her front yard provided a challenge to keep ahead of the leaves. The grove of pecan trees that separated her yard from Stephen's property gave the joy of delicious pies ahead.

On this day, October 13, which was a Monday, she had spent the morning outside, first with a rake and then squatting down to fill her basket with pecans. The leaves were raked up into three piles and ready for Stephen to burn later in the evening. He cautioned her about burning the leaves herself, and he didn't have to insist, for she remembered too well how quickly a fire could get out of control.

After eating dinner, she planned to crack and shell the basket of pecans. All the fixings for baking a pie were in her cupboard, so she would surprise Stephen with a pecan pie to take home to the family—after saving the first slice for herself.

A can of tomato soup and saltine crackers were her dinner. Then she sat down to watch the television news at noon. Paper shells pecans were easy to crack and shell so she could do this and watch the news at the same time. The set had not been turned on since Friday night. The weekend had been busy with a visit from Ruth and Jess. Sometimes, it was a relief not to watch the news and get all stirred up.

When the television came on, it was showing pictures of something terrible that must have happened. She could see smoke and fire trucks. *Dear Lord, I hope this don't mean more trouble for the black folks. I ain't heard much about that lately. Whoever it is, I pray for them. I know how bad fire can be.* Her prayer was interrupted by the announcer.

"Yesterday in the early morning hours, dynamite was placed inside the Temple which is the Jewish Cultural Center of Atlanta. The building was destroyed, but there were no injuries or loss of life. The culprits have not been identified, but a radical white racist group is suspected since the Temple has been involved with civil rights advocacy."

Then he started interviewing folks who belonged to the Temple. It was too sad for Myra to watch. Her first thoughts went to her friend, Mrs. Rosenberg, back in Glencoe. Even if Mrs. Rosenberg didn't live in Atlanta or go to that Temple, Myra knew her friend would be mighty upset.

Myra had never known any Jewish folks until she met Mrs. Rosenberg when she bought material from her to make the dress she wore to marry James. She still had the lace handkerchief

Mrs. Rosenberg gave her that day. There was a special place in her heart for the Jewish folks after she learned about the awful camps during World War II. Mrs. Rosenberg's son was killed when his plane crashed over Germany. *Dear Jesus, why do these folks that the Bible talks about so much keep havin' such terrible things happen to them? I know it ain't yore fault, but I shore pray that you help them. Amen, Myra.*

This was a time when she wished she could read the paper for herself. Stephen always read her the news that was of interest to her, but sometimes she thought he left out the worst parts. When he came over that evening, they talked about the bombing, and neither could imagine how anyone could do such a horrible thing. He said the ones guilty would be caught and punished, but that never happened.

"I shore would like to help them out. Do you know how I could send a little money to them to help build another Temple?"

Stephen smiled at the way his mama always wanted to send a little money to help. "No, Mama, I think they will get enough money to rebuild. I'm sure there was insurance. It's terrible to know that there are people out there who would do such a thing."

"I been thinkin' of Mrs. Rosenberg. I know she drives all the way to Savannah to go to her services, but this must have broken her heart. I wish I had a way to tell her how sorry I feel."

"I know something you can do that she would appreciate. Arliss will take you to the store tomorrow, and you can buy a card that says something about how you are thinking of her. Tell Arliss what you want to say, and she'll write it for you. I betcha Mrs. Rosenberg will feel better when she hears from you."

That was just what Myra did, and a note came right back from Mrs. Rosenberg.

My dear Mrs. MacTavish,

I have been so sad since I heard that our Temple in Atlanta had been bombed. I don't know how or why anyone can have so much hate in their heart. We must pray for them.

When your sweet card arrived, my heart was lifted, and I gave thanks for kind and caring people like you. Thank you for having me in your thoughts and prayers. I know we worship differently, but our prayers are the same.

I miss you very much. You are one of my dearest friends. Please come to see me when you visit Glencoe.

With friendship and love,
Leah Rosenberg

This event made Myra realize more and more the handicap of not being able to read. She wanted to know more than what she saw on television, and she knew the *Atlanta Journal* would print details.

Again, she started thinking seriously about the reading class but turned her thoughts to sewing and getting ready for Thanksgiving and Christmas. It was difficult to have so many in her house for holidays, but she wanted everyone to be together. Thanksgiving usually wore her out, and getting ready for Christmas was even harder, but she would manage

One evening in early November the telephone rang just after she finished cleaning the kitchen from supper. It was Laura James. After the usual pleasantries—how are you—fine—how are you, she got to the point of why she called.

"Mama, I been thinking about Thanksgiving and how hard it must be for you to prepare for all of us and then turn around and do it again for Christmas."

"It ain't hard for me. I been doin' it all my life. You know how yore papa always wanted y'all home with us for holidays."

"That's right, but things have changed now. Besides, he just sat back and enjoyed the day while you did all the work," Laura James said with a giggle.

"I reckon that's the truth, but I can still do it. I'll start early, and Arliss is here to help me."

"Well, Carlton and I have a plan that I think everyone will enjoy, and it will be easier on you."

"Now, don't you start tellin' me that I'm gettin' older. I know that, but I can still cook dinner for my family."

"Hear me out before you say no. How about we all gather at my house? We've got plenty of room, and everyone will be able to sit down and eat together. The young'uns will have plenty of space to run and play, and you know how the men love to be here in the country."

"That's too much for you to do with you workin'. It always takes me two days to get the food ready. Besides that, I'll miss cookin'."

"Here's the plan. I'll cook the turkey, but you must make the dressing—everybody will be disappointed if you don't. Ruth said they would bring a cured ham from the restaurant. The rest can bring vegetables, salads, and desserts. Carlton has already planned how he can set up a long table on sawhorses where everybody can sit together. You know my dining room has the space."

"That'll take all day to get the food passed." Myra did like the picture of the whole family sitting at the same table. At her little house she had to put card tables everywhere—even in the bedroom.

"Carlton's already thought about that. We'll put the food on my dining room table and everyone can walk around it and serve their plates, just like eating in the S&S Cafeteria."

"I'll do that on one condition. I get to make the dumplin's, and candied sweet tater too . . . and that you let the young'uns go around the table first. I never liked it when folks let the grown-ups go first and eat up all the good pieces of chicken. You remember yore papa wouldn't stand for that. That's why he never wanted to eat with yore Aunt Grace—that and the fact that she never cooked enough for the crowd, and we always had to eat again when we got home." Myra laughed big from that memory.

"Then it's set, and you will make the dressing, dumplings and sweet potatoes. This will be easier on everybody. I'll let everyone know."

"You musta already let Ruth know. How did you know I would say yes?"

Laura Jean giggled again and said, "I talked about it with everyone, and they think it's a fine idea. Idella was even happy about it. She can drive out here herself and not have to ride with me and Carlton. She also offered to make one of those congealed salads with cranberries and oranges in it and bring rolls from the bakery in Swainsboro. I just told Charlotte, Wallace and Arliss to add whatever dishes they felt like cooking."

"One more thing, Laura James. You make a big pot of fresh turnips."

That is exactly how Thanksgiving was celebrated that year. The dining room table was loaded down with food. Everyone planned to stay for supper and go home after dark. Ruth, Woody, and Jess would drive back to Mount Vernon to spend the night with Woody's mother and drive home to Jacksonville the next day. Woody had enough good help in the restaurant to allow him to take a holiday.

Myra's favorite part of the day was sitting with the men on the big porch after the meal while her daughters cleaned up the kitchen. The children, even Laura Jean, had a good time fishing in the pond, climbing trees and exploring the barnyard. Laura James had told everyone not to dress up, but of course, Idella and Laura Jean came dressed in their finest clothes.

Idella continually called out to her daughter, "Laura Jean, you be careful that you don't get your clothes ripped or get in that muddy water. You know how much those cost."

Ruth told her niece right away that she should enjoy the day and forget about her good clothes. She said, "If you mess up your dress and shoes, I'll buy you some more."

"Laura Jean, you mind me—Ruth is not who buys your clothes—as I remember, she never took care of anything when she was your age."

Stephen immediately tried to smooth things over between his sisters and said, "Yea, she did. She took care of staking out that old cow and bringing her home for me to milk every night."

The memory made Idella laugh and say, "Yea she did—but she squalled her eyes out every step of the way."

"And Mama switched me nearly every day. I never got away with anything. Y'all remember the time Papa made me smoke after I had tried it on my own." Ruth could never be angry with her sister. The mood changed, and all were laughing and talking again.

Near the end of the afternoon, the leftovers were brought out and all filled their plates again. It was a crisp autumn day, but everyone took their plates onto the porch and enjoyed being outside. The view of Carlton's pond was peaceful, and the soft noises of the cows and horses made the scene perfect.

Ruth had the practical idea of using paper plates, so that eliminated the cleanup. She used what they still called Papa's store-bought bread and made turkey and ham sandwiches for the children. She served the sandwiches on a paper plate with a big slice of cake and handed each a bottle of Coke. They thought Aunt Ruth knew the finest way to dine and took off to picnic by the pond.

"Laura Jean, you stay right here and eat your supper with us. You're too old to be acting like a young'un. I don't want you sitting on the ground. You'll ruin your dress and shoes. It's filthy down there," Idella warned her daughter.

Ruth could not let this pass and told her niece, "You go have a picnic. If you do soil your dress or shoes, I promise you that

I will see to it that you get new ones. Go and enjoy being with your cousins. You never get too old to have fun with your family."

"That's plain meddling in how I raise my daughter, Ruth. I want her to learn to take care of her clothes because I don't have money like you to buy more just because she was not responsible. You might want to pay more attention to your own son. He's been everywhere from the top of a tree to the hog pen."

"Idella, I only wanted Laura Jean to enjoy the time here. You should've done what Laura James suggested and not made her wear her best clothes. None of the rest of us came dressed like we were going to dinner with the queen. You don't need to worry about Jess. Woody keeps him in line when necessary."

"I can't help it that I don't have a husband making a fortune running a restaurant. I have to do it all myself."

"I know that, Idella, and I'd give anything I could to change it, but that can't be done. I was not trying to brag or hurt your feelings. I only wanted all the kids to have a good time since they don't get to be together often."

"We're leaving anyway. I don't want to drive home after it gets late. I am *alone,* you know."

Myra had her fill. She knew Ruth only wanted the best for her sister and niece. Idella's getting mad and leaving early messed up their happy holiday.

"Honey, don't go yet. It ain't that late. We all want you to stay longer," Myra pleaded.

"Don't worry about the time, Idella. I'll drive behind you to your house. Swainsboro is right on my way," BJ added.

"No, thanks. I don't need your charity, Mr. College Graduate, Big-Time Atlanta Lawyer. I remember when you were wearing

Hoover britches and crying for another piece of sweet potato, and you usually got more than your share—'cause you were Mama's babe-e-e."

By this time, Ruth was crying, Myra was crying, and Laura Jean was crying. Stephen stood up. "That's enough, Idella. No one has given you charity. All we've done is try to make things easier for you, because we love you. You need to apologize to Ruth, Mama, and BJ."

"That'll be a cold day in hell. Go to the car, Laura Jean. I've had all of this day that I can stand."

As she headed for her car, BJ followed her and drove behind her all the way to Swainsboro. He left his wife and children, so Myra hoped he planned to return—and he did.

Not another word was spoken about the incident, but the merriment was gone, and soon all left for home or wherever they planned to spend the night.

Myra didn't talk about it on the way home, but she worried that Idella might not come for Christmas. However, bright and early Christmas morning, Carlton and Laura James's car drove up with Idella and Laura Jean sitting in the back seat. It was a merry Christmas for all, and not a cross word was spoken.

Chapter X

1958

During the week between Christmas and New Year's, Myra felt unusually restless when she should have felt blessed and joyful. *Lord, what's the matter with me? Am I just ungrateful for all you provided for me? I'm 'shamed if I am. It was a good Christmas for all. Idella seemed happy and enjoyed the whole day. She didn't even mind when Ruth gave Laura Jean a new coat and them horse riding britches that she had such a fit over. Ha-ha! She got the britches but she ain't got no horse. I ain't makin' fun of my grandbaby. She shore was proud of those britches and called 'em jodhpurs. I 'spect all the young girls are wearin' 'em now, and that's why she had her heart set on gettin' a pair. Leave it to Ruth to buy such as that. The young'uns plumb showered me with presents. I wish they wouldn't waste their money, but I do believe I will enjoy that electric coffeepot and the waffle iron. Maybe my life's*

gettin' too easy, and that must mean there's somethin' I oughta be doin'.
Amen, Myra.

"Grandma, Grandma, Mama sent me to check on you. She didn't want to call in case you were still asleep. Daddy didn't have time to stop by this morning." Her granddaughter was at the door.

"Come in, Bonnie Ruth, you're just who I need to see this morning. No, no, I wouldn't be sleepin' this late, but I'm about to try out that new coffeepot and waffle iron, and you can help me figure it out. Are ya hungry? I got some good syrup that Carlton brought me. His papa made it. Now you take these books that came with 'em and read out loud to me."

"I had some cereal, but I love waffles, so does Andy, but he's off with Daddy."

Bonnie Ruth read the coffeepot instructions first, and Myra followed along and did each step. Soon, coffee was perking.

The waffles took longer because the batter had to be mixed. The little booklet had recipes.

"Grandma, there's recipes in here for different kinds of waffles—there's blueberry, pecan, and just plain. Which one do you want to try?"

"I ain't got no blueberries—the pecan sounds good, but maybe we oughta just start with the plain ones."

Bonnie Ruth dutifully read the waffle recipe, and Myra followed each step. The waffle iron was plugged in and ready when the mixing was completed.

Myra carefully poured the batter into the iron and closed it down. A light came on, and steam came out around the sides. Bonnie Ruth reminded her grandmother that the waffle would be ready when the steam stopped.

The steam stopped, and Myra lifted the lid to an evenly browned waffle. "Uh, uh . . . I can't wait. Get the butter, honey.'

"We can't eat this one, Grandma. It has to be thrown away. We can eat the next one."

"There ain't nothin' wrong with this one. It's ready to eat."

"No, Mama always throws the first one away. I don't know why, but she must know."

Grudgingly, Myra put the tasty-looking waffle in the trash and poured in more batter. The second one was ready in no time. The iron made one big round waffle with a line in the middle that could be cut for two. She had intended to let Bonnie Ruth have the first one, but she couldn't wait another minute for her first taste. They shared.

A big slab of butter melted on top, and cane syrup filled each little hole. Halfway through their second waffle, they heard someone at the door.

"Bonnie Ruth, are you here? I was worried when you didn't call to let me know your grandmother was okay." Arliss stood at the door.

"Mama, I plumb forgot. We made waffles and coffee, and then we started eatin'. Grandma's fine."

"Come in, Arliss, and have a waffle with us. There's enough batter for a few more. I do believe this electric pot makes the best coffee I've ever tasted. I *am* enjoyin' my presents."

"I shouldn't because I had a big early breakfast with Stephen, but I can't resist."

Arliss sat down and enjoyed a waffle and cup of coffee and also declared the coffee was the best she had ever tasted. The coffeepot had been Ruth's gift, and she had also given Myra a three-pound bag of coffee called Eight O'Clock.

Arliss left to finish her housework, but Myra asked her granddaughter to stay and write down the waffle recipe. She remembered all the steps in using the coffeepot and waffle iron, but she couldn't remember the recipe.

"Now, don't write every word. Just put down the things I need to put in. I know about stirrin' and things like that, and I know to turn the waffle iron on to heat up first and to throw away the first waffle. When it stops steamin', it's done. I know that too." She pulled her notebook and a pencil from the drawer. "I'll need to sharpen this pencil with a knife. It ain't been used."

Bonnie Ruth was surprised that her grandmother had a notebook and pencils. She didn't comment but started writing the recipe down in large block letters.

2 EGGS

2 CUPS MILK

1 tsp SODA

2 CUPS FLOUR

2 tsp BAKING POWDER

1/2 tsp SALT

6 TBSP SHORTENING

"Grandma, I want you to read this over with me. You can do it."

"I'll try, but all them letters don't mean nothin' to me. I never had a head for letters, but I do know my numbers."

"Just think about how you make a cake. The first thing is two eggs. Now say it with me." Bonnie Ruth read each ingredient, and Myra repeated.

"Two eggs, I'll remember that."

"Two cups of milk." Myra nodded as she looked and repeated the words.

"Next is one teaspoon of soda. I put that in small letters so you will know it is the little spoon."

"This is sodie just like I use in biscuits?" Myra asked.

Bonnie Ruth assured her, "Same thing. What do you think should come next?"

"I'd say flour, but how much?"

"That's right, and it takes two cups."

"Here's some more of them little letters. That means the little measuring spoon."

"That's right. You will need two teaspoons of baking powder and one half teaspoon of salt."

"The last one looks necessary. It's in them big letters and you need six."

"Good for you, Grandma. That is six tablespoons of shortening—that means some kinda grease. Use the big measuring spoon."

"What kinda grease?" Since the recipe called for shortening, Myra wondered if that was different.

"Mama uses Crisco out of a can, but we used lard in what we made 'cause that was all you had."

"I'll get me some of that Crisco. I've seen a woman on television usin' it to fry chicken. I been thinkin' about tryin' it. I remember the woman's name—it's Betty Crocker. Her chicken shore looked crispy and brown. What else is there to do?"

"Nothing but stir until it's smooth and pour in the waffle iron. One thing I forgot is you have to grease the waffle iron before it heats."

"I'd shore remember that. I ain't about to stick my fingers on that hot iron. Could be that's why Arliss throws away the first one cause it soaks up the extra grease. She's smart like that."

They went over the recipe several times, and soon Myra could identify all the words. Then she read it completely through on her own.

Bonnie Ruth was so happy and proud. "Grandma, you can read that."

"Lowdy mercy, I can. Reading ain't as hard as I thought. 'Course, this is all that I can read."

"I know you can learn to read. I'll help you. All the letters make sounds. You can learn to say the letters and make the sounds and then put together to make words. It's not hard."

"What I'd like is for you to learn me the letters and how to write 'em down."

"I will. We'll start tomorrow. I've got to go now and clean up my room. I left before doing that, and Mama's probably having a fit."

For the rest of the morning, Myra continued to read her recipe. Of course, she had memorized it by now, but her mind was softening about her ability to learn.

Bonnie Ruth was still out of school on holidays, so she had free time to spend. She was quite excited about helping her grandmother learn the alphabet. The days were near freezing and a good time to spend in the little warm cozy house. They started each day with a waffle and coffee. Bonnie Ruth's coffee was half milk and lots of sugar. Her grandmother never seemed to tire of waffles, and neither did she. After the first day, sausage accompanied the waffle, and that made it even better. All morning, the little house was filled with the good smell of coffee and sausage. She was thinking about being a teacher, and this was a good way to see if she liked teaching. There was no question about her going to college. Her daddy talked to her and Andy all the time about college.

Her mother never asked why she was spending so much time at her grandma's, and that was a relief. Grandma had told her that she was not to tell her mama or daddy about the reading lessons. When Bonnie Ruth asked why, her grandma only said, "Just don't." There was no reason for her to be ashamed, but it seemed like that was how she felt.

Through the rest of the holiday break, they spent every morning together. They started with the alphabet.

"Grandma, the way I learned the alphabet when I started to school was to sing it."

"Sing it!" She thought her granddaughter was teasing.

"Yes, ma'am, it goes like this—abcdefg—hijklmnop—qrs and tuv—wxy and z. Now I've learned my ABCs. Tell me what you think of me." The letters were sung to a tune.

For the rest of the week, they sang together at every chance. They even sang as they ate their waffles and sausage. Myra could not get the alphabet song out of her head and caught herself singing it when she was alone.

The song worked, and next, Bonnie Ruth printed out the letters, and Myra would touch them as she sang. When she was asked to point to a specific letter, she would sing the song in her head until she got to the right letter. It took two days for her to learn to recognize all the letters of the alphabet.

On the third day, Bonnie Ruth dotted the letters out and had Myra trace over them. She started leaving homework of a page of letters with lines underneath for Myra to practice writing. At first, these were in order and later mixed around. Myra could write the alphabet with no model by the last day. Her granddaughter gave her a test by calling out a letter for her to write. Myra's grade was one hundred.

"Grandma, I go back to school next week, and I won't have any time to help you during the week. I have so much homework that it will be hard for me to stop by after school, but I will try. Please don't stop practicing."

"Honey, you've already taught me more that I had ever hoped to learn. I'm not gonna stop until I can read the Bible and the cards my sister sends to me. Next week, I'm going to school."

And she did.

Chapter XI

1959

Black-eyed peas and collard greens simmered on Myra's stove for the New Year's Day dinner. James always declared this was his favorite of all the holiday meals. Myra thought eating these dishes was a way to get your stomach back to common food after all the fancy holiday dishes. This year, Myra would have Wallace and Grady along with Stephen and his family at her table.

She was able to see Wallace more often than the other girls, since Macon was close enough for them to come for the day on Sunday. They didn't have children yet, and Wallace seemed to have a need to be with family as much as she could. She now owned the dress shop that she had worked in since she first moved to Macon and had changed the name to *Wally's*. Myra had been there several times, and she'd have to say that it was a nice store—but the prices were too high for her. Folks in Macon seemed to have enough money to shop there. She didn't like to admit it, but she had gained weight over the years. The dresses in *Wally's* were made for slimmer folks. Anyway, Myra had always made her own dresses.

Dinner was ready at twelve o'clock, and Wallace and Grady arrived just as she was ready to put everything on the table. Grady loved to eat, especially his mother-in-law's cooking, so she knew they wouldn't be late.

"Oh, Mama, the kitchen smells like New Year's Day," said Wallace.

"Oh yea, we got it all today. Black-eyed peas for good luck and collards for money just like yore papa always said."

Stephen, Arliss, and the children followed them in. "We got Papa's real favorite this year, Wallace. I caught two 'possums. Mama's baking one and making dumplings with the other."

"You hush that, Stephen. You always try to aggravate me. I already looked in the oven, and I know a pork roast when I see it. Besides, you've got too uppity to go 'possum hunting."

It did Myra's heart good to hear them joshing like they did when they all lived at home, and she joined in the teasing. "I've seen the day when I was proud to have a fat 'possum on the table, and that day could come again, so don't y'all poke fun at 'possum," she warned.

After lingering over the finished meal and enjoying memories of other New Year's, Myra and Wallace found themselves alone for the rest of the afternoon. Stephen, Grady, and Andy went to Stephen's house to watch a football game on the colored TV.

Arliss left to visit some of the shut-ins from their church, and Bonnie Ruth went to the picture show with a friend.

"Mama, I'm glad to have this time alone with you. I've had something on my mind that I want to talk over with you."

"I hope it ain't about Idella. I've made my peace on that subject. We just have to look over it when she blows up at us like she did Thanksgiving. She's always been prideful, and seein' her brothers and sisters doin' so much better than her affects her nerves. We have to be thankful of the times, like Christmas, when she can be happy and act like herself."

"No, Mama, that's not what I want to talk about. I agree with all that you said, and the rest of the family does too. Her life is not the way she thought it would be, and that is hard for her. I never gave it a thought after she left on Thanksgiving. I want to help her anyway I can with Laura Jean, but I have to be careful not to make it seem like Idella can't provide for her daughter.

"Now that I own the store, I can send Laura Jean lots of pretty clothes that I get as samples. All samples come in small sizes and just fit her."

"Excuse me, honey, I didn't mean to take the talk away from you. My mind was on Idella and wonderin' what she is doing today. Now you tell me what you wanted to talk about."

"You know that Grady and I want to have children more than anything in the world. So far it looks like that is not going to happen for us. We went to a specialist in Macon and talked with him about it."

"Reckon it has anything to do with the spells you used to have, and all the medicine you take now to keep from having the spells?" (Wallace suffered from fainting spells until a doctor determined that she had petit mal seizures and gave her medicine to control this.)

"I wondered that too, but the doctor said that would not prevent me from getting pregnant. We have been married a long time and never tried to prevent it. The doctor said I should have conceived by now if I was able. The problem could be with me or with Grady. Unless it can be corrected, we don't want to know."

"Honey, I shore am sorry. You and Grady would make the best parents and give a young'un a good home and lots of love. I know how much you're hurtin' over that."

"Well, not so much now. The doctor suggested that we think about adoption. The more we talk about it, the more we think this is what we should do. We'd both love to be parents of a baby that needs a home."

"So when can you get started on this?"

"We have already started the paper work, but that could take a long time."

"I don't see why it should. There's always little young'uns that need a home. I bet if we all got on the lookout, we could find some pore girl that has to give up her baby."

"No, we can't go that way, Mama. We have to do it the right way through the Welfare Department. It must be a legal adoption, so we will know the child will be our own forever."

"I see what you mean by that. The only way I can help is to pray."

"Please do that, Mama. I know you'd do it without being asked. I want it for me and Grady, but I also want it for a little baby out there who needs a good home."

"I'm mighty proud of you both. Is this a secret between us?"

Wallace's face crinkled up in a grin. "No, I want everyone to know, but let me have the pleasure of telling them."

"Is the ball game over?" Wallace asked as Grady walked into the house.

"No, it's just the halftime. I thought we better head home before it gets dark. The daylight is short this time of year. I didn't care nothing about watching anyway. I just liked being with Stephen and Andy. That new colored TV is mighty nice."

Before they left, Myra couldn't resist hugging him and saying, "Grady, if there's a man on earth who would be any better papa to a young'un than you, I don't know who it would be."

He was always shy, but this time he hugged her back and said, "Thank you, Miz Mac, that means a lot to me. I pray I get the chance."

"Mama's praying, and you know how she can get things done through the Lord," Wallace said.

Myra was left with a good feeling about this. She would pray hard for a new grandbaby. It would be her grandbaby no matter who it came from.

She flipped on the TV before going to bed and was surprised to see another mob of folks gathered up somewhere. The men all had big guns and beards and didn't look at all like the civil rights demonstrators—Myra had learned this term. She couldn't make heads or tails of what she was seeing and was just before turning the television off when the announcer said,

"Today, January 1, 1959, the Cuban rebels, led by Fidel Castro, declared a victory over the dictator, Batista, and have taken over the capital of Havana. Batista and his family have fled the country."

"Cuba, Cuba—now where have I heard of that? It ain't around here. Looks like it ain't even in our country. I hope the right side won. Why does there have to be so much ill will among folks. I'll just go to bed and pray on that.

Dear Lord Jesus, my girl shore needs some help in gettin' her a baby. I know there's some pore girl out there who needs a good home for her child. Even if she is my daughter, I can recommend that you won't find a better mama and papa than Wallace and Grady. If you could hurry it up, I would appreciate it. I want that new grandbaby while I got enough time left to enjoy it. Also, whatever was on the television tonight looked like those folks had been at war. I pray that the right side won, and those folks will have a better life. Thank you for a new year. If I get through it without sickness, I will be most grateful. Thank you for the happy time I got to have with my table full of good food for my family to enjoy. Amen, Myra.

Chapter XII

1959

School started back the Monday after New Year's Day, so Myra thought there was a good chance the reading class would resume also. She slept little the night before and was excited but scared at the same time. *Shucks, if I don't like it, I don't have to go back. I don't care what those ladies might think.*

Monday morning was sunny and clear. The temperature was just above freezing, but she had a warm coat, hat, and gloves. Heavy cotton stockings would keep her legs warm on the walk to the church. She was encouraged by the sunshine.

Just as she sat down to eat a quick breakfast, Bonnie Ruth ran in. "Grandma, I got to hurry to catch the bus, but I brought you a present." She handed Myra a funny-looking little wooden thing with something inside it that looked like a razor blade.

"What's this?"

"Grandma, it's a pencil sharpener. It will trim your pencils into a sharp point that's better than a knife can do. Give me your pencils, and I'll show you."

Bonnie Ruth sharpened all three pencils quickly, and Myra was impressed at the sharp points.

"I shore thank you, honey. I can use this. I do like to write with a sharp pencil."

Myra found a cloth bag that she used for embroidery thread, emptied it, and put her notebook, pencils, and pencil sharpener in it. Now she did feel like she was going to school.

She was ready to leave but then remembered the class didn't start until afternoon. That was disappointing because it was hard to wait and to find something to fill her time. She also feared that a visitor would come before she left. Bonnie Ruth was the only one who knew her plans to go to the class, and she wanted to keep it that way until she felt less nervous and worried that she would fail.

Eating dinner never crossed her mind—she was too excited. She would leave home in time to talk with the teacher before anyone else arrived. She needed to explain how little she knew about reading—or anything except cooking, cleaning, sewing, and of course, picking cotton.

The side door of the church was where she had seen the ladies entering. It was locked, so she decided to knock. A smiling lady about the age of Arliss opened the door.

"Hello, come right in. I hope you are a new student. I am Christina Laurens, one of the instructors."

"Pleased to meet ya, Miss Laurens. I'm Myra MacTavish, and I've come to see about tryin' to learn to read."

"Please call me Christina, Myra. You are not going to try to learn to read—you *are* going to learn to read."

"Hello, Myra, I am Julia Greenberg, the other instructor." She was standing behind Miss Laurens. "We are so happy to have you join us. Glad you came early so you can get your workbooks and supplies before class starts." This lady somewhat reminded Myra of her old friend in Glencoe, Mrs. Rosenberg.

Myra sat at a long table and looked through the three workbooks and a thick book called a dictionary.

"How much do I owe ya? I might not have enough on me today, but I can leave the stuff here and bring all that I owe tomorrow."

"You don't owe a cent. The supplies are part of the program, and it's all free," Julia said.

"I'd shore appreciate ya tellin' whoever paid for it, that I thank 'em." Myra knew the money had come from someone.

The rest of the class came in together, and several of them lived in the Projects across from Myra.

"Miz Mac, I'm so happy that you decided to come. As smart as you are, I know you'll learn fast—probably get ahead of me, and I been comin' for over a year—'course I had to take some time out when I hurt my back." Mrs. Martin was genuinely pleased to see her neighbor.

"I thank ya for tellin' me about it. I just had to make up my mind to try it even if I might not be able to learn."

"Now stop that kind of talk. You have already done the hardest part," said Mrs. Greenberg.

Myra was confused. So far, she hadn't done anything. "I have?" she asked.

"Yes, the first step, making up your mind to come, is the most difficult. We are all friends here, so let's stop this Mrs. I am Julia. This is Christina. You are Myra, and everyone else tell her your name."

One by one, they called out, "Bertha," "Callie Jane," "Lillian," "Bessie Mae," "Tot," "Florence," "Eula," "Ruby Nell." Last was the woman that Myra had only called Miz Martin, and she said, "Hazel."

"I'm pleased to meet all of you. I didn't get to go to school long enough to have school friends, and now I do." Myra smiled for the first time.

"Let's get to work. Myra, since you are just starting, Christina will work with you one on one."

"Come, Myra, let's find a spot in another classroom. I can't wait to get started." Myra followed her out the door. It was nice to know everybody's given names, but Myra knew she would not be able to call the teachers by their first names. That didn't seem proper.

"We will start with workbook one on the first page."

Myra was glad to see that someone had already written her name on each of the books. She would hate to lose one.

The first page was the alphabet. The teacher was delighted to see that her student was proficient in the alphabet and could identify all letters and write in a straight neat way.

"You are way ahead, Myra. Did you learn this when you were in school?"

Myra laughed and said, "I didn't learn nothin' in school except how to crochet. (One of Myra's early teachers decided that since the little girl did not get to attend often enough to learn reading, she would teach her to crochet.) I just learned the alphabet last week. My granddaughter, Bonnie Ruth, taught me."

"She was a good teacher. I think we are ready to move on to the sounds these letters make." She separated the alphabet cards into two stacks and put the small stack (vowels) aside. First, she asked Myra to call the name of each of the letters. Then she placed the letters B, C, D, F, and G in front of Myra. For more than an hour, they practiced the sounds of each letter. Next, she turned the letters over, and on the back was a picture of a ball, a cat, a dog, a fish, and a goat. After Myra said the words, the teacher made the sound of the first letter; Myra quickly identified the sound with the picture.

She was so pleased that she clapped her hands, and Christina gave her a big hug and said, "Are you ready to read?"

The next page in the workbook had the pictures from each card. Underneath was a straight line and the letters that made the rest of the word:

_____all _____at ___og ___ish ___oat

After looking at the picture, Myra had no problem putting the right letter into the space. By changing the first letter, she quickly realized that she could turn *ball* into *fall* and *fish* into *dish*. She laughed loudly and said, "This ain't hard a bit."

On the next page, the words *I see a* was written many times with a line beside it. Myra then made sentences writing in the words that she knew.

By the time the class ended, Myra had learned the sounds of all the consonant letters. Her homework was to continue making sentences by adding words to *I see a*. She knew she could do this. She also had learned the word *see*.

She walked home with the ladies from the Projects and found that she enjoyed their company. They chatted like school girls about their day, the instructors and even made little jokes.

After a quick bite of leftover ham between a cold biscuit, Myra set to work. She had been too nervous to eat anything before leaving for school. She wrote and wrote in her notebook and delighted in all the words she was learning. Her notebook was almost filled. At this rate, she would need to buy a new supply of notebooks soon.

"Grandma, Grandma, unlock the door." Bonnie Ruth was home from school and was eager to see if her grandmother had kept her pledge to go to the class.

"Come in, honey, you're just who I need. Take this money and run down to the store and buy me as many notebooks as it will cover. No, wait, let me get the carton for you get us some Cokes and a bag of Cheese Doodles. Put two cold ones in the carton. I'm ready for recess."

Bonnie Ruth hurried to the store and brought back six notebooks that only cost a quarter each. She was eager to hear about her grandmother's first school day and also loved this special time with her and sharing their secret.

They sat on the sofa beside the little heater, and Myra told her all about her the class and proudly showed off her work.

"Grandma, you've done real well. You write so neat. Let me write out some more words for you." Using the same pattern of the workbook, she wrote out ____*an*. This was harder, but Myra experimented with the letters, and wrote *can, Dan, fan, man,*

Nan, pan, ran, tan. When she correctly made a word, Bonnie Ruth read the word aloud, and Myra repeated the word several times.

They were still working when Stephen walked in the door. Myra gasped because she had hoped to keep the secret until she got more confident.

"What're y'all doing? Playing a game?" Stephan asked.

"Tell him, Grandma, tell him. He won't laugh. I know he won't."

"Tell me what? Are y'all up to something?"

Myra gathered her courage and said, "Stephen, Bonnie Ruth is trying to help me learn how to read. If it's keepin' her from her studies, I'll make her stop."

"Daddy, I'm keeping up with my homework, you know that. I'm gonna tell you the rest. She went up to the Presbyterian Church this afternoon and started taking a class to learn to read."

Bonnie Ruth was shocked when she saw tears come to her strong father's eyes. "Mama, don't you even think about quitting. I have never been any prouder of you, and it makes me so happy to know you have this chance. I always hated to hear you put yourself down and say that you were dumb. You are the smartest woman I know. You aren't educated because you never had a chance to go to school, but you have been plenty smart—just think about all you have done. I want to help you, but Bonnie Ruth is probably the better one to do that. There is one thing I won't put up with. You aren't walking up there in the cold anymore. Arliss will take you every afternoon and pick you up when it ends."

By this time, Myra was crying too. She tried to think of a way to thank her son, but all she could think to say was "It don't take but a few minutes to walk to the church. Arliss don't have time to take me and pick me up. Besides, I walk with the ladies from the Projects."

"Mama, you always astonish me. Arliss can easily take you and the others in our car. There is plenty of room for all of you. You might have to crowd up, but it's a short ride.

"Now, I think it is time to close school for the day. Put your books away. I'll be back in a few minute to take all of us to the Dairy Cream for supper. This is Monday night when they sell those big hamburgers for ninety-nine cents. We're gonna celebrate."

Before she closed her eyes, Myra wanted to share the day with Jesus. *Dear Lord Jesus, what happened to me today was somethin' I never thought I would do. I'm thankful that I finally made up my mind to try the readin' class. Thank you for the kind folks I met there. I'm gonna do my best to learn. If I can learn, the first thing I will do is read the Bible. There's more I oughta say, but my eyes are gettin' heavy, so I have to say good-night. Amen, Myra.*

That was the end of Myra's first day of reading class.

Chapter XIII

1959

For an old country woman who had never spent a full week in school, Myra took to reading like it was second nature. By the end of January, she had completed the first workbook and started reading the one-page stories that were in the second workbook. She never realized so much pleasure came from reading. The stories kept her interested, and she often read her favorites over and over. There was a funny one about a hen that thought the sky was falling and ran to tell the others. Myra thought that sounded just like a hen, if hens could talk.

The television was only turned on to watch the evening news. She let the folks in the stories solve their problems on their own. Most nights she cooked a quick supper and ate while she watched the news. Now that she was aware of happenings in the world, she wanted to keep up. Mrs. Donovan never came to visit again and barely acknowledged her greeting when they met in the store. Some days after they got home from school, Hazel Martin came, and they studied together. She and Myra were becoming special friends. One would read a story aloud, and the other would correct. They also read words on flash cards and practiced until they learned every word.

Stephen kept his word and did not tell the others. He didn't discuss it with her either because he knew she was shy about her reading. Bonnie Ruth continued to study with her grandmother and kept her father informed of the progress she was making. Arliss drove the school bus of four ladies to and from the church each afternoon.

Both instructors were amazed at Myra's progress. By the first of March, she had caught up with the classmates who had started before her. Two months later, she had completed all three workbooks and was now reading anything she was handed. It seemed as if she had known many words but did not realize it until she started the class. Handwriting improved along with her reading. Spelling was more difficult, for she wrote a word the way it sounded and found this was not usually correct. This did not deter her, and she kept a spelling list to learn.

Her time was consumed with homework and reading books. After watching the evening news, she read the old *Atlanta Journal* she had bought before starting the class. This increased her reading ability, for she read every part of that paper, even the classified ads. A new world opened to her. Any word that she couldn't determine, she wrote down to ask Bonnie Ruth. The old paper was getting worn thin.

The pictures of the black folks and a policeman on the front page of that old paper had intrigued her to buy it. Later on the news, she heard they were trying to sit down at a counter to eat with white folks. It was somewhere in Carolina. Now she could read the details in the paper. There was still a lot to learn, but reading would make that possible. Her challenge was the promise to God that she would read the Bible. She had not been successful because so many of the words were hard to pronounce and different from words she had learned. This was disappointing, and she had to confess to God that after trying her best, she could not read his word. *Oh Lord, I hate to own up to this after I bragged so about learnin' to read the Bible. I've tried, but I just can't read most of the words. Forgive me for lettin' you down. Amen, Myra.*

James gave her the Bible after the war when he started selling for the Georgia Novelty Company. The merchandise he received to sell each week always contained beautifully bound leather Bibles with all the words of Jesus printed in red. Since his customers could only pay a small amount weekly for their purchases, Myra often thought of how dear these Bibles were to folks who had so little. She loved to open the Bible and look at the pages, even if she could not read the words. This brought memories of her papa reading stories from his old worn Bible. During the time the family moved so often, Papa's Bible was lost. *Wonder if I could read better from Papa's Bible. He read the words easily. Even if I couldn't read it, I'd shore love to hold it in my hands and know he had held it in his hands.*

She turned to the pages in the back where James had written down his and Myra's names, their dates of birth, and wedding date. His writing was so smooth and kind of fancy. She loved to run her fingers over the writing. The entry of his death date was in a different handwriting. She wondered which child did that—sounded like Laura James.

Now that she could write James's name, she wrote it over and over in her notebook. Was she showing off for James? It still gave her pleasure just to say his name, and writing it gave her added satisfaction. When Ruth first started courting Woody, she did the same thing and wrote his name over and over. Myra thought Ruth was silly to do this, but now she was doing the same thing. *Silly old woman*

The classes continued through the summer, and Myra never missed one. She learned new words every day and started looking up meanings in the dictionary. As new students came in, the instructors assigned Myra to help them just like Christina had helped her. Her method of teaching letters was the same that Bonnie Ruth had used with her. It worked, and the instructors told her to forget about using the books until the student learned the alphabet. Myra felt so comfortable with reading that it seemed like there had never been a time when she could not read.

Mother's Day had always been a time when all the family gathered and treated her like she was somebody special. Every year, she told them not to go to that trouble but still looked forward to the celebration. There didn't seem to be anything special to celebrate about the fact that she had raised a family of six, and they never went hungry a day or had to pick cotton. The children seemed to think it was a reason to celebrate, and that made her proud and thankful. She wanted to tell the whole family about learning to read but still felt too shy to mention it to them.

As the classes progressed through the summer, Myra thought of ways to provide little treats. A pound cake or cobbler appeared at least once a week along with a big jug of iced tea. The mid-afternoon break turned into a party with everyone laughing, talking like good friends, relaxing, and enjoying being together. They were enjoying school days that they never experienced when they were young.

By the end of summer, she was competent enough to stop attending the class and continue learning on her own, but she did not want to give up this enjoyable time. Instead of being part of the class, she read at home and came in early to seek help from the instructors when needed. She was assigned to work with anyone who had just entered the class or was having difficulty. She had to admit that she was quite proud to have learned enough to teach others.

Here I am thinking I'm a teacher, but it does feel good to help someone. If I do say so myself, I think I am doing a pretty good job. I might have made a good teacher if I'd had the chance.

The family always had a get-together when the weather cooled off in the early fall. It was a time to spend together and catch up. Fall brought back childhood memories of the time when cotton picking was over and Papa had a few dollars to buy everyone new shoes and stock up on rations for the winter. On good years, there would be some extra treats like a bag of candy or cold drink from the store. She had told these stories to her family many times, but they never tired of hearing.

They gathered at Stephens's home in early October. This was also near the anniversary when she and James were married. This year would have been forty-eight years if James were still living.

After the big meal that was prepared by the children, everyone gathered in folding chairs in the pecan grove behind Stephen's house. The day was sunny but cool and pleasant under the shade of the trees. When Stephen called everybody together, Myra had a feeling they were up to something. She hoped they hadn't wasted their money on buying her a present. She had everything she needed or wanted.

BJ stood up, and after saying a few jokes about his sisters, he got real serious and started to talk.

"Mama, this is close to the date that you and Papa married. We are all so thankful that you are our mother. None of us would be sitting here with the good life that we all have if it were not for you. We all remember there were times when Papa didn't do the best he could, but there was never a time when we did not know that he loved us and loved you. So here's a toast to the anniversary of Mr. and Mrs. James MacTavish."

All raised their glasses of iced tea and said, "To Mama and Papa."

BJ continued, "You had to spend your childhood working and helping your family instead of going to school. Now you have made up for that. Yes, we all know about you learning to read—nobody told your secret—but we figured it out when we started seeing books all around your house. Our hearts burst with joy to know you will never again say, 'I can't read.' We talked about the best gift we could find to show you how proud we are of you.

"Stephen wanted to give you a million dollars, but you don't care about money. So he put his cash back under the mattress.

"Laura James wanted to give you a milk cow, but Stephen said not in his backyard.

"Idella wanted to give you a car, but we were afraid you'd stay on the road all the time, and we'd never see you.

"Wallace was going to give you a bunch of dresses, but you like to make your own.

"Ruth thought about sending you on a cruise, but she didn't have time to go with you.

"Of course, I thought of the best thing of all. I was going to give you a little dog like Jip, since you enjoyed having him in your house so much. (Jip was their dog when BJ was very young and lived in the country with no playmates.) That didn't work because there's just not a dog around that compares to Jip. Well, we were stuck."

As he went through the list, everyone was laughing and enjoying his remarks. Myra was beginning to wonder if this meant she was getting nothing.

Finally, Laura James stood up with a big wrapped package. "I think we did find the best gift of all. Mama, you know that was a bunch of foolishness from BJ. No way would Carlton let me give away one of his milk cows." This brought on more laughter and jokes.

Myra opened the package placed in her lap and found a beautiful Bible. Before she could start protesting that she had tried but could not read the Bible, Laura James started to explain.

"Mama, I know you had trouble reading Papa's Bible. This is a Bible that you can read. It is called the *Revised Standard Bible*. That means it has been written in words like we talk today. You had trouble because Papa's Bible was written the way people talked back in ancient times. It is also in large print. Try it."

Laura James opened to the first chapter of Genesis and handed the Bible to her mother. Myra wiped her glasses on her apron and studied the page for a minute before starting to read.

"In the beginning, God created the heavens and the earth. The earth was without form and v-o-i-d . . ."

"That word is void, Grandma. It means nothing," Bonnie Ruth added.

"If it don't mean nothin', then why is it in the Bible?"

"Grandma, it means the earth had nothing on it."

Myra continued, "And darkness was upon the face of the deep—I reckon that means the waters—and the spirit of God was moving over the face of the waters—yep, I was right about the waters. And God said, 'Let there be light,' and there was light. And God saw the light was good. And God separated the light from the darkness.

"Let me catch a breath," she continued. "God called the light day and the darkness he called night. And there was evening, and there was morning."

No one said a word until she finished chapter one of Genesis, but tears were falling from everyone's eyes, and then they started clapping loudly.

"Mama, you've done some remarkable things without an education. Now that you can read, you're gonna be hell on wheels." Only Ruth would say such as that.

The family clapped again, and all chorused, "Yes, you will." Andy added, "Watch out, world. Here comes Myra."

"James, what do you think about me reading? I could shore have been a bigger help to you if I had learned long ago."

. "Mama, you talk to Papa all the time. Does he ever answer?" Wallace asked.

"He just did, honey. He said, 'Old Gal, we shore did raise some fine young'uns.'"

When the day ended and everyone left for home, Myra continued reading her Bible. She sat in the swing as long as there was enough light and then moved inside to sit beside a lamp. Then she took it to her bed.

Dear precious Lord, thank you for my young'uns who know me better than I know myself. It must be that way with you too 'cause just when I need yore help, I find it. I'm so proud to have this Bible. I might fail, but I promise I'm gonna try to read every word—if I can just live that long. It's a mighty big book. Thank you for the gift of rest and sleep. It's always good to lay my head down after a big day like today. Amen, Myra.

She closed her eyes and was soon fast asleep.

The next morning, the *Atlanta Journal* appeared on her porch and continued every morning for the rest of her life.

Chapter XIV

1960–1961

Reading consumed Myra's time. She had an insatiable appetite to read as if she were making up for all the years when she could not even read the newspaper. She and her sister, Dolly, in New York City had a regular correspondence. Reading the words that Dolly wrote made her sister seem much closer. She continued to ask Bonnie Ruth to check over her writing so she wouldn't write something that she didn't mean. Once her granddaughter made a correction, Myra never made the same mistake again.

The "Book of Genesis" was slow reading. She was most interested in reading the stories that Papa had told her, but these were hard to find in such a big book. Arliss attended a study group at her church and owned a concordance of the Bible that gave the pages of passages and stories. She looked up Myra's favorites and placed a card on the page where each story began.

Soon, Myra was reading about David and Goliath, Daniel in the lion's den, King Solomon's suggestion that the two mothers who were both claiming the same baby should divide the baby in half, and Noah and the ark. Mary, Joseph, and the birth of Baby Jesus was her favorite. She was surprised and somewhat confused to learn that the story was written in more than one of the Gospels, and that each story was different. She talked this over with Arliss and realized that different people would never tell the same story exactly the same. Reading these precious words always took her back to her childhood in Sullivan's Corner when she played the part of Mary in the Christmas pageant.

Cold winter days that once seemed so long now passed quickly when she was lost in a book. Soon it was June, and she had to start spending time in the garden. She scheduled her day to spend time on both of her loves and went to the garden early every morning.

The Atlanta Journal often confounded her. There was so much that she did not understand since many of the articles were about events that happened before she started reading the paper. Some of it she knew from television. One thing that she always read over several times was any article concerning the civil rights movement. Young black folks were still trying to sit down in restaurants. Another group was riding on buses and trying to use the white restrooms. Many were going to jail and being mistreated. Myra still did not understand the right or wrong way to try to get better treatment for black folks, but she knew that turning dogs and fire hoses on them was an ungodly thing to do. She listened to Stephen and could tell he was troubled, but he never defended either side.

She scanned the *Journal* every day and clipped out articles or pictures of these events and stored in her shoebox. Somehow, this made her feel that she was at least doing something. It was a relief to put some of her thoughts on the garden. She always felt peace when she could get her hands in the ground.

The telephone was ringing as she walked up the steps with her apron filled with green beans and fresh-dug potatoes. *Who was calling this early in the morning?*

"Mama, it's Wallace. I'm sitting here holding the prettiest thing I've ever seen in my life."

"What're you talkin' about?" Myra wasn't excited. Wallace always acted this way over a new dress, shoes, or such.

"I didn't tell you until now because I wanted to be sure it would really happen. You know that we have been working with the welfare about adopting a baby. Last week, they called with good news. A thirteen-month-old baby boy was available for us. There was only one question. This little baby has a twisted foot, but she said it can be fixed by wearing a brace for a while. Grady and I weren't concerned about that, and we knew this was our son. He came home with us yesterday."

"Will he be able to walk?"

"Oh yes, he will wear the brace at night until his foot is straight, and then he will go to a therapist to help him learn to walk better."

"Praise God that the little fella can be helped. My prayers have been answered. You and Grady deserve this baby. Tell me about him."

"He's the sweetest little thing—got a lot of black hair—he's small for his age, but he'll catch up."

"Is he doing all right with his eatin'?" (Myra had nursed all her babies and knew Wallace could not do this. Therefore she wondered about it but didn't know how to ask).

"Everything is fine. He takes formula from a bottle and is eating baby food. He has an appetite. He hardly cries at all. I think he has never known what it was like to have someone take care of his needs, so he just doesn't bother to cry. He is smiling at me right now."

"I know how proud you and Grady are. I can't wait to see him."

"We don't want to travel with him for a few weeks until he's adjusted to us. I'm going to ask Stephen to bring you here to see him."

"Hey, Grandma, you got ya another fine grandson." Someone else got on the phone.

"Ruth, are you there already?"

"I couldn't wait. As soon as Wallace called to tell me they were getting him, I got in the car and headed to Macon."

"That sounds like you. You can be a big help. Now put Wallace back on the phone."

"I'm right here, Mama," said the new mother.

"What's his name gonna be?"

"There was never any question about his name. He is James Grady Findley."

"That's a right fittin' name. Yore papa would be honored to have a grandson carryin' his name, and you added Grady's name. What will we call him?"

"Why, James, of course—now, you don't tell the others. I want to hear their voices when they hear the news. I did call Ruth first. She had offered to come and help me with him until I get used to tending a baby. I'm thankful for I shore needed her."

Baby noises and cooing could be heard in the background, the sweetest sound in the world.

"I'm hangin' up. You better tend to yore young'un."

"I will, Mama, I will. Come to see us soon."

Tears streamed down Myra's cheeks. "Why am I squallin' when I'm so happy?"

These were tears of relief. Her heart had ached with her daughter's heartbreak at not being able to have a baby.

Dear Lord in Heaven, you have done the right thing—not that you don't always—just that sometimes we don't know it right away. This little boy will have all the love and care in the world. Aside from havin' him to love and raise, they are helpin' a little fella who needs extra care. I know they're up to it. I praise you, Lord, and thank you for all your goodness and love for old Myra. James, are you listenin'? If you are, I know you're mighty happy. Every time I call his name, James, I will think of you. Excuse me for lettin' James butt in, but I couldn't seem to help it. Hope that wasn't a bad thing. Amen, Myra.

Stephen hurried to Myra as soon as he heard the news. He was as excited as she had ever seen him. All his life he held a soft spot in his heart for his little sister, Wallace. He knew she had a harder time than any of the others because of the seizures. Folks called them fits and treated her like she was strange. Now she owned her own shop, a nice house in Macon, had a good husband, and at last her own son. He had always believed that good would come to folks who were deserving, and his little sister deserved much good in her life.

"Mama, I can't wait to see that little fella and see Wallace and Grady with him. Let's go over Sunday. It doesn't take long to drive to Macon. We can leave after church and stop on the way for some dinner. We won't stay long. How does that sound?"

"Sounds just right. You call and tell her. Now I have to buy some presents for him."

"I'm going to wait until we see what they need. I want to buy him something useful, like a stroller."

"You're gonna let Bonnie Ruth and Andy go with us, ain't ya? They'll be as excited as we are to see their new cousin."

"Of course, Mama. They wouldn't miss this for the world."

When they arrived Sunday afternoon, Grady, beaming from ear to ear, met them at the door and led them to the screened back porch.

Wallace was sitting on the porch, and little James was standing up holding on to the sides of the play pen. Of course, it was filled with toys.

"Lord, look at that pretty little boy. He's pulling up and trying to walk." Myra glanced quickly at his little twisted foot. "Hand him to me. I got to get my hands on him."

Grady put him into Myra's arms, and she kissed him and said, "Come here to yore grandma, James." The baby looked up and gave a big smile. These two were bonded for life. He was passed from lap to lap and ended up falling asleep snuggled in Arliss's lap.

It was hard to leave, but Myra knew that she would be able to have plenty of time with this grandchild. That caused her to regret how little she got to see Laura Jean when she was a baby—and she still didn't get to be with her as much as she wished.

On the drive home, the talk was all about little James. Myra had a thought on his foot. "You saw how he walked around the playpen draggin' that foot. I betcha it got twisted because he walked around sideways in his bed at that home. Pore little thing, probably hardly ever got out of that bed or had anyone to hold him. I 'spect there was so many babies bein' kept there that the folks workin' couldn't get around to them often."

Stephen nodded and said, "That's a thought—could have caused it to be deformed. You can bet it will get fixed soon because he will have the best care they can find. It's a blessing that Wallace and Grady are there for him."

"He is fine-looking with that dark hair and eyes. His skin is a little darker too. I betcha he might have Indian blood like me. Wouldn't that be somethin'?" Myra added.

"I noticed that too. No matter what kind of folks he came from, he is all ours now. He is a Findley and a MacTavish. Ma, I'm proud to know I came from Native Americans. Andy keeps reminding me that this was their country first. He thinks that might help him in his campaign for governor." Stephen chuckled but was always supportive of his son's ambition.

Chapter XV

1962

All seats in the auditorium of Swainsboro High School were filled, and folks were having to sit on the bleachers that were used for basketball games. This wasn't a problem for Myra, Laura James, Carlton, Stephen, Arliss, Bonnie Ruth, and Andy, for they arrived an hour ahead of time and were waiting when the principal unlocked the door.

Idella came alone and was surprised to see her family. She had expected to be the only family member to see her daughter graduate. LeGrand had been unable to attend Laura Jean's activities during his illness, but she knew he would not have missed this occasion. She did not think of him often, but tonight, she missed his presence beside her. When she walked in and started looking for a seat on the bleachers, Stephen stood up and pointed to the seat saved for her. Of course, she should have known they would attend the graduation of their beloved Laura Jean.

Idella was late because she and Laura Jean had a fuss just before time to leave. Laura Jean left and walked to the school carrying her cap and gown, but Idella waited a bit to calm down from the argument.

The dispute had started when Idella mentioned the generous amount of money her daughter had received as graduation gifts and demanded that she save it until she went to business school in Macon in the fall. She did not have the means to send her daughter to college as LeGrand had planned. She could finance a year in business school only if Laura Jean lived with Grady and Wallace. Since Wallace worked full time in the shop, this would be a help to her with little James as well as saving money on living expenses. Laura Jean was not included when this arrangement was made, and Wallace was skeptical that her niece might have other plans.

When her mother brought up the subject of business school, Laura Jean exploded, "I am not going to business school. I have prepared for college, and I will do anything I have to do to go to college and get a degree."

"There's no way on earth I can pay for that, and you know it. If your daddy had lived, he would have sent you to GSCW, but I can barely keep up with the bills now. You ought to be thankful to go to business school and have the chance to learn a way to earn a living. You probably can get a job in the bank or maybe with one of the lawyers when you finish. You're smart, and they'd be glad to hire you."

"You don't have to make plans for me. I refuse to spend my life like you as somebody's helper. I'm going to be a writer, and I already know how to type. I'm leaving as soon as I get back from the senior trip. I'd skip that except I helped raise most of the money to pay for it, and I do want to go to Washington DC."

"You're leaving—where the hell do you think you're going?"

"To Atlanta—that's the only place in Georgia that I would live."

"Where will you live? Where do you think you can go to college and pay nothing?"

"Mama, you've always tried to run my life, but this is too important for me to obey you. I have been investigating this for a long time. I applied and received a scholarship to Georgia State that will pay my tuition. They will help me get a part-time job to pay for my living expenses. I can get a room in the YWCA that is close enough to the college for me to walk."

"You've been doing all this conniving behind my back . . . ." Idella couldn't say more, for Laura Jean grabbed her graduation robe and ran out to walk the two blocks to the high school. Idella bawled until her eyes were red and puffy but then realized that she had to rush to the school to see her only child graduate.

Myra could tell her daughter was upset and had been crying. Maybe it was just sadness to see her little girl grow up. When the processional started down the aisle, Myra's heart burst with pride. Graduating from high school was not as unlikely an accomplishment as it was in Myra's day, but she continued to look on it as a rare opportunity.

Idella and Laura James graduated from Glencoe High School before the Depression. She still felt sad that Stephen,

Ruth, and Wallace did not have the chance to graduate. Stephen dropped out of school and went to work to help the family. When they had to move to the country, the school was too far away for the younger girls to walk, and they had no other way. BJ was lucky enough to miss that time and not only graduated from high school but the University of Georgia and law school. Even if the other three had to drop out of school early, she had to say that they had done very well in their lives.

James, they got all that from you. You was a smart man, and I wish I coulda been more of a helper to you. Maybe we wouldn't have fussed so much if I hadn't been so ignorant. James was always included in her thoughts.

This was a night to be proud of her granddaughter. Laura Jean was valedictorian of the class and gave a speech that she had written herself. Myra listened to every word she said about reaching for your dreams and letting nothing stop you. As her daughter was speaking, Idella started to cry silently.

Laura Jean received several awards that were medals or certificates. The awards were for good citizenship, being the valedictorian, having the highest grade in history, and for being the editor of the newspaper. The last award was handed out by the bank president. He first talked about how the bank wanted to honor students who could be leaders and encourage them to continue their education in college.

The bank president continued and said, "The National Bank of Swainsboro is proud to award a one-thousand-dollar scholarship to the college of her choice to—Laura Jean Porter!"

The entire auditorium of people stood up and clapped. The family joined the folks standing and clapped until their hands were sore. Idella remained seated for a moment and then rose and joined the clapping.

After the recessional, the graduates lined up in the hall to receive congratulations. There was a long line to Laura Jean, and most were heard to say, "Your daddy would be mighty proud of you."

Myra watched with pride and knew how proud LeGrand would be of his daughter. He was a smart man with a good education and would have chosen college for his daughter over business school. Idella's wish was to keep Laura Jean close by and for her to learn a way to earn a living. A business course had enabled Idella to work and support them after LeGrand died. Myra did not know which would be the most helpful, but she couldn't get the words from her granddaughter's speech out of her mind. "We must always reach for our dreams and let nothing stand in our way." *How will that turn out for my granddaughter?*

When the last folks finished congratulating the students and left the school, the family got into their cars and returned to Idella's house. Laura Jane had brought her niece's favorite pound cake, and Carlton stopped at the Dairy Queen and bought several flavors of ice cream. They meant to have a celebration for Laura Jean. It started out that way but turned quickly into a tense situation.

Stephen wanted to know more details about the scholarship, and Laura Jean was eager to share, for she knew her uncle respected her ambitions.

"The Georgia State scholarship will pay my tuition, and the thousand dollars from the bank will help pay for my books and fees. The college will get me a part-time job, and maybe I can get a second job in a store on Saturdays. If I go to summer school every year, I could graduate in three years plus one summer. I will do that unless I need to work. The bank will give the money directly to Georgia State, and I can draw on it as needed."

"I'm impressed at how you have taken care of this on your own, Laura Jean. I know you'll make it. A girl that won all the honors that you did *should* definitely go to college." Stephen looked right at Idella as he spoke.

"You don't forget that if you get in a tight spot, there's folks you can call on," Carlton added.

Idella kept quiet as long as she could. She didn't want to start a commotion, but she was upset that they all seemed to know more than her mother about what was best for her daughter.

"That's fine for you to say, Stephen. You'll be able to send your young'ens to any fancy college they choose, but I would struggle to send her to business school for a year, and I can only do that if she lives with Wallace. I despise that old man Thompson from the bank. He had no right messing in my affairs. He's always got something up his sleeve. I don't trust him at all."

"Mama, he didn't just pick me. I applied for the scholarship. The principal called the four seniors with the highest grades into his office and told us that we could apply for the scholarship. I filled in the forms and wrote an essay about my goals in life."

"Why didn't I know anything about you applying for a scholarship?" her mother asked.

"I didn't tell because I didn't really think I would get it. Larry Snooks from Lexsy wants to be a preacher, and I thought for sure that would win over someone wanting to be a writer. Also, I knew you would pitch a fit—just like you're doing now."

"Well, Missy, you're not going to Atlanta, and that's final. The way you're acting, you're not going anywhere." Idella had to make one last attempt, but she knew she was defeated.

Stephen wanted to turn the tide to a more positive outlook and said, "I have an idea, Laura Jean. Let's call your uncle BJ and tell him about the scholarship and see if he has some advice for you. He knows all about that college and living in Atlanta."

"Do that, Stephen. It'd be good to know BJ will be close by if she needs him." That thought set Myra's mind at ease.

"Well, that's a long-distance call, and I can't pay for you to talk long."

Stephen had expected this remark from his sister. "Don't worry, Idella. I'll ask the operator for the charges and leave the money to pay for it. I'll dial him right now."

BJ was delighted to hear about the scholarship and encouraged Laura Jean after she told him her plans. During the time they were talking, Idella went out to the porch so she would not hear the conversation.

The call ended with Myra and BJ talking, and he made her feel comfortable with her granddaughter's plan. Stephen walked onto the porch and sat down in the swing with his oldest sister.

"Idella, I know it is hard to have your baby leaving you all alone, but you've got to think about her. She's so smart and deserves this chance to go to college. I wouldn't hesitate a minute if it were one of my young'uns. BJ said that is a fine school and as good as the University of Georgia, but it's new and not as large. He said that is the best place for her to go if she wants to study writing. Living in the YWCA is a good choice. It stands for Young Women's Christian Association."

"I know what it means, Stephen. I may be poor, but I'm not dumb."

"Nobody ever thought that you were, Idella. Sounds like BJ wants to take her under his wing and advise her. He said he would come down the weekend after she gets back from the senior trip and take her to Atlanta. He'll help her get registered for the summer session and moved into the YWCA. Now I will say one more thing, and then I will hush. That little girl has gone through some hard times in her young life. She has earned the right to live her life as she chooses. I want you to promise me that you won't fuss with her anymore. Let the last week she'll be at home with you be a happy memory."

Idella broke down then, put her head on her brother's shoulder, and cried. She was defeated and now had to make peace with her daughter.

Chapter XVI

1963–1964

Laura Jean's first year of college fulfilled her dreams and aspirations. Georgia State was not the ivy-covered buildings of a picturesque college with football, antebellum sorority houses and carefree undergraduates. Ironically, the main building was located on Ivy Street and had originally been a garage with ramps for hallways. The ramps were very practical locomotion for busy and focused learners. It was a place for students obsessed with the desire for a college degree and willing to forgo the amenities to attend an affordable college by working a part-time job. It was the perfect fit for Laura Jean. She fell in love with Atlanta and the opportunities offered, and the city seemed to love her back.

Living in the YWCA with girls her age changed her personality completely. She became outgoing and fun loving.

Her grades—except for math—were all As, just like high school. She found the courses fascinating and had an insatiable appetite for reading books of all kinds. English classes were her first love because these involved writing, and her professors immediately recognized her talent.

She had an afternoon job as a file clerk for an insurance company and Saturday job selling children's clothes at Rich's. Her two salaries provided enough money to pay for her room and meals eaten in school cafeteria or one of the small grills around the campus. She had found a lot of cheap places to eat in Atlanta and dined regularly on Krystal burgers (which at that time cost twenty-five cents). Life was good for Laura Jean, and she was excited about her future.

Relations with her mother were strained, at best. Actually, she could never remember a time when she and her mother were in agreement. Memories of her father were shrouded by his illness and feelings of regret that she had no recollections of a warm family life. She often thought of him and wondered if they might have grown closer if he had known her when she was more mature. Somehow she felt this would be true.

Love was never lacking in her life and was expressed by her aunts, uncles, and mostly her grandmother. She secretly adored her mother and knew that her mother felt the same, but neither had ever learned to express this comfortably.

Her mother often played the piano in the late afternoon. Laura Jean usually did not recognize the haunting and melancholy tunes, and sadness would permeate the house. This could have been an opportune time to sit beside her mother and show love and support, but she never entered the room to interrupt the solitude.

Dislike for piano lessons remained an unspoken contention between them. Her mother felt Laura Jean did not appreciate the opportunity to learn to play the piano. Laura Jean had no interest but suffered through an hour of practice at home each afternoon and an hour lesson each week with the disagreeable instructor who had no patience for an unmotivated student.

Finally, after five years of unproductive lessons, her father stepped in on her behalf. He had never commented on the piano lessons, but he must have taken an interest that Laura Jean did not realize.

"Idella, this is enough. If she has not developed an interest in learning the piano in five years, it is not going to happen. I can't blame her. The little girl has no talent, nor the love for music like you. Let's give her a chance to find what she does enjoy and can do well."

That was the end of a career in music for Laura Jean, but she continued to feel that she had been a failure and disappointment to her mother. This was another memory of her father that showed they were compatible and that he was involved in her life.

In sophomore year, she had her first course in journalism and found her vocation. Her sights were set on getting an internship with the *Atlanta Journal* which could lead to a job on the staff.

Visits home were infrequent and brief. She worked at Rich's as much as possible when she was not in school. With their sewing skills, Myra and Laura James supplied her wardrobe.

Packages would arrive wrapped in grocery bag paper and tied with string. These packages tugged at Laura Jean's heart and kept her stylishly dressed. Laura James worked in a woolen mill and was able to buy short pieces of wool flannel called mill-ends from the company outlet. Since Laura Jean was so small, the mill-ends were adequate to make skirts from expensive wool flannel and sometimes enough for a dress. Wallace continued to give her store samples of blouses and sweaters. When she was home, Carlton usually slipped her a twenty-dollar bill. Every few weeks, she received a letter from Ruth containing a ten-dollar bill. All the family did whatever possible to help and encourage her.

BJ kept in close touch, and she went to his house occasionally on Sunday. Once she had a throbbing toothache and suffered until finally calling her uncle to ask what she should do. He immediately took her to his dentist, and Idella never received a bill. Life was good.

November 22, 1963, Laura was completing the first semester of sophomore year and already studying for exams. After her last class of the day, she ate a grilled cheese at Walgreen's lunch counter and walked to her afternoon job.

Back home, Myra had a cold and cough so was taking it easy on her couch with the television for company. She was thinking about Thanksgiving and being with all of the family. It was a good day.

At 1:40 p.m. EST, Laura was engrossed in filing and out of touch with any news events. Myra was semidozing on the couch with the television in the background when she became alert to the voice of the man who gave the news every evening.

Here is a bulletin from CBS News. In Dallas, Texas, three shots were fired at President Kennedy's motorcade in downtown Dallas. The first reports say that President Kennedy has been seriously wounded by this shooting.

Another bulletin from CBS News, President Kennedy has been the victim of an assassin's bullet in Dallas, Texas. It is not known yet whether the president survived the attack against him.

The newscaster came on live, sitting at a desk just like he did on the evening news. He looked directly at Myra and all the American people.

We have a report from our correspondent Dan Rather in Dallas; he has confirmed that President Kennedy is dead. Evening anchor man, Walter Cronkite, removed his glasses and wiped his eyes.

Myra had the same feeling as when the sheriff came and told her that James had been found dead. *No, they're wrong. This can't be true. I just saw him this morning on the news gettin' off a plane with his pretty wife in her pink coat and his bushy hair blowin' in the wind.*

Laura had no access to television, so the news came to her from a coworker. The office reacted in shock and disbelief. The office manager gathered everyone to verify the horrifying news and to dismiss them for the day. As she ran to the YW, it seemed like all of Atlanta was running home. The staff and residents of the YW were gathered in the reception room glued to the only TV in the building. All were crying as they watched the replays of the events over and over. Laura wanted to be alone and went outside to sit on the steps. *What would happen without this man whose heart was filled with caring? He offered such promise for a better life for everyone. Is all hope gone for us? Will life ever be the same again?*

Laura was not eligible to vote in 1960, but she felt the fervor of the campaign and cherished his every word. She truly believed that he was the one who could make a difference. *Now he was gone.* For the next days, she sat in front of television at every opportunity and felt her heart break over and over.

Myra grieved in front of the television through all the coming events and saw rerun after rerun. She remembered the hurt she felt when President Roosevelt died. His death was a personal grief for her because that president had put food on Myra's table when it might have not been there without government commodities. This president was young with little children and had so many plans for helping folks in need. *Why, Lord, why, do the ones who are trying to do good have to be taken?* There was never an answer for that question.

Thanksgiving came soon after the funeral. The family gathered at Laura James and Carlton's as planned. It was a somber holiday but a time when families needed each other.

The first two years of college were filled with work and studies for Laura. (She had dropped the Jean from her name.) She had a few dates but none that interested her and was content to return to the YW after work and concentrate on her studies. Sundays were spent exploring Atlanta and taking advantage of the museums, libraries, and culture of the city.

Junior year brought the first step to her future goal. She was accepted by the *Atlanta Journal* as an intern. The pay was slightly higher than her former jobs, but working hours were increased. When she first stepped into the press room, it took her breath away. Even though her assignments would be minor and mainly running errands, she had found her destiny. She was under the same roof as two Pulitzer Prize winners of the sister paper, the *Atlanta Constitution*. This was a sacred place for a girl from Swainsboro, Georgia, whose only experience had been writing for the high school newspaper. *Not unexpected—she always knew it would happen.*

Life threw her an unexpected curve. She had little interest in or time for dating, but suddenly she wasn't sure about this. Ian Wilhelm, senior intern on the sports desk, entered. His reporting on high school sports was already getting him bylines, and he actually had a desk. She was delivering messages that required a signature of receipt when she stopped at his desk. He typed away, ignoring her, so she waited until he reached a stopping place. She was beginning to wonder if she should speak up when he looked up from his work and said, "Do you need me to sign?" She looked into the bluest eyes she had ever seen and could barely squeak out "yes."

He scribbled his name and then asked, "Now how do I learn your name? I don't deliver messages." Was he making fun of her lowly position, or did he want to know her name?

"I'm Laura Porter. I've only been an intern a week."

"Are you from Georgia State or that little country school down the road (University of Georgia in Athens)?" Again, she wondered if he was serious or just making fun.

"I'm a junior at Georgia State."

Then his face lit up in a big grin, and his blue eyes twinkled with pride and said, "I'm a senior at Georgia State. I graduate in June."

He returned to his typing; no good-bye was said. Laura didn't know what was happening, but she hardly controlled the

giggles coming out of her. His name stuck in her mind—Ian—
Ian—Ian. She had never known anyone with that name.

Interns worked late on Saturdays to get out the Sunday
edition. This meant giving up her Saturday job at Rich's, but the
hourly pay balanced out. The newsroom was always humming
with activity, and she loved the excitement and clamor of getting
out the week's largest edition. They were dismissed one by one
according to the need for them. It was also a casual night with
lots of jokes and laughter.

Laura was sitting in the group of interns waiting for an
assignment when she was surprised to see Ian walking toward
her. Two weeks had passed since she had met him.

"Hey, Laura, I just finished writing up the Bass-Grady game
that I covered this afternoon. I'm going to get some Krystals and
celebrate. Want to join me?"

"I can't. I'm still working."

"You're not working—just waiting around on the payroll.
Nobody will miss you. The paper's put to bed. Go clock out and
meet me in the lobby."

Laura was nervous about leaving without being dismissed,
but Ian must know since he had been there two years and was
already a reporter. She grabbed her jacket and clocked out.
Several other interns were leaving at the same time, so she felt
less worried about being fired.

Ian was wearing a leather jacket like pilots wear with a scarf
around his neck. She had never seen a man wearing a scarf,
but it was appealing. She was surprised when he took her hand
as they dodged the traffic to cross the street to the Krystal.

The crisp fall air filling her lungs was a welcome treat after the smoke-filled news room.

He steered her to an open booth and said, "I love these little burgers. I could eat them every day. How many do you want?"

"I love them enough to eat every day too. They're so good and cheap. Get me two and a Coke." She brought a dollar bill from her wallet to hand to him.

"No, no, this is my date, not yours." As he stood at the counter waiting for service, she tried to figure out that comment. Was this a date—just for him and not for her—was it a date or just two fellow interns relaxing after getting out a large edition of the paper?

He came back with a bag stuffed full and two Cokes on a little tray. She watched as he spread a feast on the table—six little burgers, two orders of fries, and two slices of banana cream pie along with the Cokes.

"I got a lot 'cause I haven't eaten since breakfast. It has been a fast day for me in both ways."

Again she did not understand what he meant. She had a lot to learn.

"Eat up. I've been intending to get to know you better ever since we met, but I haven't been able to catch up with you at work or school."

He continued to say things that she couldn't figure out. Sitting across the booth and hearing him talk gave her that bubbly giggly feeling again.

"Now I want to know the following things: where are you from? How do you like working at the *Journal*? What are your plans for the future? And most important, do you want to go to the Lowe's Grand with me on Sunday afternoon?"

Laura laughed at his reporter-like questions and answered likewise, "Swainsboro, Georgia."

"I've heard of Swainsboro, but I don't know exactly where it's located."

"In southeast Georgia, halfway between Macon and Savannah. Where are you from?"

"I'm more southeast Georgia than you. I'm from Waycross, right by the Okefenokee Swamp. Now answer the other two questions."

She was surprised to learn he was also from a small town in southeast Georgia. "Answer to number two is yes, I love working at the *Journal*. It's what I have dreamed of doing all my life. Number three is I want a staff position on the *Journal* and eventually to write a novel. The last answer is I would love to go to the show with you. What are we going to see?"

"*The Birds.* Have you seen it? It's Alfred Hitchcock, and I love his pictures. You're not afraid of birds, are you?"

If she had been honest, she would have said yes, but she didn't want to miss the chance of sitting in a theater with Ian. Truthfully, she was deathly afraid of any type of fowl. This started when she was chased by her grandmother's rooster.

"It's a date then. I don't have a car, but I can pick you up at the YW, and we can walk up to Peachtree. Now I will walk you home."

"Ian, I love to walk, but how do you know where I live?"

"That's a secret that I will never tell." Again, his remark confused her.

"Where do you live?"

"In a rooming house on Tenth Street. I take the bus to Five Points, and then it's only a few blocks to Georgia State. That's how I get to school every day."

"How do you go to the ball games you cover?"

"The cameraman and I use a *Journal* car. I'm saving to buy a car. That's something else that I want to tell you. I only need two courses next semester to graduate. I will take night classes and work full time as a reporter."

"That's wonderful. That means you will be on the staff when you graduate."

"Yes, but that will have to be delayed for two years. I'm in ROTC and will be commissioned in the army as a second lieutenant when I graduate. Then I have to serve two years active duty. Being in ROTC kept me out of the draft. Also, I draw a little money for being in the reserves."

They walked down the night streets of downtown Atlanta and started a conversation that never seemed to end. Ian listened when she talked, and she opened up more than she had ever done in her life. She told him all about her family, her father's illness and death, the conflict she had always felt with her mother, and how thankful she was to have this chance for a different life. Sharing her feelings with Ian seemed natural.

He talked about his mother, father, and two sisters like he had enjoyed his childhood. He said his father was proud that his son could go to college and would not have to follow his father's footsteps and work for the railroad all his life.

"When I got my first byline, they framed it. My sisters both married young and have children. They never wanted to leave

Waycross, but I knew I had to be in Atlanta to do what I planned. Now tell me about your book."

"Well, there isn't anything to tell. I can't seem to find a story. Is a novel in your future?"

"I've been gathering research for years on the Negro Baseball Leagues, especially the Black Crackers. I have talked with a lot of the players, and there are some good stories. I work on it every Sunday if I don't have too much studying to do."

"That will be a great book. You should talk with my Uncle Woody. He played with a traveling team when he was young, and sometimes they played black teams."

"I'd love to meet him. Laura, I haven't spent much time dating since I've been in Atlanta. I was always studying, working, or just didn't have the money to spend. I want to be with you more, but I warn you that the best I can offer is a Krystal and a picture show every once in a while."

"You know I love Krystals. There's a lot we can do that doesn't cost money, and I enjoy walking."

"I've never met a girl like you. It feels like we are walking on the same path. Maybe we will publish our books the same year."

Laura snickered at that and said, "You will publish. They won't publish blank sheets."

"Now you listen here, Miss Laura Porter, you and I come from a state that produced some of the most famous writers. Think of Margaret Mitchell. My rooming house is near the apartment where she lived and wrote *Gone with the Wind*. When I walk around Tenth Street, I can just imagine her running down the sidewalk with all those wonderful words in her mind."

As they walked, he had held onto her hand; and several times in passing people, he put his arm around her waist as if to protect her. She wanted to pull him close to her and never let go.

"What is the curfew?" he asked while looking at his watch as they neared the YW.

"Eleven o'clock on Saturday nights."

"You have forty-two minutes left. Let's sit on the steps and talk until then, unless you are tired or cold."

She was shivering in her light jacket but could feel the heat from his body and that more than warmed her.

At one minute to eleven, he kissed her on the cheek and said, "Sunday afternoon, two o'clock." He waited until she was safely inside and then walked down the steps.

From her third floor window, she looked to see if he was out of sight, but he was still standing in front of the YW looking at the door she had entered.

Is this what love feels like? I know it's too early to say such, but I sure do like the feeling I get when he touches me. This is new to me. Shucks, he might not even like me after the first date. If I spend time with him, will he leave me? I couldn't stand that. Grandma, I wish I could ask you.

She knew what Grandma Myra's words would be: *Listen to yore heart, girl.*

Chapter XVII

1964

On their first date at the Lowe's Grand Theater, Laura didn't have to confess that she was afraid of birds. Ian discovered immediately when she buried her face in his shoulder. By the scene of the birds getting into the house, she was shaking.

"I'm sorry about choosing this show. You should have told me that birds frighten you. We don't have to stay." Ian was distressed.

"No, I don't want to leave. I want you to see it. Just don't pay me any mind."

"Are you sure? I don't want you to have nightmares."

"I won't, and I do want to see the ending."

Although she was terrified and knew she would have nightmares, it was worth anything to keep her head snuggled on Ian's shoulder. It was even better when he put his arm behind her back and pulled her over closer.

He whispered into her ear, "No more birds for you, my lady. Now let's get one thing straight—no more fibbing to me about anything."

As they walked along Peachtree headed to the YW, she told him the story of her grandma's fighting rooster and how he chased her and her cousins.

"You should put that in your book. Maybe the reason you can't get started is that you're trying to write about things you don't know anything about."

"No one would want to read about my d-u-l-l life."

"Well, I liked that story you just told me. Give it a try."

Holding hands seemed the natural way for them to walk. His hand felt soft and warm, and his fingers were strongly interlaced with hers. Strong, warm, and soft—that was Ian.

The next few weeks were filled with more dates, long walks, meeting between classes for a Coke, and after the first date, kisses and more kisses.

Grandma Myra always expected her to be home for the family's annual holiday celebrations. The one person in the world that she never wanted to disappoint was her grandmother. The newspaper would be on a limited staff of interns during Thanksgiving, so she could ride down on the train on Wednesday night and stay until Sunday. She would love the family time with her grandmother, aunts, uncles, and cousins but felt anxiety about the extra days she would have to spend in Swainsboro. Her mother would pump her for information about her activities, and she was not ready to talk about Ian.

The *Nancy Hanks* ran a daily round-trip from Savannah to Atlanta with a stop in Wadley which was near Swainsboro. Her mother received scrip from the railroad as payment for giving space in the paper for the train schedule. Laura had a pass to travel on the train until the scrip was depleted. The downside of riding on scrip was that she could not reserve a seat. She had to roam through the cars looking for an unoccupied seat. Usually, the trip could be started in a seat reserved for someone boarding at a station beyond Atlanta. This luck lasted until the seat holder boarded. Then she looked for a seat vacated by someone who departed at a station beyond Atlanta.

Holidays were hectic and crowded with college students headed home. On these trips, she had often spent most of the journey in the restroom which fortunately had a little sitting area. On the rare times when she had extra funds, she could stake out a stool in the club car and order a BLT and pot of tea. Drinking several cups of tea allowed her to occupy the stool longer.

"What are your plans for Thanksgiving?" Ian asked during the week before.

"I'll go home like I always do. Are you going to Waycross?"

He beamed because he had good news to share. "I've been assigned to cover the Shrine Bowl game between U of Georgia and Georgia Tech freshmen, and I can't refuse that. How would you like to go to the game and watch me at work?"

"I don't know. My family will be disappointed, especially my grandmother." This is what she said, but her heart told her to stay with Ian.

"I promise you a good Thanksgiving dinner. After the game, I will take you to a little restaurant on Tenth Street that is advertising a special holiday dinner with all the trimmings. Then we can be together all weekend."

No way could she refuse a chance to see Ian at work covering a game and to share their first holiday together. Her answer was "Yes." Telling her mother would take courage. Lying was the only alternative. Grandma Myra had a warning about lying. She often told her grandchildren that a lie would always *come back to bite you.* Laura had always honored that warning, but this time she would fabricate her reason for missing Thanksgiving and give an explanation to her mother that sounded reasonable and worthwhile. Since every minute over three on long-distance calls was costly, she was thankful the conversation would be short. Nothing upset her mother more than wasting money.

Laura dialed the number, and her mother answered in the syrupy voice she used when the caller was unknown.

"Hello, Mama, I will talk quickly. I just want to let you know that I won't be home for Thanksgiving. I have a chance to work at Rich's on Friday and Saturday for their big sale. I can use the extra money, so I can't pass this up. I am sorry and will miss the family. Please explain to them."

"No, I'd rather you come home. Your grandma will have a fit if you don't. You can get by without the money."

"Mama, my expenses get higher every semester, and my bank scholarship money is running out, so I have to start saving every . . . ."

"Your three minutes are up," the operator cut in to say.

Both hung up without saying good-bye to avoid the extra charges. Laura was relieved to get by without more arguing. She told her second lie about the scholarship money and was surprised at being able to think that up so fast. Actually, the scholarship money would last through the year. Then she had to start worrying about financing her senior year.

Thanksgiving morning, Ian, the cameraman, and his girlfriend picked her up in a green car with *Atlanta Journal* painted on both doors. In small letters underneath was *"Covers Dixie like the dew."* A card in the window read PRESS. Laura was impressed to be riding in an official press car.

"Tip and Gladys—Laura" was Ian's introduction.

Fans wearing red and black or white and gold were already filing into Grant Stadium, home of the Georgia Tech Yellow Jackets. Ian and the cameraman would spend the entire game on the sidelines, but they had seats for the girls in the lower section of the stadium on the Tech side. This was Laura's first experience at a college game. She knew nothing about football and only went to her high school games when she had worked at the concession stand.

When the game started, she watched intently, but her eyes were not on the action. She followed Ian's every move on the sidelines. At halftime, he raced up the bleachers bringing hot dogs for Laura and Gladys and wolfed down two himself.

When the game ended, she didn't know who won until all the folks in red and black yelled and clapped. Then she realized she could look at the scoreboard and learn the score. It was Georgia 10 and Tech 7. Now she could talk about it with Ian and say it was a close game.

After the game, the four of them went to the restaurant on Tenth Street for their Thanksgiving dinner. This was her first double date. It was fun to be with the other young couple. Both of them had regular jobs at the *Journal*. The cameraman filmed sports, and his girlfriend sold classified ads. They were all *Journal* people and felt a camaraderie together.

Ian was right about the dinner being just like home. A long table was filled with turkey, ham, dressing, vegetables, and desserts. Waitresses continually filled glasses with sweet tea and passed hot rolls. A wave of homesickness came when she did not find dumplings on the table. This would be her first holiday meal without Grandma Myra's dumplings. This quickly subsided as she watched Ian fill his plate with a little of everything. They laughed, joked, and all ate too much. Ian kept an eye on his watch and too soon said, "We have to head to the office to get our coverage turned in by the deadline."

Tip drove at the speed limit down Peachtree to the *Journal* office. Everyone raced up the stairs to the newsroom. Tip selected the shots he chose to use in a short time. Ian spent much longer at his desk working on his coverage. (She had learned from him to call it sports coverage instead of article.) She spent the time exploring the newsroom and identifying all the top reporter's offices.

It was almost eight o'clock when he called to her. "Laura, come and check this over and tell me want you think. When I saw all those kids in wheelchairs lining the field, I knew I had to do more than just write up a game." He handed the typed sheets to her.

STRONG LEGS RAN
Ian Wilhelm
Atlanta Journal Staff Reporter

Strong legs ran and kicked and passed and tackled. Weak legs sat in wheelchairs on the sidelines.

Bulldog and Yellow Jacket fans filled the bleachers. This rivalry was bitter, and the outcome of any competition between the two could break the heart of the loser—but not today.

Emotions filled the hearts of every fan in the stadium at the Shrine Bowl game on this Thanksgiving Day.

The final score did not matter. This was a game where there were no losers.

It was also a well-played game between freshmen.

The article went on to describe the game and how the scores were made or not made, the good tackles, and the usual report of a football game.

"Ian, this is beautifully written. I can't hold back the tears. You put your heart into the writing." This was a side of her boyfriend that she had not seen.

"They may reject it and ask me to rewrite and just cover the game, but I had to do it this way. That's what the game means. It's all about those kids and the help they receive at Shriner's Hospital."

They started walking back to the YW by way of Hurt Park, which was near Georgia State and in the center of the city. They felt at home in downtown Atlanta. Even though both were from small towns in rural areas, they were city folks now.

"Let's sit on one of the benches," Ian invited. With the full moon hanging low and the sky filled with stars, there could not be a more romantic evening for what he had to say. He pulled her close and then started to talk.

"Laura, I had made up my mind that I would not even think about getting serious with a girl until after I graduate and finish my army time. Then you came along. I want to be with you all the time. Everything I do, I wonder about what you would think. Laura, there's no way out. I'm falling in love with you."

Laura was overwhelmed. How do you judge if you are really in love or just love being with someone who makes you feel like you are walking on bubbles? She knew she loved her family and had a special tenderness for her grandmother, but she didn't get these same feelings. Is loving and being *in* love different?

"Well, say okay or nod or something." He was honestly disappointed when she did not respond. *Should I have waited longer? Maybe I have really scared her away.*

He got his answer when she pulled his head down and led him into the longest and most intense kiss ever.

"Ian, I don't know what love between a boy and girl is supposed to feel like, but I do know that I love what I feel for you."

"That's enough for now. You are the most beautiful, special, and exciting girl I have ever known. I can't be thankful enough that 'of all the newsrooms in all the world, you turned up in mine.'" They both laughed and shared the memory of seeing *Casablanca* together at the Art Theater.

Ian's write-up was on the front page of the sports section the next day. On Monday, the sports editor stopped by Ian's desk and said, "Well done. There might be a spot for you to write a weekly editorial for the sports page." Ian was on his way.

For the rest of the autumn, they enjoyed the glorious time of falling in love. They were so close that one of them could start a sentence and the other could finish. No matter where they went on a date, they always ended up sitting in a secluded spot to kiss and caress. Ian always said "I love you" before leaving her at the door, and soon she was replying "I love you too." Life was wonderful for two young lovers who had the world before them.

Both had to make plans to spend Christmas with their families. Laura was hesitant to tell her family about Ian, but he had told his parents everything about her and even sent a picture taken by Tip at the Shrine Bowl.

Chapter XVIII

1964

Laura rode home on the train to spend Christmas with her family. She carried a Rich's shopping bag of inexpensive presents for everyone. Ian had suggested that they save their gifts and celebration until both returned to Atlanta. They did not leave for home until the day before Christmas Eve so they could enjoy the *Journal* party together, and both planned to return on December 27. Being apart was too difficult.

The time in Swainsboro was usually tense for Laura and her mother, but this holiday was better. They shopped together and picked out a new outfit for Laura's Christmas gift. Then Idella looked at her daughter's scuffed loafers and decided they must go to Robert's Shoes also. Her mother had heels in mind, but Laura convinced her that she did not wear heels to work and wanted loafers. Idella grimaced but agreed.

Walking down the sidewalk to the car, Idella looked proudly at her daughter and said, "Laura Jean, I want you to wear your new skirt and sweater to Mama's on Christmas. You have become a really pretty young lady. Your eyes are the same blue as your father's, and that blue sweater sets them off perfectly."

The compliment came as more of a surprise than the gift. Her father had not been mentioned in years. Laura tried to picture him in her mind, but all she could bring up was the photograph that hung in her mother's bedroom. It did not show the color of his eyes. This made her wonder if she had inherited more of his traits than his eyes. She knew he was studious, enjoyed deep conversations with his friends, and read continuously. *Huh, not unlike me.*

On Christmas Day, Myra's small house was overflowing when the entire family gathered. After the big dinner and gifts, Ruth winked at her niece and said, "You sure seem happy, Lady Bug. I think you have something to tell us. Has the love bug bit you?" Her aunt was teasing but also curious.

"No, I'm just happy to be here with all of you. I don't even have a boyfriend."

"Sugar Pie, I hope you do have a fella. Just remember what Mama always told us, 'Don't let him look you straight in the eye 'cause that's where your trouble starts.'" Ruth chuckled.

Everyone laughed at Myra's tale of the first sex education she ever received.

"It shore didn't take me long to learn different. Look at this bunch of young'uns sittin' here." Myra joined them in laughing at that memory of her Aunt Nannie's advice.

The day after Christmas, Laura was in her room listening to records and thinking of Ian. Her mother came in with a surprise. "Laura Jean, you have a visitor."

When Laura walked to the front room, she was shocked to see Ian standing just inside the door. She had never told him the address. How did he know how to find her, and why had he left Waycross a day early? She was thrilled to see him—but how could she explain Ian to her mother?

"Ian, I'm surprised to see you. How did you get here?" She introduced him and tried to make her voice sound as if he were simply a school acquaintance, but she could not hold back the big smile on her face.

"I will show you if you'll come outside." He was careful with his words since her mother was standing beside them, and she had not acted at all cordial to his visit.

In front of the house was a small shiny black car. She could not make out the model.

"You know I have been saving my money, and my daddy's Christmas present helped me out a little. This is a Henry J, a car made by Henry J Kaiser, the man who makes Kaisers and Fraziers. It's the car of the future and gets twice the mileage of bigger cars. The dealer gave me a good buy on it since it's not brand-new, and I was paying cash. Come on, let's take a ride. Do you want to come with us, Mrs. Porter?"

Idella certainly did want to join them and learn more about this young man who seemed to know her daughter so well.

The car was compact and didn't have any of the extras of other cars. Behind the back seat was an open space that took the place of a trunk. With Laura's directions, they drove around Swainsboro. Not a word was said except "turn here."

When they returned to the house, Ian let his purpose be known. "After I got the car, I couldn't wait to show it to you. Instead of riding to Atlanta on the train tomorrow, I thought you could ride back with me today."

"I don't think that's a good idea. It's a long drive to Atlanta, and you would be driving after dark. No, she has to stay until tomorrow and go back on the train." Idella was set on this.

"Ma'am, my car has good lights and is in top shape. I wouldn't ever do anything that might cause a problem for Laura."

Idella took that as a fresh remark but only said, "My answer is still no."

"If you don't want us to go this afternoon, I'll spend the night at one of the motels I noticed when I drove in on US One. Then we can leave early in the morning."

Idella was wise enough to know a lost cause. "There's no need to do that. I have an extra bedroom, and you can stay here."

"I don't want to be any trouble."

"It's too late to think about that," Idella quipped.

The conversation stopped when Laura James and Carlton drove up. They both wanted a little more time with their niece.

"Aunt Laura James and Uncle Carlton, this is my friend, Ian Wilhelm. We work together at the *Journal* and both attend Georgia State. He spent Christmas with his folks in Waycross and stopped by to offer me a ride back to Atlanta tomorrow."

Both were a little taken aback, but Carlton responded with, "Good to meet you, Ian. That's thoughtful of you. That train will be mighty packed tomorrow."

Laura James looked him over and found him acceptable for her niece since he was nice-looking, well dressed, and spoke politely. "Yes, it will be much easier for her to go to Atlanta in your car than going to Wadley to catch the train."

Carlton was always curious about cars and asked, "That's a fine-looking automobile. What kind is it? I don't think I've seen one like that."

Ian gave the explanation of the Henry J and especially emphasized the high miles per gallon and the fact that he had paid cash. Carlton went out and looked the car over and even checked under the hood.

"Mr. Larson, would you like to drive it?"

"Yes, indeed." Everyone except Idella got into the car to make another trip around Swainsboro. Idella said nothing and walked back into the house.

Laura James and Carlton spent a few hours, and Ian felt comfortable to laugh and talk with them. It was clear that he had won over these family members. On the way home, Carlton said, "That's a good boy. I'm glad she seems to like him."

"I like him too. Idella wouldn't like Jesus Christ if she thought he was trying to court her daughter. We have to start looking for his articles in the *Journal*. Sounds like he has a good future ahead of him. I like that he's from Waycross and not way off somewhere," Laura James agreed with her husband.

Early the next morning, they packed Laura's things in the car and headed back to Atlanta. Laura was leaving with her sweetheart, and Idella was left at home alone.

New Year's Eve was celebrated with a special candlelight dinner at an Italian restaurant. Laura had her first glass of wine and found she not only enjoyed the grapey taste but the warm feeling it gave her. The second glass was enjoyed even more. Now was the time to exchange presents.

Ian's gift to her was a gold heart on a chain with a card that said, "A symbol that you have captured my heart."

Laura gave him a book about Shoeless Joe Jackson and a card that said, "Thank you for loving me."

Chapter XIX

1965

New Year's Day 1965 found Myra alone. Alone doesn't mean lonely. Sometimes, the loneliest place is in the middle of a crowd. In the first years after James died and even sometimes now that he had been dead for twelve years, she found herself feeling alone in the midst of a family celebration. Folks could be all around and trying to make her happy, but James was not there. *Will I ever stop missing him?* She didn't want to stop because she cherished the memories—even the painful ones.

Lordy, Lordy, the things I do think about sometimes just downright shameful things to think. Lord, I hope that ain't a sin. Somehow I don't think so, or you wouldn't have made men and women with these feelin'. Anyway, I thank ya that I can remember my James and feel the love just like I did when he was livin'. Amen, Myra.

Her hands had become so stiff and achy that she had to give up needlework. This was like taking a part of her life away. When she sat down, her hands didn't know how to be idle. Stephen's doctor said she had arthritis, and that came with old age. He prescribed pills that helped a little, but she didn't like the sleepy feeling that came with the pills. At least her walking wasn't affected. She knew a few ladies in the Projects who were crippled with arthritis and could hardly get around.

Christmas had been happy for all. Laura Jean looked beautiful and happier than Myra had ever seen her. She had not noticed until this visit that as her granddaughter got older, she looked more like her father, LeGrand, with his blue eyes and thick black hair. *She musta got his brain too because she was doing so well in college and had a job at the Atlanta Journal.*

Laura Jean had blushed and dropped her eyes when Ruth kidded her about having a fella. That was a sure sign that she did. Myra remembered how shy she had been about folks knowing she and James were sweet on each other. Myra hoped that her granddaughter did have a fella and that he was a good boy. The girl was old enough and knew her mind. Idella would pitch a fit, but she'd have to get over it just like her brother, Will Rob, did when she started courting James.

Idella was another story. In some ways, she seemed sour on life. Even when she was a child, she expected to always have her way. She jumped into marrying an older man to get away from the hard times of the Depression. LeGrand made good money and built them a nice home. Idella enjoyed being one of the society ladies of Swainsboro. That all ended when LeGrand had heart trouble and wasn't able to work for years before he died. Idella had to take over and make the living. After that, she just closed down and couldn't find joy in anything, even her daughter.

Myra always felt like she was walking on eggs when she was with her. She couldn't talk and share with her oldest like she could with her three other daughters. Maybe it would help if Idella could share with her sisters, but she had too much pride to do that and resented the success they had achieved. Myra knew they had all worked hard for everything they owned and enjoyed.   It wasn't a matter of luck. Stephen was up before daylight every day and worked as hard as a field hand. Woody had bad knees from his war injuries and sometimes had to roll around his restaurant kitchen on a little stool with wheels. That didn't stop him from feeding hundreds of folks every day, and Ruth was always there helping. Laura James and Carlton had started with a few acres and by their hard work now owned a big farm. Carlton still worked on the farm just as hard as he did when he first started. Laura James had a well-paying job as a supervisor at the woolen mill in Dublin. She left home before daylight to get to work. Grady had done well as an electrician. He had been smart to take advantage of the GI Bill to learn a well-paying trade. He and Wallace were a good team and saved to own a nice home in Macon and the dress shop. BJ worked all day and went to law school at night for many years. Yes, they deserved their good life and did not deserve their sister's scorn.

Reading replaced sewing as her favorite pastime. Arliss introduced her mother-in-law to the library, and they went every two weeks to check out new books. Myra's favorites often reminded her of childhood days. Sometimes, this made her sad.

Her all-time favorite was *Charlotte's Web*. She read it first because the words were easy to read. She kept checking it out and always cried when Charlotte died. That was life. She had spent many years going through the seasons of life and watching people and things age and reach their time. When she was a young girl living with her family, and even when she met James, she was in the springtime of her life.

In the spring, all life is new, and winter seems far away. Now winter seemed to come around before she could snap her fingers. She enjoyed the changing seasons. Spring, summer, and fall were pleasant, but winter was comforting. Sleeping under a soft quilt, sitting by a warm fire, setting a pot of soup on the stove to simmer, and the feel of crisp cold air were comforts. There was no need to dread the winter. Charlotte, the spider, died, but new life came, and the pig loved again.

The librarian often picked out books that she thought Myra would enjoy. One day as Myra hesitated in finding a new book, the librarian suggested *To Kill a Mockingbird*. The title appealed to her because she liked mockingbirds. When they were young, her brothers often shot bob whites with their sling shots. Enough small birds could provide a filling supper when smothered in gravy, but they never shot a mockingbird. Late every afternoon, she and her brothers used to hear a mockingbird sing from a tree branch. The mockingbird copied the songs of all the other birds and filled the air with sweet music at the end of the day.

The book was not just about mockingbirds as Myra had thought. It was hard to read, but she kept reading. To her, it seemed almost like reading parts of the Bible. It made her think of Rosa Parks and her own black friend, Rosa. The newspaper still showed Rosa Parks's picture now and then, but there was a lot about that young preacher, Martin Luther King Jr. She continued to cut out and store the clippings in a shoebox. Her box was getting filled. Somehow it made her feel a part of what they were doing.

The Bible was always by her chair, and she read from it every day. She had stopped trying to read it from front to back. The stories that Papa used to tell were in the Old Testament, and after reading the ones she remembered, she found the rest of it hard to read, especially all the begets.

In the New Testament were the stories of Jesus, and this is where she always turned. She repeatedly read the letters of Paul. In all his traveling and writing to folks about Jesus, she wondered if he ever wrote to his mother. Surely he had a mother who worried about him doing all that traveling and telling folks what they might not want to hear.

Civil rights demonstrations continued. This had become less painful for her to watch, and she decided if they kept at this, it could make a difference. These demonstrations started peacefully but usually did not end that way. Myra had some feelings for both sides, but she did know that folks should not be treated badly just because of the color of their skin. Her own mama seldom left the house because folks shunned her and called her a squaw. Her papa's family had disowned him after he married. Since childhood, she had resented her mama for not taking better care of the family, but now she understood how sad life had been for her one-half Creek Indian mother. She had given up her family and culture to marry and never had the comfort of being around people who accepted and respected her.

Some kind of war was starting up again on the other side of the world. She couldn't tell if the United States was mixed up in it or not. When she asked Stephen about it, he only said, "I sure hope not."

Well, James, here I sit wasting the first morning of the New Year just sittin' and thinkin'. Time to get goin' if I'm to eat collards today. Good thing I soaked the black-eyed peas last night and started 'em simmerin' this morning. I don't want to leave anything out and take a chance of having a bad year. Stephen and his family had gone to visit Arliss's sister in Florida. That meant they wouldn't be eating Myra's good-luck dinner.

It seemed a shame to have all that good food and no one to help eat it. She had never learned to cook black-eyed peas for just one person, so there was plenty to share. She walked over to the Projects and went door to door inviting folks to join her for dinner. Five ladies took her up on the invitation, and they spent the afternoon telling tales of the old days. Her day was complete when BJ, Ruth, and Laura James called to wish her Happy New Year.

Laura James ended her talk with a proposal. "Mama, I always feel lonely after the holidays, and the bad weather is depressing. How about Carlton coming over tomorrow and bringin' you to our house? We'd both enjoy your company."

Myra could see through her daughter's reasoning and knew she was concerned about her mother being alone in a time that could be lonely. That was Laura James's way of letting her mother know that she would not be a burden for them. Myra was ready to say no until she thought about sitting by the fire with pine logs crackling, cooking a hearty dinner, and eating with Carlton while Laura James was at work. She could have a good hot supper ready when her daughter got home in the evening. She loved Carlton like a son, and he treated her like a mother since his had been dead for a long time. She enjoyed going to their church because real old time Gospel hymns were sung, and they often went to the picture show on Sunday afternoons.

"I can't go tomorrow, but have him come the day after. I'll have to come home in two weeks because my library books are due."

Chapter XX

1965

Atlanta was covered in a rare snowfall on New Year's Day. Snow clung to the trees and was almost knee deep. Buses were not running. Ian called Laura at the YW to say he was walking from Tenth Street to be with her. He couldn't bear the thought of not sharing this rare event with his sweetheart.

When he reached Five Points, he saw Laura walking toward him. They ran together, embraced, and then danced around in the snow, laughing and feeling the sheer delight of being a couple in that special moment. They chased each other to throw snowballs, and both fell on their bottoms in the snow which brought on a case of giggles for both. Two kids from South Georgia having a snow experience they had only seen in movies.

"Let's go to Hurt Park and build a snowman, Ian."

The snowman's body was fine, but he looked a little bare without eyes or mouth. Laura suggested he needed a scarf, hat, and pipe

"Well, he's not getting my scarf. Give him your hat," Ian laughed.

By now, they were both soaked and cold but not ready to give up the snow. They cuddled on the steps of the city auditorium and said "I love you" over and over along with many kisses.

Back at the YW, there was an urn of coffee and doughnuts set up in the warm lobby, and they spent the rest of the day playing endless games of Scrabble. By nightfall, the buses had started running, and their fairy-tale day had ended

Ian was now working full time at the *Journal* and spent many evenings covering various sports events. Usually, Laura accompanied him and carried her textbook along to read as she sat at a high school basketball game. Studying and working intensely to make her name known as a reporter did not leave time for the leisure of watching a game. Ian understood and was glad to have her near to wink at during a time out.

She diligently turned in articles, but none were ever published. Ian kept encouraging her to find unusual stories. One night, they went to the emergency room at Grady Hospital, and she wrote about what it was like there on a Saturday night with all the different illnesses, crying children, and accident or fight victims sitting crowded together waiting to be treated. It was a touching human interest story, but she had little hope of seeing it in print. After turning in this article to one of the assistant editors, she watched to see if he read it, and he did. Not only did he read it, but it appeared in the paper the next day.

Buried in the inside pages of the local section was *A Saturday Evening in Grady ER* by Laura Porter. She was so proud and sent clippings to all her family. Ian framed it and told her that no matter how much fame she achieved as a reporter, she should always display her first published article.

Spring would bring Ian's graduation and army commissioning. They were having long talks about their future. Both knew their love would last forever, but they would have to be apart while he completed basic training and she completed her senior year. Future plans included the *Journal* and both completing a novel. A few weeks before graduation, he surprised her with an engagement ring. Her mother had not been told about their serious relationship or future plans—now it was time to tell someone. Laura decided that Aunt Ruth was the best choice to smooth the way with her mother. So she wrote a letter to her aunt.

Dear Aunt Ruth,

You were right at Christmas when you said I looked so happy that I must have a sweetheart. I had been dating this wonderful boy, Ian Wilhelm, and I was already crazy about him. I know that I want to spend the rest of my life with him.

He graduates from Georgia State this year and will have to go into the army for two years. After that, he has a good future in journalism.

He has asked me to marry him, and I said "yes." We share so many goals in life and enjoy everything we do together. I know you will like him.

Did Mama tell you that he came by after Christmas and gave me a ride back to Atlanta? He tried to be friendly, but she was plain icy.

I always looked at you and Uncle Woody as the way people in love should act.

You are always so happy to be together. My dream was to find someone to love and love me as much as you and Uncle Woody love each other.

I know Ian is that person.

What do you think?

Love you lots,
Laura Jean

A letter came back which showed Laura that she had made a good decision about writing to her aunt first.

Dear Laura Jean,

Your letter made me so happy. There is nothing like being in love, and it sounds like you have found your true love. I knew I loved Woody the first time I saw him, and I love him just as much today.

Ian sounds perfect. I can't wait to get to know him. If he loves you, I will love him just as much as I love you. You and Mama share the same spot in my heart. I have always been proud of the way you set out to make the life that you want and let nothing stop you. (You know what and who I mean.)

Thank you for sending the clipping. I have it framed and hanging on the wall at the restaurant so I can brag about my niece.

I haven't seen your mother since Christmas, but Wallace called and told me about Ian stopping in Swainsboro. She said your mother's only comment was "he's all right." Now, honey, that ain't bad for her.

Here is what I think. Hang onto that boy. He is a keeper. You need to let the family meet him, especially your grandmother. We will all be in Fitzgerald for Mother's Day. Bring him down then. I promise to make everyone behave.

Love you lots more,   Aunt Ruth

Laura felt relief after Ruth's letter. She had been uncertain about how her aunt would take this sudden news. If Aunt Ruth would be the one to spread the news, she knew it would be fine with all—except maybe her mother. A phone call would be too awkward, so she would write a letter.

She showed Ruth's letter to Ian, and he smiled as he read. "I can't wait to meet that lady. We will drive down for Mother's Day."

Before Laura composed the letter to her mother, she was surprised to receive a call. It was, of course, only for three minutes. That was enough to convey that Idella looked forward to their visit. Laura gave a long sigh of relief. Aunt Ruth had fulfilled her purpose well.

They drove to Swainsboro on Saturday afternoon to take Idella with them to Fitzgerald the next day. Her mother was in a rare good mood and gave Ian a warm welcome. Aunt Ruth had paved a smooth road.

The little house was filled, and many were sitting outside under the pecan trees on this pleasant Sunday in May. Two charcoal grills were filled with chicken, and dinner would be eaten outside. Ian was readily brought into the family circle and felt right at home. He hugged Myra and told her how happy he was to meet her at last since Laura had told him so much about her. "I love your stories, and I've told Laura that these are the stories she should write."

He won a staunch ally in Myra. Her greatest compliment was always "He's a good boy." The same way she described Carlton, Woody, and Grady.

BJ was impressed to meet Ian. "I'm happy to get to meet you, Ian. I always read your articles in the *Journal*. I like the way you write and mention things other than how the scores were made. I really liked the one you did on the Thanksgiving Shrine Bowl. My son, Brian, and I were at the game. We usually spend Thanksgiving with Mama, but Brian asked to go to this game. I was proud that he had that concern, and I choked up when I saw those kids in wheelchairs. They were having the time of their life."

"Thank you, sir, I am proud of that article. I was afraid they'd want a rewrite and just coverage of the actual game, but my editor congratulated me and told me they might want me to do a sports editorial once a week. That is what I'd really like to do."

Stephen listened and then added, "I usually just scan the sports page, but I'll start reading it more. I wish I had read that article."

"Thank you too, sir, but you also must start watching for articles by Laura Porter. I know they are impressed with her writing."

The rest of the family made an effort to have time to get to know Laura Jean's fiancé. They made a fine-looking couple. Ian was medium height with neatly cut blond hair and blue eyes. Laura Jean was short and came just to his shoulders. Her black wavy hair fell softly at her shoulders. The aunts were very impressed with the engagement ring. It wasn't a large solitaire, but the Tiffany setting made it sparkle.

On the ride back to Swainsboro, they chatted about the day and family members. Idella joined in the talk and seemed happy that Ian and her daughter were in love. She was pleased that he was college educated and had a promising future. Secretly, she was relieved that he was a young man with his life ahead of him. She did want the best for her daughter.

Chapter XXI

1965

Ian's parents and two sisters came to Atlanta to see him commissioned as a second lieutenant in the U.S. Army and receive a degree in communications from Georgia State University. Ian was graduating cum laude (with honor) and was also a distinguished military graduate.

This was their first introduction to Laura, although Ian had told them all about her and sent pictures. Ian's mother knew her son was seriously in love, and this would be her daughter-in-law and mother of her grandchildren.

Laura was included in the family celebration, and she felt like she had known them forever. The Wilhelm family's pride in Ian was evident in their smiles and hugs for him. These were South Georgia folks who didn't try to put on airs. College graduates were rare in their family, and they knew their son was destined for greatness.

Laura had often heard Grandma Myra's memories of her uncle BJ's graduation from the University of Georgia. He was the only child in the family who had been able to go to college. Now she would be the next to receive a degree.

Ian was handsome in his army uniform with the shiny gold bars on the collar. Their plans for marriage would be delayed until he finished training in whatever branch of the army he was assigned. He had applied for acceptance into the Signal Corps as a communications officer but wouldn't know his post until he received orders in a few weeks. Until then, he could continue full time at the *Journal*. Their plan was to be married after Laura's graduation, and he received a permanent assignment. Neither wanted an elaborate wedding, just the two of them and a priest.

As the Wilhelms said their good-byes, Ian's mother pulled Laura aside to say, "Laura dear, I am thankful and pleased that you and my son are together. I have prayed every night that he would find the right girl to be his wife. When I see the two of you looking at each other, I know that he has found her. You must come to Waycross soon. We want to show you off and have the rest of the family meet you. He will be coming home before he leaves for the army, and you must come with him."

Laura blushed and said, "Thank you. I appreciate that. I'd love to go home with him, but that will depend on work."

"No, I said come. They will give you the time off if you ask. I know they think highly of both of you." The lady was determined.

Laura's ambition received a boost when she was accepted to be a senior intern with the *Journal* during her last year of college. She was also given a full-time job for the summer. She found a small apartment in the home of a widow. Since she would be making more money through the next year, she could afford the extra rent. This meant she had to ride the bus to work and school, but she didn't object to that. An apartment would give her more time to be with Ian during the weeks before he left. She could cook their dinner every night. Of course, he would never spend the night. Both had agreed that was not the way they wanted to start their marriage. Life was good.

Orders came three weeks later that Second Lieutenant Ian Franklin Wilhelm had been assigned to the Signal Corps and was to report to Fort Dix, New Jersey, on September 1.

Ian was exhilarated. The orders gave no indication of what he would be doing, but he knew the Signal Corps dealt with communications, and that meant writing. The date gave him more than a month to be with Laura and continue at the *Journal*.

The apartment on Piedmont Avenue opened a new world of pleasure for them. They drove home in the little Henry J through the rush-hour traffic and usually stopped at an A&P to buy groceries for their dinner. Ian was as much into cooking as Laura, and they browsed magazines for recipes or came up with a concoction of their own. Both enjoyed the results of either. Ian never tired of spaghetti, and this was on the menu every Saturday night. He would arrive by ten o'clock on Saturday morning and prepare the sauce to simmer on the small stove in the kitchen which had once been a closet. After dinner, they often went to a movie at the neighborhood theatre or visited

Piedmont Park. Once they drove up to Lake Altoona for the day to swim in the lake and bask on the sandy beach. There were lots of laughs, lots of kisses, and lots of temptations. They kept their vow to wait until marriage, but Ian was the stronger.

They often sat outside on the steps and looked at the stars and changing moon. One night, Ian told her, "When I am at Fort Dix, I'll look at the moon every night at nine o'clock and know that you're looking at the same moon. I'll feel that you are close."

"What about the nights when there's no moon?"

"There's always a moon, darling, even when you can't see it. The moon is always there. You can see it in your heart when all your eyes see is a dark sky. I think that's called faith."

Laura had regularly attended church in Swainsboro until she started to college. Her father had been a leader in the church, and a memorial window was dedicated to her grandparents. Her parents always sat by that window. Everyone in the little church usually sat in the same pews year after year. When she was small, this made her feel special and wish she had memories of her Porter grandparents. Her grandfather died years before she was born, but Grandmother Porter died when Laura was three. She and her parents lived in the Porter home with her grandmother, and Laura was born there. Somehow, even though she had no memories of Grandmother Porter, she felt that they were alike. She had not attended church at home or in Atlanta since she graduated from high school. She knew her mother still attended occasionally.

Ian went to early service at a large Episcopal Church every Sunday. He never talked about his church, but she knew that he felt a deep faith that filled him in a way which she envied.

Near the end of July, they arranged to have a Friday and Monday off from the *Journal* and drove to Waycross. It was a strange but happy feeling to be in the place where Ian had grown up and meet his family and friends. She slept on the single bed in his tiny bedroom. The walls were covered with posters and awards. It had not been changed since he left. Quite different from her bedroom. The first time she came home from Atlanta, the room was as sterile as a hospital room. All her memorabilia was packed away in a box and put in the storage house (which used to be her play house).

Her mother had painted and redecorated the room. The only thing familiar was her little dog, Pee Wee, who was now sixteen years old. She was surprised that her mother had taken over his care and seemed to have grown attached to him. When she came home for Thanksgiving of sophomore year, her mother told her that he had died. She had waited until Laura came home to tell her the sad news. Laura cried alone in her bedroom over Pee Wee who had shared her bed and her dreams.

Ian took her to visit his former teachers, the shoe store where he had worked during high school, and all his family members—which seemed like a large part of Waycross.

They drove out to the Okefenokee Swamp because she had heard tales of it all her life. The parking lot was filled with tourist. They looked at some of the gators and snakes on exhibit, but she declined a boat tour through the swamp. The damp musky smell of the *Land of Trembling Earth* filled her nostrils and made her fearful of being on the swamp water in a boat. Ian didn't mind and told her tales of his high school job operating one of the tourist boats

They stopped on the banks of the Suwannee River which flowed through the swamp. It was mystical, and thoughts of the song made her feel sad.

Sunday morning, the entire family dressed and went to early church. They didn't ask Laura if she wanted to go—they just assumed that she did.

Walking into the little tabby church was another world for Laura. Ian told her not to worry but watch and follow him. Before sitting down, the entire family kneeled on the little pull-down kneelers, so Laura joined them. They stayed a long time, so she did too and tried to pray, but she did not have any words. When they stood, tears were running down the faces of the family, including Ian's. They knew the insecurity of serving in the military at this time.

The service was different from any she had experienced, and she was touched to see Ian so much a part. She even listened to the sermon and found it intriguing. During the prayers, the priest called Ian's name and asked that he be safe during his service to the country. She had only thought about him being away and how much she would miss him. Now she realized he could be in harm's way. Vietnam was in the news a lot, but so far, the United States was not at war.

When they kneeled for the communion prayer, she found herself repeating "Oh, God, keep Ian safe" over and over. Ian had told her that she did not have to take communion if she chose not, but when the cup and bread was raised, she found herself in line behind Ian.

What's happening to me?

On August 31, she drove Ian to the airport to take a plane to Newark. Before leaving the car, he handed her the title to the Henry J that he had transferred to her name. He was wearing his uniform which emphasized that he was really leaving for a different life that did not include her. After a few long kisses and vows to call and write, he disappeared into the tunnel leading to the plane, and she returned to an empty apartment.

After the workday, she had the challenge of filling empty hours. This was an unknown experience, since until now her schedule had been filled with Ian, work, classes, and studying. After spending so much time with Ian, she had lost contact with any friends that she might call to join her for a movie or dinner.

Maybe now was the time to get started on her novel. She had talked it through with Ian, and he kept suggesting that she write about what she knew. Her mind brought up every memory of growing up in a small Georgia town; there were lots of details but *no story*.

She opened the portable Underwood that she had owned since high school and typed the first sentence: Margaret was a girl of the sixties who knew what she wanted . . . No more words came. She ripped the paper from the roller, balled it up, and threw it at the wall. "Damn, I can't even begin. I can write about something I see on the streets of Atlanta, but I don't have a book in me."

Her time in the apartment continued to be lonely. She and Ian exchanged long letters every day, and he called on Sunday morning. Laura used the phone of her landlady since she did not have one of her own. They only talked on Sunday morning because the phone was free to talk as long as they wanted. Her landlady went to church and out to lunch with a friend every Sunday and invited Laura to use the phone during that time.

Ian's letters were filled with his classes, daily schedule, and learning about sending out press releases. This was intermixed with how much he missed her and loved her. Laura's were similar filled with newspaper gossip and her love and longing for him. Every letter was at least two typed pages, since both *were* writers.

They were committed to her finishing senior year and graduating. Ian would finish his six-month military schooling at the end of February and would receive a permanent assignment. He would save his leave time to attend her graduation and suggested they go to Hawaii to be married and spend their honeymoon. He would have saved enough of his pay to finance the wedding and honeymoon. This would also eliminate conflict from either family about a big wedding. Thoughts and dreams of marriage and Hawaii kept them happy. Life was good.

Both kept their pledge to look at the moon every night at nine o'clock. On a cloudy night, Laura always remembered that just like the moon, Ian was there with her.

One Sunday morning when she felt especially lonely, she dressed and caught the bus to the church that Ian had attended. She felt shy but took a pew and knelt to pray.

Dear Lord, I haven't had much experience with you, but you mean a lot to Ian. He is the best person I have ever known. I wish I could find the true faith that he has. I love him so much. I could not bear to lose him. So, God, I ask you to keep him safe and bring him back to me. I promise that I will come to church and do whatever it takes—I don't know what I should do—but I'll try. Amen, Laura Porter.

On the way out of the church, she picked up one of every booklet in the rack and spent the afternoon reading about the Episcopal Church.

Chapter XXII

1966

Ian's two-day pass for Christmas was not enough time for a trip to Georgia. Both Laura and Ian were disappointed but agreed it was not practical. Since his training would end in late January, he could take a short leave before reporting to his next assignment.

One week before the end of his school, he received orders and called with the news.

"Babe, I've got my orders, and it's a big surprise, not what I expected but a great opportunity for me to make a name for myself."

"Tell me quick. I hope it's close enough to visit you."

Ian gave a stilted chuckle and said, "I'm afraid not."

"Tell me—don't keep me in suspense."

"I will still be a part of the Signal Corps but assigned to an army unit in Vietnam to write press releases on the action going on there. It's a one-year assignment, and after that, a stateside duty to complete my service."

Laura could not comprehend why he would be going to Vietnam. She also was at a loss to understand why he was excited about being far away from her. She was terrified at the thought of him being anywhere near the fighting she saw nightly on television. She said nothing, but he could hear her sobbing.

"It won't be bad. I'll be there as a reporter. I won't ever carry a gun. These people are fighting for their freedom from the Communists, and our country is only there to support them.

"Think about it, babe, my press releases will be going all over the world. My name will be known. I don't want to be away from you, but there is one bright spot. I will get R&R at the end of six months, and we can spend it in Hawaii. You can meet me there, and we will have our wedding just like we planned. I'll miss your graduation, but we'll make up for that in Hawaii. We'll talk about it more when I get home next week."

Ian could make anything sound positive and exciting. By the time they finished the conversation, she was proud of his assignment and looking forward to Hawaii.

When he arrived in Atlanta on leave, he told her more about the opportunity and what it would mean for their future. She did understand his reasoning and tried to remain optimistic.

Laura took a week's vacation, and they divided the time between Waycross and Atlanta. The time ended too quickly, and again, Laura watched Ian disappear into the tunnel to board a plane that would take him to Seattle to board an army transport plane that would take him to Vietnam. They kept up a cheery banter until time for the last kiss when they held each other so tight they could have cracked a rib.

Letters between them crossed the world daily. Both tried to exhibit good morale. Ian did not include details of his movements with U.S. and South Vietnamese troops. He knew the only way to adequately cover the action was to be a part of it. He was usually at a safe distance, but he desperately wanted to show the truth of the involvement of the United States. Laura pictured him sitting behind a typewriter and far from harm's way. That is how he presented his daily activities to both his parents and his fiancée.

During the winter semester, Laura worked full time at the *Journal* and in the evening took the final two classes needed for her degree. She was earning her stripes as a reporter and was being given increasingly stronger assignments. Her articles and byline had appeared on the front page several times.

Thursday, April 4, 1968, had been a busy but satisfying day for both Laura and Myra. Laura had covered a session of the state legislature. The business of the day was cordially conducted, and several issues pertinent to small farmers were passed. Speaker of the House George L. Watson was a Swainsboro native and good friend of her father. During recesses, he always took time to visit the press section to say hello to Laura. This increased her standing with the press corps.

Since it had been a slow news day of legislation, she was inspired to write her article on Mr. George and the respect he was afforded by his colleagues. This was not front page but printed in a prominent spot along with a photo of the speaker of the house in charge of the gavel. The day ended with a feeling of accomplishment. After her nightly bowl of soup, she stretched out on the couch to finish the day with the evening news but turned off when coverage of Vietnam was shown. In her mind, she had to believe that Ian was safe and only reporting and nowhere near the fighting.

Myra's day had been equally fulfilling. Trees were budding, and all the yard was beginning to show signs of green. Spring always brought new life and hope. She spent time looking over the blooms on the potatoes and garden peas in Stephen's garden. It wouldn't be long before she would be enjoying her favorite vegetables. The afternoon was filled with a visit to the reading class at the Presbyterian Church. Arliss drove her over, and one of the instructors brought her home. She had worked with three students and felt each understood the sounds better. Now she was reclining in her chair and also watching the evening news. She also turned away when fighting in Vietnam was shown. Laura Jean had assured her grandmother that Ian was only reporting and not in the fighting. All the same, Myra worried. Bullets sometimes hit the wrong target.

Laura's graduation would be in a few weeks. She planned to receive her degree in the mail and not bother with marching in the graduation processional. Since Ian could not be there, she wasn't in the mood. Inviting her family to attend did not seem important. Uncle BJ's call made it very clear that she was wrong.

"Hey, Laura, I need to check with you about your graduation. I haven't heard anything from you, and I need to make plans. I know your mother and Laura James are planning to come, and they will stay at my house."

"No, Uncle BJ, I don't plan to go to the ceremony. They don't have to come."

"Listen here, young lady. You are going to be a part of the ceremony. Your mother and aunt deserve to see you get your degree. You can't take that privilege away from them."

Laura was startled that he felt so strongly and surprised that her mother and aunt wanted to attend. "If you think they'll really come, I will do it."

"I know they are coming, and so am I. It will be a MacTavish celebration. You know you are only the second in the family to graduate from college."

This touched her heart, and she consented.

The day before graduation, she and BJ met Idella and Laura James at the train which arrived at noon. She was surprised and pleased to see her mother so excited. They stopped for lunch at the Varsity, dropped by Laura's apartment, and then went to BJ's house in Buckhead for the evening. Laura returned to her apartment after dinner and would meet them at the ceremony in the city auditorium the next morning. Graduation was at ten o'clock.

Laura's mood lifted when she got into the line in her cap and gown and heard the strains of "Pomp and Circumstance." She was pleased with herself, and being a graduate of Georgia State University, an *Atlanta Journal* reporter, and the fiancée of the man of her dreams was far beyond her expectations.

After the ceremony ended and graduates marched out of the auditorium, her aunt, uncle, and mother smothered her with hugs and took many pictures. Laura basked in their pride for her being the second family member to become a college graduate.

Next, they enjoyed a long celebratory lunch, compliments of Uncle BJ, and then Idella and Laura James boarded the evening train back to Wadley.

Idella had much to brag about her daughter. She would be sure to have a picture and write-up in the next issue of the *Blade*. Many Swainsboro folks were interested in keeping up with Laura Jean.

A bouquet of yellow roses were delivered shortly after Laura returned to the apartment. The card read, *So proud of you. Only two months until Hawaii. All my love, Ian*

Her every thought was filled with Hawaii and counting the days until she was with Ian again. She started planning the trip wardrobe and looking for a suitable wedding dress—or maybe she should wait and buy a Hawaiian wedding dress. She was so ready to marry Ian that she would wear a croker sack. Life was good.

Chapter XXIII

1966

The date was set for both Laura and Ian to leave for Hawaii on August 6, three weeks to go. Reservations were made. Wardrobe was ready. Ian had searched out all things necessary for a Hawaiian wedding. He had a two-week R&R. The *Journal* happily arranged for a two-week paid vacation for Laura. The newsroom had given her a shower. Wedding day would be on August 8. Ian had located an Episcopal priest on Maui. Honeymoon details were his secret, but he had researched every possibility and made elaborate plans. Laura was receiving calls from the MacTavish family and the Wilhelms to congratulate the couple and wish them much happiness.

Monday morning, she sat at her desk typing up notes from a Friday night assignment. She was tapped on the shoulder and looked up to see the newsroom editor beside her.

"Laura, come into my office with me." He looked very somber.

Seated in the editor's office were the sports editor and the managing editor of the *Journal. Am I getting fired?*

The managing editor spoke, "Laura, we have some tragic news that we must tell you. I want you to read the news release that we just received." He handed her a copy right off the wire.

U.S. Army Signal Corps Fort Dix NJ Second Lt Ian Franklin Wilhelm was killed on July 16, 1966, by sniper fire in the Mekong River Delta of South Vietnam. He was a Signal Corps communications specialist attached to an army unit to provide press releases to the military on action being carried out by the United States. He was an outstanding officer of the United States Army.

When she reached the word *killed,* she screamed and fainted. She came to with all three editors fanning or wiping her face. A crowd from the news room had gathered by the door. Her first words were "Does his family know?"

"Yes, an envoy was sent from Camp Stuart to tell them personally before the news was released" was said by someone.

The sports editor cradled her in his arms and said, "We are all heartbroken. He was so fine, and we had great plans for him. Watching your love grow was such a pleasure. Now what can we do for you?"

"You are on paid personal leave as of now and take as long as you need," said the managing editor.

"I want to go home. Call my Uncle BJ. He's in my address book."

Someone appeared with a shot of whiskey which Laura refused.

In no time, BJ appeared in the newsroom. His office was only a few blocks away. He held his niece close and talked to her in a soft voice that no one could hear.

"I'm taking you home with me. Charlotte can go to the apartment and get the things you need."

She didn't refuse. She needed his strong arms and big shoulders. At BJ's home, she took a sleeping pill and went to bed. Maybe if she slept long enough, she would find this was only a nightmare. While she slept, BJ called all the family. They were shocked and devastated.

When she awoke after dark, BJ was sitting on the bed beside her. Charlotte brought in a plate of scrambled eggs and toast, but Laura shook her head and fell back on the pillow in sobs.

BJ spoke over the sobs, "Honey, this is hard, hard, but there is one thing you must do, and that is call Ian's parents."

"They already know."

"I know that, but you need to speak to them." He wanted her to learn more and about any arrangements.

"The number is in the little address book in my shoulder bag."

BJ dialed the number and handed the phone to her. Ian's sister answered the call and said her parents just couldn't talk yet, but they had thought of her first of all. The conversation was mainly sobs on both ends. Between sobs, Laura did hear that they would let her know as soon as they were notified when the body would arrive in Waycross.

He's not a body—he's Ian—don't call him a body. It's the body I love and have held so close.

BJ suggested driving her to Swainsboro. That was the last place she wanted to be. He offered for her to stay with them until she received word of . . . He hesitated as he tried to think of a less painful word to use and finally selected "the arrival."

She refused all offers and said, "I'll stay in my apartment and return to work until I leave for Waycross."

"That isn't necessary. They don't expect that. Stay with us. You need to be with the ones who love you," her uncle stressed.

"They love me. Uncle BJ, I appreciate your help and know that you love me, but I think the time will be easier on me if I'm working." That is just what she did.

Eight days later, Ian's sister called to tell Laura that Ian's *body* would arrive at Hunter Air Force Base in Savannah in five days. It would be escorted to Waycross by an honor guard. They were planning the funeral two days later. She apologized that her mother or father had not talked to her. She said they couldn't talk without breaking down in sobs, and that would only cause Laura more pain.

"I'll drive down the day before the service." Laura avoided using the word *body*. He would always be Ian and still alive somewhere just like the moon on a cloudy night.

Ruth called to tell her niece that she had reserved a motel room in Waycross and would meet her there. If there was any time Laura needed her aunt, it was now. Ruth well remembered the fear and grief when she got the message that Woody had been wounded in World War II. Thank God he lived through the war.

Both arrived at the motel about the same time. Ian's sister had asked Laura to meet the Wilhelm's at the funeral home.

When they arrived an hour before the visitation hour was set, Laura was embraced by every member of Ian's family and told how much he had loved her.

An American flag draped the casket. She walked to the casket alone and put her head down on the flag. It felt hard, and the flag was scratchy. This was not her Ian. When she had snuggled her head on his chest, it felt like her grandmother's feather pillow but also sturdy like it could hold her forever. Tears would not come. There was nothing to cry about. Ian was not dead. He was just behind the clouds and would appear again.

At the funeral service the next day, Laura and Ruth walked with the family in the processional following the cross and the casket. Laura looked straight ahead until Ruth took her arm and slightly turned her body. One pew and half of another was filled with Idella, Myra, Stephen, Arliss, Bonnie Ruth, Andy, Woody, Jess, Laura James, Carlton, Wallace, Grady, BJ, and Charlotte. Her family had done the only thing that they could do—stand by her. Two pews were filled with coworkers from the *Journal*. They ranged from the managing editor to copy boys. All were there to show their love for Ian and Laura.

Before the casket entered the church, the white pall used by the church for funerals replaced the flag that had draped the casket in the funeral home. The service followed the Book of Common Prayer, and the priest called him "our dear sweet boy who grew up with us, lighted our candles, carried out cross, knelt at our altar, and so often made us laugh. We knew he was destined for greatness. Now he has answered a higher calling." The priest also said that Ian was a man of love—for his God, his family, his country, his church, and for his dear Laura.

During the kneeling time before the Eucharist, Laura tried to pray but her only word were *"Why, why, why?"*

As they processed out to walk to the little graveyard behind the church, the congregation sang *A Mighty Fortress Is Our God* and then *God Bless Our Native Land.* Six soldiers in dress uniforms carried the casket. After exiting the church, the white pall had been removed, and the American flag returned to cover the casket. At the close of the committal, the flag was folded and presented to his mother, and *Taps* was played.

Laura bid Ian's family good-bye and promised to stay close to them. They didn't have to ask for they would be in her heart forever. She knew they needed privacy in their loss and so did she. She would go back to the apartment and grieve in her own way.

The MacTavish family gathered in a group around their beloved Laura. Words were clumsy for a loss so great.

"What are your plans, honey?" Stephen asked.

"I don't know. It doesn't matter anymore," Laura whispered.

"She's coming back home until she gets over her grief," Idella said.

"I'll never get over it, Mama, and the last place I want to be is in Swainsboro. I appreciate you wanting to take care of me, but I want to be alone."

"You need to do what feels best to you, honey, but remember yore grandma is here for you if I can help." Myra understood her granddaughter's need.

Ruth had other plans. The Henry J was parked at Ian's sister's house, and Ruth had asked the brother-in-law to take care of it for a few days.

"Well, the first thing we have to do is go back to the motel, change our clothes, pack up, and get your car." Ruth tried to use words that would not make Laura think she was being told what to do.

The Henry J had been left in the driveway at Ian's sister's house. They put everything into Ruth's car, and Laura thought they were headed to get her car. Ruth had other plans and turned onto Highway US One.

"Where are you taking me? I need to get my car and start back to Atlanta."

"Nope, we're going to the beach. You've never been to our beach house. There's no better place than the beach to think, walk, and cry. You can have the privacy you need. Woody has stocked it with food and turned on the air. I'll stay if you want but leave you alone if you prefer. I'll be close by if you need me."

There couldn't have been a better plan. Ruth's beach cottage was comfortable and not too large. After she had shown Laura around and was assured that being alone was what her niece sincerely desired, Ruth went home to Woody and Jess. Before leaving, she showed Laura the stocked bar and brought out a bottle of Frangelico liquor. "This tastes so good, baby, and it will give you a good night's sleep which is what you need right now."

Laura nodded with no plan to open the bottle. She wandered around the house for a while and finally fell asleep on the couch fully dressed. With no alarm clock, she slept soundly until a dream of Ian swimming away in the ocean jarred her awake. It was one o'clock in the afternoon. She pulled off her clothes and staggered to the shower. After standing under the hot shower until it turned cold, she dressed in shorts and a T-shirt that had belonged to Ian and sat down in a rocker on the front porch. The roar of high tide crashing against the beach muffled her thoughts but did not keep away the image of Ian's casket being lowered into the ground. Over the sound of the surf, she thought she heard *Taps*.

What do I have left that I care about? Nothing. If Ian is beyond the clouds, maybe if I walk to the horizon, he will meet me there.

She ran to the shoreline and started walking toward the horizon. She walked until the water reached her shoulders. The rough high tide kept knocking her over. She thought about relaxing and letting the tide take her under, but something always made her stand up. Over the noise of the surf, she thought she heard singing. It sounded like one of the old timey hymns that her grandmother sang to her when she was small. The words were *"Flying away when life is over."*

Did Ian fly away? Suddenly, she did not want to go under the water; she wanted to fly to him. Then over the singing, she heard her grandmother's last words, *Remember that your grandma is always here for you.* She couldn't give her grandmother any more grief than she had already suffered. She turned and let the incoming tide wash her ashore and raced to the house to shed her wet clothes and wrap in the big terry cloth robe that had been lying across her bed. She closed the doors to keep out the sound of the surf and realized she was hungry after hardly eating since she had collapsed in the editor's office. She found cheese, apples, and crackers and decided to try one of Uncle Woody's beers.

For the next week, she spent her time walking on the beach, talking to Ian about what she should do, and crying until she was exhausted. She ate no-cook meals from the stocked refrigerator and pantry. She thought she had finished all the beer until she looked in the storage room and found a whole case. On the fifth day, she made a phone call. "Aunt Ruth, come out. I need to talk."

Ruth was ready to go at a moment's call. She dropped Jess off at the restaurant and picked up a bag of Krystal hamburgers. She found Laura sitting in the porch rocker.

"Honey, I'm so glad you called. I'm here for whatever you need. Let's enjoy these burgers and have a beer. What would your grandpa James think to see us sitting here drinking beer?"

This brought a small laugh and the comment, "He'd say, 'Where's mine?'"

They ate the burgers, rocked, and watched the tide roll in until Laura suggested a walk on the beach. She was wearing her watch and waiting for nine o'clock.

"Ian and I always looked at the moon at nine o'clock when we were not together and shared this time. Even when he was in Vietnam, we did. Of course, the time was different. He was watching when it was night for him and day for me, but that didn't matter."

"That's a wonderful memory, honey."

"It's not a memory. I do it every night."

"Tonight is really cloudy, so the moon might not be out."

"That's the best time. We can't see the moon, but we know it's there. I can't see Ian, but I know he is near."

Ruth pulled her close, and they walked the beach under the full moon that appeared through the clouds. Laura would start talking when she was ready which didn't happen that night.

When Ruth woke, Laura was already sitting on the porch and sipping coffee. She got a cup and joined her.

"Aunt Ruth, I will never love again. Ian was my soul mate. I'll never want anyone else. What will I do with the rest of my life?"

Ruth knew better than to insist that she would love again. Her niece wasn't ready to hear that.

"You've got to go on with your hopes and plans for the future. Ian depends on you to do that. He had faith that you would be a great writer. You can't let him down."

"Not without him to help me."

"Just like you said about the moon, he's near and will inspire you."

"I have to tell you something, but please don't tell anyone else. Ian and I did not wait to have a wedding. The last week we were together, we just couldn't wait any longer. We knew we would be married soon, and it seemed like we were already married. I am so glad now. In my heart he is my husband." She looked up to see her aunt's expression and knew by the tenderness in her eyes that she approved.

For the next two days, they talked continuously, walked on the beach, sat by the surf, rocked on the porch, ate meals prepared by Ruth, and cried. Laura had so much pent up inside her, and it wasn't all about Ian. It was time to deal with everything. Ruth remembered Laura from childhood as being somber and having a barrier around her feelings that no one could break through. She understood some of the reasons but had no idea of the depth.

The barrier cracked, and long-felt emotions started spilling out. Her first confession revealed how she had never felt that she fit in anywhere except when she was alone with her grandparents or aunts.

"What about your parents?" Ruth knew the answer but wanted her niece to express these feelings.

"It always seemed as if I was the problem that made them both dissatisfied with their life. I know that my mother was never happy, and Daddy was more connected with his work and older friends. I knew about his other children, but they never told me about them. I just learned by eavesdropping. That made me feel like there was something wrong with me. Why did they marry? They sure weren't connected like Ian and I. I know Daddy was too old for her, and she must have been frustrated because she was stuck in a life that was not fulfilling. That wasn't my fault."

"Of course, it wasn't your fault. The age difference was a hardship, and then your daddy was sick for so long. I do know one thing. They both loved you with all their heart, and they cared for each other in their own way."

"It was fun to be at Grandma's with all of you. I remember on Christmas Day that Mamma, Daddy, and I would get to Grandma and Grandpa's house just before dinner and leave as soon as the last gift was given from the Christmas tree. When I was little, I would cry and beg to stay, and they'd get mad with me for crying and say that I didn't appreciate all the toys from Santa. I hated the drive home because they would always have a fuss, and I would cry and think about the fun Bonnie Ruth and Andy were having."

"Honey, I am so sorry. I wish I had told Idella that I was keeping you there until I left whether she liked it or not—but she still wouldn't have agreed."

Ruth related some of the background of the courtship of Idella and LeGrand. She described the family's hardships during the Depression and how her sister had so much vanity and determination to make her life better. LeGrand came along just at that time. He was a fine-looking man, well dressed with money to spend and driving a new Packard. As to his older children, Ruth could say nothing. She remembered how they had ignored Laura when they came for LeGrand's funeral. Ruth could not imagine having a little sister and not wanting to know and love her.

"All I can say about the older children is they must be heartless to turn away from their father and not acknowledge you. They are the losers, and you should never feel responsible for this part of your daddy's life."

Laura had question after question and expressed her confusion and feelings of guilt. Bringing the past into the open was the only way to move forward.

After sharing the depths of her soul to her aunt, Laura was ready to attempt the healing process. It was time to go home and acknowledge her fear of a future without Ian. Despairs of her childhood were now more acceptable and not a yoke of insecurity.

The next morning after stopping at the restaurant to check on Woody and Jess, they headed to Waycross for Laura to retrieve her car and start the journey back to a different life. Grieving for Ian would take time, but now she could expose herself to the suffering of losing the love of her life before they had started their life together. Her grief would be healing and not shadowed by hurts from her childhood.

"Baby, this has been a valuable time for both of us. Your love with Ian was the way love should be, and your grief for him is cleansing.

"Now, here is something that you must do. Make peace with your mother. She needs you, and you need her. Get to know her as a person. Get to know the Idella that I idealized my whole life. I know you will like her. You are like her in many ways— ambitious, determined, and proud. Those are good traits if you keep them in control. Stop in Swainsboro on your way back. Let the past go and just talk to her as a friend. I think she is waiting for that.

"The other thing you must do is stop in Waycross and spend time with Ian's family. They need to keep a tie with you. There are many things that you both will want to share. Promise me that."

"I will. I had already thought about stopping in both places. I will take your advice about Mother. I have always longed to be close to her like I am to you and Grandmother."

"You will be."

After the short drive to Waycross, Ruth left Laura at the Wilhelm's home and headed the white Buick convertible south to her husband and son. Laura spent an evening of closeness and comfort with Ian's parents which was filled with stories of their beloved son.

Chapter XXIV

1966

During the three days Laura spent in Swainsboro with her mother, the estrangement was bridged. Ruth had given sound advice. The past was left in the past, and they developed a friendship on an equal basis. Laura discovered that she actually enjoyed her mother's company. They shared their loves and losses, and for the first time, she realized that there had been a caring bond between her parents.

Overwhelming sadness and fear of life without Ian returned on the drive back to Atlanta in the Henry J. Ian had been so proud of the car, and she never let it slip that she thought it a strange vehicle with an even more unlikely name. She had a light moment when she recalled how he always referred to "the Henry J" vs. "the car."

What should she do? Was there anything of value left in her life? Through the next painful weeks, she went to work, did her assignments, returned to the apartment, and closed out the world. Invitations from coworkers were declined, and conversations were limited to work related. She knew they were trying to help, but she was not ready for help. She feared if her grief waned, then Ian would be lost to her forever. Sleep was fitful at best. Food was only a necessity. Weight loss and circles from loss of sleep attacked her appearance.

Her journalism suffered. She completed each assignment thoroughly but without the passion that had won her front page and bylines. A first-year intern could do as well—was the *Journal* only keeping her because of Ian? She didn't care if they terminated her—she didn't care about anything. Her mother came for a weekend and was crushed to see the state of her daughter. Desperate measures were needed, and Idella knew where to turn.

The next Friday afternoon, when Laura returned home, a white Buick convertible with a Florida tag was in her driveway. She knew the visitor, but she did not expect the accomplice. Laura walked into the apartment carrying her bag of meager groceries for weekend meals and heard a familiar greeting. "You come in here, sugar pie, and hug yore grandma."

The brightness in the little rooms startled her and good food smells filled the air. Her guests had taken the liberty of drawing the curtains and opening the windows. How could they be cooking in the tiny kitchen which had originally been a closet and furnished only two pots and a frying pan? They seemed to be preparing a meal.

"Ruth, you keep an eye on the dumplings and finish up the rest, while I have a few words with my grandbaby."

Laura did not know what to expect, but she did want to sit close to her grandmother on the couch and lay her head against her soft bosom. Myra pulled her close and patted her and said the comforting words Laura had heard in her childhood. Her most cherished were "It's gonna get better. It's gonna get better. Grandma's here now."

Instead of sobbing as she expected, she felt so secure and warm in her grandmother's arms that she fell asleep for a bit. She woke to see the little table for two where she and Ian had eaten was set and ready for diners.

"Come on and eat these good dumplings that you've always loved, and there's a pulley bone too," Myra said as she led her granddaughter to the table and sat in the chair across from her. Ruth brought out their plates—Laura had no bowls—filled with the steaming chicken and dumplings, butterbeans from Myra's freezer, potato salad, thin little hoe cakes of cornbread, and of course, sweet iced tea. Myra had prepared the food at home and found a way to warm it in the closet kitchen. A buttery pound cake waited on the counter. Since there were only two chairs, Ruth sat on the floor to eat. Laura relished her first full meal since the news of Ian. After supper, Myra was ready to talk.

"Now, baby girl, you're hurtin' so bad that you think it'll never end. When yore grandpa passed, I thought for shore if I just gave up, that I'd die. I just sat there awaitin' for the Lord to take me. I waited almost a month, but he wasn't ready for me. If I couldn't die, I had to do somethin' so I got busy livin' again.

I can't say my sorrow changed, but I knew I had to keep puttin' one foot ahead of another.

"There's somethin' ahead for you. You've got the gift and a love for writin', and it's a shame not to put to use the gift the Lord gave you. You get up every morning and say, 'Dear Lord, here I am ready to do thy will.' Promise me that you'll do that—just try and see what happens."

"Grandma, I'll try, but I just don't know the way."

"Don't you fret about knowin' ahead of time. The way'll come."

"Okay, ladies, the serious talking is over, and now it's my turn." Ruth got their attention. "Tomorrow, we're hitting Rich's as soon as the doors open. First, we'll go to the hair salon where those fancy French men work. We could all—you too, Mama—do with a new hairstyle. Then we'll shop till we drop—pack up all those old dark colors and come out dressed for living. We'll eat dinner in the Tea Room where they serve those slices of roast beef that you can cut with a fork. This is my treat."

Both Laura and Myra protested Ruth spending so much money on them, but she insisted, "Woody makes money every day—and I spend it." The next day followed Ruth's plan, and with the new hairdos and clothes, all were eye catching as they walked down Peachtree Street.

When the white convertible pulled away on Sunday afternoon, Laura had a direction. She didn't know where or what it would be, but she would be patient and wait to learn. Every morning for the rest of her life, she started the day with Myra's prayer. She customized it, and said, *I'm here, Lord, show me the way, and I'll try to follow.*

Chapter XXV

1966–1967

Christmas presented a dilemma. Laura did not want to cause the family holiday to be a somber day but knew if she spent the time alone in Atlanta, they would be even sadder. A solution turned up when a college friend suggested that they spend this time in an inn in the mountains of North Georgia. The friend was recently divorced and shared Laura's need for a quiet time, free of festivities. This turned out well. Both enjoyed long walks in the scenic area, reading beside the huge lobby fireplace, old movies on TV, and the elaborate meals served by the inn. Surprisingly, the family had agreed to her plans and calmed any feelings of guilt.

A few months into the New Year, Laura was called into the office of the managing editor. She knew for sure this would not be good. They had given her time because of Ian, but she knew her work had been lacking. She had expected to be fired but not by the managing editor.

"Come in, Laura, and close the door. (This did not sound good.) I have a special assignment that only you can do justice." *Does special assignment mean I will be put on the obituary desk or writing up weddings?* She expected the worse.

The editor shoved a manuscript box toward her. A note attached was in Ian's scrawl handwriting.

> *Property of Atlanta Journal*
> *If this is left behind, please see that it gets to them.*
> *Second Lieutenant Ian Wilhelm*

"Laura, this arrived two weeks after his death. We had asked him to write some columns for us during his tour of duty. We had not received any until now, but he was writing. I have read every page, and this tells a story that must be published. We are considering running it as a series for the Sunday editorial page with his byline."

She was so choked up just to see his handwriting that she had no comment.

"To do this, we need your help. Ian wrote it as a reporter to be run as news articles. We think it should be written as his own story. The facts, his impressions, his emotions are all there. Ian's heartfelt concern must be captured."

"What can I do? I will never be able to write with the sensitivity of Ian. He felt so intensely."

"And so do you, Laura. You have just never let the writer come out. I am giving you this assignment. Personalize it, put it into first person—*You* know Ian's voice better than anyone—speak for him."

"I will do my best. Thank you for caring that his work is read."

The editor simply handed her the box and said, "Get busy."

She went to her small office, closed the door, and started to read. Ian seemed to be sitting beside her and directing her thoughts. His words made the reader feel as if they were walking with him through the mud and hearing explosives going off all around.

Small faces with big wondering eyes looked at him as he passed. The smell of fear mixed with the smell of gunpowder. Hands reached out for a bit of food. He was almost face to face with the enemy. Homes and livelihoods were destroyed. Vietnamese, with all their possessions strapped to their backs, were on the move in hope of finding safety. Babies were crying constantly. Bands of small children who had been separated from their parents roamed on the outskirts of the battlefield. Day after day after day, nothing changed except the body count.

As the pages progressed, Ian's tone moved from determination to do the job, to questioning the value, to desperation at the hopelessness of the endeavor.

Laura read for three weeks and only added pronouns or structure to his words without changing his point of view. He told of an actual war that folks at home only viewed as fighting between two factions in a far-off place. He gave Americans a firsthand look.

The first article of the series received overwhelming interest. Readers responded with letters and calls. "My View from

Vietnam" by Second Lieutenant Ian Wilhelm filled a reserved spot on the editorial page every Sunday for ten weeks.

Near the end, the editor called Laura into his office with the glad news that twenty leading newspapers had picked up the series for syndication. There was champagne and much merriment in the newsroom that evening. Laura took no lauds—the praise was for Ian's words.

At the end of syndication, a New York publisher offered a book contract with the stipulation that Laura write an introduction and work in their editorial office as needed.

Ian's journalism would live forever between the covers of a published nonfiction novel.

Laura was off to New York with a salary and expense account from the publisher. Perhaps she had found her direction.

Chapter XXVI

1968

The first few months in New York seemed like a role in a play to Laura. Everything was different from the script of her former life. It was as if she had learned all the lines and was ready to go on stage, but suddenly her role was changed. When the curtain went up, there was no choice but to assume the new role.

Work on Ian's book began immediately, and she was immersed in his elegant words which touched hearts and souls. Her work was quite different than preparing articles for newspaper publication. This would be a story with a plot and characters. After a few sessions with the staff, it was as if Ian was channeling the words through her. The story took off immediately, and all were pleased. She was treated with respect and readily accepted as a colleague by all.

The efficiency apartment supplied by the publisher was convenient and comfortable for her needs. She occasionally accepted an invitation for a drink or dinner with her coworkers, but usually she returned to the apartment and prepared a simple supper to eat as she watched the news.

Thursday, April 4, had been a hectic but satisfying day for Laura. It was one of those days when hours were spent finding the exact words to express the character's emotion. Today, the character had been herself as she had listened to Ian explain his assignment to Vietnam. Near the end of the day, the lines fell into place. Now at home, she had shed her tailored business suit for jeans and one of Ian's T-shirts, ate her nightly bowl of soup, and stretched out on the couch to finish her day with a glass of wine and the evening news.

Myra's day had been equally fulfilling. She had enjoyed an early morning walk through her yard and Stephen's large garden and orchard. April showers in the late afternoons would soon bring a showcase of blossoming trees and flowers. She looked forward to seeing fruit trees and berry bushes blooming and knowing that soon she would be making the jams that her family loved with their biscuits. Stephen had already promised that he would send one of his workers to pick the peaches and blackberries. Then she could make the jams, even if she had to sit on a stool to stir. She walked around her yard and admired the new green leaves and small buds. April was always filled with promise.

In the afternoon, Arliss drove Myra over to the Presbyterian Church to visit the reading class. Instead of dropping her mother-in-law there and returning later to pick her up, this time she stayed for the entire visit. She invited the ladies from the Projects to ride home in her car. Myra enjoyed the extra time with her school friends. It had been a satisfying day for an old lady. Now she was reclining in her chair and watching the evening news.

The broadcasts were abruptly interrupted with a bulletin. *An attempt on the life of Dr. Martin Luther King Jr. was made as he stood on the balcony of the Lorraine Motel in Memphis, Tennessee. Shots were fired at 6:01 p.m. He was immediately transported to Saint Joseph's Hospital.*

Both Laura and Myra sat dazed and watched as the shooting replayed over and over on their television screens. Surely, he was only wounded. Look at the times he had almost been killed. He was Dr. King and infallible—not so this time.

The next bulletin flashed onto the screen. *Dr. Martin Luther King Jr. was pronounced dead from a fatal bullet at 7:05 p.m. at Saint Joseph's Hospital in Memphis, Tennessee.*

Laura immediately turned off the television. Another senseless killing was more than she could bear. He was gone. *Did he take hope with him?* Her thoughts shifted back to her church school teacher telling the class, "They could kill the man, but they could not kill the message."   The teacher was speaking of another man who was killed senselessly at another time and in another place. This did not take away the sorrow, but it did offer hope.

Myra scolded Dr. King as if he were one of her children. "What were you thinkin' comin' out on that balcony and wavin'? You knew better. There's always been somebody hidin' in the bushes awantin' to kill ya. Lordy, Lordy, why didn't you stay inside where you oughta been?" This wasn't grief but anger at an intolerable act.

Then she pictured his wife and four little children and hugged a pillow as she cried alone for Dr. King and all the injustices of life that she did not understand.

Life moves on, even in the saddest times. Myra continued her work with readers, and Laura continued putting life into the story of another slain hero. Both continued their prayers for peace and justice for all.

Chapter XXVII

1970

The sixties had been filled with heartbreak and turmoil. Myra hoped the new decade of seventies would bring peace and comfort. Arthritis was now her adversary and had kept her inactive through the cold months. This made her even more thankful for her ability to read.

May fourth was a pleasant spring afternoon. The warmer weather had lessened her arthritis, so Myra decided to walk over to the Presbyterian Church to look in on the classes. She needed to lean on her cane, but if she did not rush, the walk was comfortable. Teachers and students greeted her with excitement and asked her to listen to several new readers.

Julia Greenberg, one of the instructors who had first worked with Myra, stopped her as she was leaving and said, "Myra, come over to my desk before you leave. I have something to share with you."

A check for three hundred dollars was placed on top of the desk for Myra to see. It was designated for school supplies and signed by Stephen MacTavish. She never mentioned the check to her son, and he never mentioned it to her. That was the way with Stephen, but her heart was filled with pride.

After the walk home, she stretched out in the recliner to read the mail and fell asleep and didn't wake until time for supper. The rest felt good and didn't harm a thing. Wasting time like that used to bother her, but now she enjoyed the pleasure of a good nap. It was nearly time for the news. She wasn't very hungry, so she scrambled an egg to eat with toast and tea while she watched the news.

When the picture came on the TV screen, the news had already started and was showing some fighting with soldiers shooting at what looked like a group of young white boys and even girls. At first, she thought it was a civil rights demonstration. This upset her, for she hoped these times were getting farther apart.

Then the announcer said, "An antiwar demonstration at Kent State University in Ohio left four students dead and nine wounded after National Guard troops opened fire on the demonstrators. The students were protesting the United States escalating their involvement in the Vietnam War.

Oh dear God, this can't be true. Our own soldiers shootin' our own young college students. Most of 'em looked 'bout the same age as Andy. I don't know what to think. According to Ian's writin', we shouldn't be in this war and killin' our boys and them folks who just want to grow their rice. But the government must think different. Lord, help me to be on the side of right whatever that might be. There's families that love them dead and hurt young'uns, and I pray for 'em. After such a happy day, I come home to find the world is still in a mess. I ask yore help for—all of us. Amen, Myra.

Laura saw the same news coverage of Kent State and was greatly disturbed. *I cannot believe it has come to this.* Her mind filled with thoughts of Ian and the distress he would have felt. This reinforced the justness of his words. *Does it take the blood of our youth to touch our conscience?*

She experienced a jumble of emotions. More senseless killings, combined with the raw memories of Ian, wilted her and brought doubts of her own worth. *Am I contributing to anything of value? I earn a lot of money and enjoy being in publishing. Working on Ian's book is of great value, but that will end, and then what will I do? Somehow I must do more.*

The ringing phone disturbed her thoughts, and thinking it to be a telemarketer, she almost ignored. The voice she heard after her hello brought a smile to her face.

"Honey, I hope I ain't botherin' ya or takin' ya away from yore supper."

"Grandma, I am always happy to talk with you—just surprised that you are calling. I hope nothing is wrong."

"I just can't quit thinkin' about that shootin' of them college students. They were just young'uns. Probably they were in the wrong in some way, but they didn't need to kill 'em. I can't make no sense of it."

"Neither can I, Grandma. It's all so wrong. The only positive is that this might open people's eyes to demand changes."

"Ain't that what Ian wrote about? He shore predicted it right."

"Yes, he did, Grandma. History will prove him right, but now, only the young people seem to care."

"I'm prayin' that right will come out. Now I won't keep ya. Are you takin' care of yoreself and eatin' right?"

"I am trying to eat a better diet. Now that I have a bigger kitchen, I am doing some cooking. I need to buy a cookbook. Can you suggest one?"

Myra had to laugh at that request. "Baby girl, I ain't never opened a cookbook in my life. I just had to try to make somethin' out of whatever little I had."

"Well, you always made the best food in the world. I wish I had watched and learned from you, but it's not too late."

"Wallace uses cookbooks all the time, and she's a mighty fine cook. I'll tell her to recommend one to you. Now ya get some rest, and ya might want to pray about that shootin'. All them young'uns had families, so add them to yore prayers."

They said their good-byes, and Laura was left missing her grandmother but feeling the closeness between them. They might be two generations apart, but their hearts were as one.

A week later, she found a package in her mailbox from Wallace. She was pleased to receive *Betty Crocker Cookbook* and *Cooking for One*. She could always count on her aunts.

Life settled into a comfortable pattern for Laura. She and New York were compatible. Completing Ian's book in his voice was her goal. She became accomplished at editing and found this challenging. She couldn't declare that she was happy, but she was not unhappy.

Chapter XXVIII

1971

"My granddaughter is working in New York City. Never would have thought I'd have three of my loved ones livin' way up there," Myra mused.

Her only acquaintance with the large city was what she had seen on television and read in letters from her sister, Dolly. The rest of the family seemed mighty proud of Laura Jean, so it must be a good thing. She prayed every day that her granddaughter would not get lost or have her pocketbook stolen like Rosa Parks did when she got arrested. She also prayed that the change would help her get through the grieving. *Lord, I do pray for my baby girl. She's carried a lot of heartache for her short life. I don't know nothin' about the way she is livin' now, so I place her in yore hands. Amen, Myra.*

Laura felt right at home in the big city. The subway and hordes of folks were not frightening as she had expected. Her confidence in discussing Ian's work with the editors was a surprise. Working with accomplished professionals did not intimidate her. The respect they showed for Ian's writing gave her the incentive to turn the manuscript into a novel of value. She spent her days working with copy editors, and they usually took her suggestions and treated her as a cohort.

Invitations to deli lunches were accepted, and she enjoyed finding herself caught up in ongoing conversations about writing. After the subway ride to her efficiency apartment in a building with a doorman, she opened a can of soup and sat in front of the television watching mindless comedies. Life was different, but so was Laura.

Myra filled the winter months with reading and television. She was often visited by a student from the reading class. Word had spread that Myra could explain the letters and sounds simply enough for anyone to understand. The sweetest words she could hear was when someone said, "I get it now." She read the *Journal* cover to cover with her morning coffee. She did miss seeing stories in the *Journal* written by Laura Porter. Idella assured her that the work Laura was doing now was more important than a newspaper story. She never missed the evening news and tried to keep up with what was happening. Most of the news was about the war in that place where Ian lost his life. She couldn't understand what was happening, except that there was too much killing.

The family gathered on Mother's Day as they had done since the children started leaving home. Idella always rode to Fitzgerald with Laura James and Carlton. This year, they brought the greatest gift that Myra could wish—Laura Jean was also in the car. She had not been home since leaving for New York. Myra couldn't stop hugging her and sat as close as possible all day. She was beautiful and seemed thankful to be with her family. Stephen had barbequed a whole hog, and the trimmings were brought by the children. Ruth and Woody brought a new treat, a wash tub filled with boiled shrimp on ice. Dessert was a churn of homemade ice cream and Laura James's chocolate stack cake. Myra had been forbidden to prepare even one dish.

After the bountiful noon meal and showering Myra with gifts, all gathered around Laura Jean to question and hear all about her life in New York. She was delighted with their interest and enjoyed telling about progress of the book.

"I sit with the editors and sometimes explain the exact meaning of Ian's words. It will be an amazing story, and the publishers expect it to be a best seller. I am writing the introduction, which I hope explains the soul of Ian." She could finally say this without crying.

Being MacTavish, the question of money arose. They did not understand how she would be paid and who would get the money for the sale of the books.

"At this point, I am actually employed by the publisher. My contract calls for the same salary I received at the *Journal* but with a cost of living adjustment. My apartment lease is paid by the publisher. I think they use this apartment often to house contributing authors like me. I feel very fortunate. I really spend little money, so I'm even saving. I did, however, splurge on a plane ticket to Atlanta for this special day to be with my grandma.

"Ian's parents are the owners of the book, and when sales are made, they will get a royalty—that's a percent of the sales. I am thankful for that. They live simply but could always use the money. I am sure they will help his sisters' children attend college. Ian would want that."

"What will you do after the book is published?" Wallace wanted to know.

"Probably I will go on a book tour. I'll still be on their payroll and will love the chance to represent him."

"Where will you go? Reckon you'll come close enough for us to be at one of the places?" Bonnie Ruth asked for she would love to see her cousin at a book signing. Bonnie Ruth was now in her senior year at the Georgia Southern University.

"I don't know. I think it will start in Atlanta. If I have my way, the tour will include Waycross, and that would be close."

All were excited and vowed they would go to Atlanta if necessary.

They extended the day as long as possible, but all left after a supper of the plentiful leftovers. Everyone went home except Ruth, Woody, and Jess. They spent the night with Myra. Ruth and her mother sat in the swing for several hours and enjoyed reviewing the day.

"Mama, we did a good job when we went to see Laura Jean and helped her start her life again. I'm so proud of my niece. After this book tour ends, I hope she gets started on her own writing. Most of all, I so hope she will be ready to find love again."

"I pray for that, but we can be thankful that she has come this far. My greatest joy today was seeing how happy she and her mother seemed together. Idella told me in the kitchen that they haven't had a cross word since they spent the time together after Ian's funeral."

"Now that is saying something where Idella is concerned," laughed Ruth.

Idella had been a concern for her mother and entire family. She was bitter and unhappy in her life. Her husband's death left her a young widow with a child to raise in a small town with few opportunities. For so long, she had seemed to resent the happiness of her family and even resent her child. That changed when she saw her daughter go through the heartbreak of losing her beloved fiancé. She and Laura became close and shared a strong bond. She was proud of her daughter's success and finally recognized that this reflected on her also.

Myra went to bed with a contented happy feeling that she hadn't had in a long time. She couldn't change the bad things going on in the world, but she could rejoice that her family was strong, well, and had good hearts.

Chapter XXIX

1971

Since childhood, Laura James had admired and tried to emulate her older sister. Even now, she felt humble around her and tried every way possible to support Idella and make her life more pleasant. They chatted on the phone every evening. Since there were no long-distance charges, Idella was open to an extended conversation. The talk was usually about family news and mainly Laura Jean. Thankfully, the mother and daughter were establishing a better relationship. Idella's comments showed pride rather than irritation. The fall days were getting shorter, and Laura James knew her sister would enjoy the company of a telephone call in the dark early evening. The phone rang and rang until she was almost ready to hang up when her sister finally answered.

"Idella, I was about to give up on you and figured you'd gone out."

"You know I never go anywhere in the evening. I was stretched out on the sofa with a cool cloth on my head, so it took a few minutes to get to the phone."

"Are you having another headache?"

"I've had it all day. It's the worst I've ever had. Aspirins usually help but not this time."

"Do you need me to come and see about you? I can."

"No, there's no need for you to come. I think I'll be better if I can just get to sleep."

"If you're not better in the morning, please go to the doctor. I still think you should let us take you to the headache clinic at University Hospital in Augusta and find out what causes these headaches."

"I know what causes them. It's being overworked and underpaid."

"You go on to bed, but call if you need me—even if it is late night."

Laura James and Carlton were early risers, so they went to bed soon after supper. Usually, she fell asleep as soon as her head hit the pillow, for she worked hard all day in the mill and kept up with her chores and cooking when she got home. The talk with her sister was disturbing, and she could not sleep.

"Carlton, wake up. Something is not right with Idella. We better go see about her."

"She said she'd be all right tomorrow after restin' tonight. Wait and call her again first thing in the mornin'."

"No, I want to go now." She was out of bed and putting on her clothes.

Carlton knew when his wife was worried about her sister, it was best to go immediately. The drive was only ten miles, but all the way, Laura James kept urging him to hurry. He kept his foot on the gas at the speed limit and didn't protest.

When they arrived at Idella's house at ten thirty, the lights were still on; and surprisingly, the door was unlocked. Laura James ran through the house, calling, "Idella, Idella, where are you?" Before Carlton could reach his wife, he heard a scream and, "Oh my god, no, no, no!"

Idella was crumpled across the bed in the room they called the sleeping porch. (This had originally been a screened porch, but later, windows were installed to use as a bedroom.) He leaned over her and found a pulse, but her eyes were closed and mouth open. Laura James continued to sob and say, "No, God, we can't lose her. Carlton, do something quick."

"She's not dead. There's a pulse. We've got to get her to the hospital and get a doctor there. Who's her doctor?"

"Dr. Ellis Phillips, I'll have to look up his number."

"Tell him how bad off she is and to meet us at his hospital." This was the same doctor who had delivered Laura Jean. He was in practice with another doctor, and they ran a small hospital. Only nurses would be on duty during the evening.

Carlton lifted Idella in his arms, and Laura James scrambled to find a blanket to put around her. She sat in the back seat and held her sister as the car sped through the dark streets. Dr. Phillips arrived as they were carrying her into the hospital, and he yelled for someone to bring a gurney. The nurses and attendants were all standing by the door. The gurney was whisked into an examining room, and the doors closed.

"I better call Stephen."

Carlton shook his head and said, "No, not yet. Let's see what the doctor has to say first. Don't give up. She could come around."

Dr. Phillips finally came out. (It was less than ten minutes but seemed like hours.) "I am so sorry to tell you, but she has suffered a stroke. She has stabilized, but we won't know how serious this is until she is awake."

"Is she in a coma, doctor?" Carlton wanted to comfort his wife, but he knew she must be prepared for the worst.

"Yes, but she is comfortable. A coma is just a deep sleep. You know, Mrs. Porter was one of my first patients when I started my practice, and she has stayed with me. I think the world of her."

"I remember that you delivered Laura Jean, and Idella had a hard delivery. She always said that you saved her baby." Laura James recalled.

"I don't know about that, but it was a long, hard delivery. I remember how proud Mr. Porter was of his new daughter."

"What would have caused this? She had headaches a lot, but I thought she was in good health." Laura James tried to search for some clue that she might have missed, but she knew that Idella did not always tell everything to the family.

Dr. Phillips thought for a minute before answering. "Her blood pressure has been much too high for several years. The first time she came to me complaining about dizzy spells, I took her blood pressure, and it was in the danger zone. I prescribed medication, told her to stop smoking, eat a better diet and relax more. She was always in a hurry. She took a few of the pills but stopped when she felt better. Office visits like this went on for years. No telling how many bottles of blood pressure medicine she bought and never finished taking."

"That's Idella. She always thought she knew best. I begged and begged her to stop smoking. Our papa died of a stroke," Laura Jean cried softly as she spoke.

"Every time she came to my office, I told her the same things, but she never listened. You mentioned your father. Hypertension is hereditary. All your family should be careful to avoid the things that increase your chances for a stroke or heart attack."

"My sister, Ruth, smokes, but she is the only one in the family. I will tell them all what you told me."

At that moment, a nurse stuck her head out of the door and called, "Doctor." He quickly walked into the room and came out hanging his head and getting his composure for the statement he must make. "I am so sorry. She had a seizure and died. I know this is hard to accept, but there was little chance that she could live. If she had lived, she probably would have been unable to talk, walk, or care for herself."

Laura Jean seemed stoic after crying for so long. "She wouldn't have wanted that. As my mama would say, 'The Lord took care of her.'"

"What can we do to help you, Mrs. Larsen? My nurse can contact the funeral home. I'm sure she would want us to call the same that she used for her husband."

"Thank you, doctor, it would help to have the funeral home called, but I want to go home and make calls to family from there. Laura Jean is in New York, so we have to let her know to come home."

The nurse spoke for the first time, "I am so sorry to lose my good friend. We went to church together. I will call the pastor and her close friends and neighbors."

Dawn was just breaking when they arrived home. Laura James patted her husband's shoulder and said, "Thank you for being so strong for me. I couldn't have gotten through without you, and I know your heart is breaking too.

"Mama always says, 'There's joy in the morning'—but not this morning." Then she began the sorrowful task of informing her sisters and brothers. Stephen would have the hardest task of telling their mama.

Arliss and Andy accompanied Stephen across the backyard to give his mother the terrible news. As expected, Myra was sitting in the swing with the unopened *Atlanta Journal* in her lap and watching the sun move up in the sky. How could he break up her peaceful solitude with news that would break a heart that had been broken and patched so many times?

Myra always expected Stephen in the early morning but was surprised to see the other two. "Well, this ain't my birthday, so to what do I owe this nice surprise?" From the look on Stephen's face, she knew to expect the worst.

"Mama, in all my life, this is the hardest thing I have ever had to tell you." His voice was interlaced with heavy sobs. "Idella had a stroke last night. Laura James and Carlton found her about eleven o'clock and got her to the hospital. The same doctor that delivered Laura Jean was with her, but she had a seizure and died about twelve o'clock. The doctor said there wasn't any way to save her, and if she had lived, she would have been helpless."

Myra listened and took in every word. It couldn't be a nightmare. She knew she was wide awake, but it couldn't be true—daughters don't die before their mamas. She wanted to say something, but her mouth wouldn't speak.

"Mama, Mama, are you all right? I know this is an awful shock. It is to me. Arliss, call Dr. Patterson and ask him to come over. He can give her something for her nerves."

"No, don't you call no doctor," she said emphatically. "I don't want to be doped up. I need to feel the pain of losing my firstborn. I won't go crazy. I'm the mama, and my family needs me. I know you mean well, son, but if I take a pill, I'll have to wake up from it, and nothin' will have changed." Streaks of tears streamed down the face of Stephen as he gathered his mother in arms.

"I know, I know. We will hold together. Wallace is on her way and will help you get your things together to go to Swainsboro."

Stephen felt his mother's suffering but knew her strength.

"Has Laura Jean been told? Pore little thing has lost everyone she loves." Myra's heart reached out to her granddaughter.

"BJ has taken care of that. She will get a plane to Atlanta, and he will meet her and bring her home. They should be in Swainsboro by supper time."

The family had gathered at Idella's home when BJ and Laura Jean arrived. It was like the death of LeGrand all over. Cars lined both sides of the street, and most of Swainsboro came to pay respects. Neighbors stayed in the kitchen to receive the abundance of food that was silently left by church members, neighbors, and friends.

They did not know what to expect from Laura Jean, since she had so recently gone through the death of her fiancé. She had become closer to her mother in recent months. Idella visited her daughter in New York at Laura Jean's expense, and she bragged and bragged to them about the visit and seeing the Broadway musical, *Grease.*

Woody stuck his head in the door of the bedroom where they were gathered and said, "BJ and Laura Jean just drove up."

They were anxious to see her but knew that first she had to accept the sympathy of the folks gathered on the front porch and in the living room.

When she came into the room, she went straight to her grandmother and snuggled in her comforting bosom. Myra petted her and said the same soothing words that she always had for sorrow. "Grandma's here." After that, Laura Jean was quiet, reserved, and dignified. Idella would have been proud of how well she handled accepting sympathies and fielding questions. Myra could see that all the best in her firstborn came out in her daughter. She could also see a lot of LeGrand in her.

The funeral home plans were made the next morning, and the funeral held a day later. Like LeGrand, Idella had also preplanned and paid for her funeral. She had expressed her wishes about burial many times. Laura Jean agreed that her wishes were to be honored, and she would be buried in the MacTavish plot in the Glencoe cemetery. Swainsboro folks were a little surprised at this, for she was a leading member of the community. Laura Jean finally announced to someone and the word spread that although her mother had loved Swainsboro, Glencoe was always her home. She did not include that her mother had also vowed that she would not be buried in the Porter family plot and be on the other side of LeGrand from his first wife.

The service was a celebration of Idella's life and filled their sorrowing hearts with pride and thanksgiving. Several church leaders and one of her friends spoke and shared the many acts of kindness she had done and the esteem she was given by her church and the town. The family saw a different side of her than just their sister, mother, or daughter. After the service, as the family silently walked to their cars for the procession, they all proclaimed how little they had really known about their sister's life.

Myra thought on that before saying, "That's the way with families. We don't see what's right under our nose until some outsider points it out." All agreed.

The procession did the same as with LeGrand. They slowly circled the courthouse square, and the townspeople lined the streets paying respect. The only difference was that the hearse headed out US Highway One to Glencoe instead of to the city cemetery.

A crowd had already gathered at the funeral tent in the Glencoe cemetery when they arrived. Myra was overwhelmed to see so many of the MacTavish and Stuart families. Grace was the only member of James's immediate family who was still living. She was there in a wheelchair along with cousins from every other family member. Mrs. Rosenberg stood on the edge of the group, and a little away from the tent was Rosa. After the committal, most of the folks came to give condolences to Myra. Rosa hung back not knowing what to do until Ruth went over and brought her to Myra.

In the family plot, a place was reserved for Myra beside James. Their infant baby was buried on the side that would be for Myra. Below these sites was the grave of Myra's brother, Jesse, who was killed at Pearl Harbor. Idella's casket was lowered into the ground beside her uncle Jesse. Another MacTavish was back in Glencoe soil.

BJ and Laura Jean stayed a few days after the funeral to get Idella's affairs in order. After all the bills were paid, there was little inheritance, except the home and automobile. Laura James and Carlton offered to take care of the sale of house and disposal of furnishings. Laura Jean only wanted a few items: her father's desk, her grandmother Porter's rocking chair, books, pictures, and for an unknown reason, the porch swing. These would be stored at Laura James's until she returned to live in Atlanta. The car was only a year old and was the first new car that Idella had ever owned. All were surprised when she splurged to buy the little Plymouth. Everyone insisted that Laura Jean keep it and leave with BJ until she returned to Atlanta. Since this would leave two of her cars in BJ's garage, she bravely decided to give the Henry J to her cousin, Brian, who had just received his driver's license.

Laura drove the car to Atlanta and returned to New York the next day. The publication date of Ian's book was near, and she was scheduled on book tours. She was thankful that she would be busy after leaving home and family.

A buyer for the house came forward in a few weeks and was willing to pay the listed price in cash. BJ advised her to sell and not have the worry of keeping up an empty house. Carleton and Laura James were relieved and thought a cash sale should not be refused. Since the deed was already in Laura Jean's name, the sale went through quickly, and she received a check for ten thousand dollars. This would be a good nest egg for her future.

Chapter XXX

1972

MUD AND GUTS

Ian Wilhelm

1940–1966

Published Posthumously

The first copy off the press was presented to Laura. She held it as if she were cradling a tiny bird. A faint picture of GIs wading through a rice paddy wearing helmets and fatigues with machine guns across their chests splashed across the khaki and green of the cover. Title and author were in bold black. This image told the story. Ian's picture in dress uniform and a brief biography were on the back cover. Laura had written a summary of his life and ended with "He lost his life in Vietnam on July 16, 1966."

Middle pages were pictures of Ian throughout his life; as a child of three, high school football player, paddling a canoe in the Okefenokee, sitting at his desk at the *Journal*, working the sidelines at a football game, he and Laura in casual clothes on a park bench, and a copy of his article on the Shrine Bowl game. His mother contributed the photos. Laura insisted on including the article.

The dedication was "To those who will not come home and the ones who love them." After consulting with the family, Laura chose these words:

Introduction

LAURA PORTER

Ian Wilhelm was always a planner. As a young boy, he planned his day, jotted it down, and crossed off each item when accomplished. He planned to excel in school, to be the first in his family to attend college, and to become a sports reporter. All were checked off. As a cub reporter for the *Atlanta Journal*, his day was mapped out in the small spiral pad that was a fixture in his shirt pocket. He never planned to be a soldier. He never planned to serve in Vietnam. He never planned to die in a rice paddy. Life takes sharp turns that cannot be preplanned in a notebook.

After receiving his degree from Georgia State University and being commissioned into the U.S. Army, he had to serve on active duty for two years to fulfill his ROTC scholarship commitment. He regarded the fearful assignment to Vietnam as an opportunity. Vietnam was not forefront in the news. American troops were there only as advisors, caring big brother, to help the people retain their independence from communism. Throngs of students had not yet taken to the streets to protest the futility of this conflict, which would take so many lives needlessly. Ian wanted to go there to help the people and to represent the United States honorably.

Plans were still a part of his agenda. He was assigned to the Signal Corps to write news bulletins for military distribution. Realizing the day-to-day realities of the fighting, the disasters ahead, and the suffering of the people, he knew there was more to write. He looked into the terrified, confused faces of the civilian Vietnamese who only wanted to harvest their rice and live in peace. Ragged, hungry children looked at him in fear. On his first patrol, the body of the soldier walking ahead of him was blown to bits by a buried explosive. This was not a short-term advisory mission. It was a war that would only escalate.

Ian's assignment was to report. He did not carry a gun. His only weapon was a small tape recorder to document all that he saw, thought, and feared. His news bulletins let this be known to the military, but he knew the story must also be told truthfully to the folks at home. To do this, he put himself in harm's way and followed the fighting. He waded through the rice paddies, suffered the heat, filth, mud, and guts scattered in his way. He was never deterred, for he knew he was serving his country.

In his taped notes was a comment made to him by a wounded comrade who said, "I never heard the bullet." Probably Ian did not hear the bullet as he talked into his recorder. The sniper hit his mark, and the life blood of a Southern boy from Waycross, Georgia, drained out in a rice paddy on the other side of the world.

What became *Mud and Guts* started as contributing articles to the *Atlanta Journal.* The promising journalistic career of Ian Wilhelm was cut short, but the contribution he made to all Americans will last for generations to come and be a legacy for future military actions.

PS. Another well-designed plan of Ian's was for R&R in Hawaii to wed his fiancée. (That would be me.)

A week after publication, *Mud and Guts* was on the top ten of most of the book lists. The country was hungry to read an explanation of this conflict. There had been a major escalation of U.S. troop involvement. Antiwar demonstrations were taking place on college campuses throughout the nation. Public opinion began to question why the U.S. was involved in this war.

The publishers knew immediately they had a best seller and possibly a movie. They suggested to Laura that Ian's parents should obtain an agent to ensure their wishes and best interests were respected. A highly trusted agent was recommended by the publisher. He and Laura went to Waycross to assist the Wilhelms who were overwhelmed by the attention and welcomed help. However, they would only agree to sign if Laura was included as manager of the book. When Laura gave them an estimate of the amount of money they could receive from the first printing, they were astounded.

"This is all mighty good, but I'd trade it all to have my boy back," Ian's mother said.

"So would I, Mrs. Wilhelm, but he will live on through his words." Laura knew this to be true.

"We'll have enough to pay off our mortgage on the house and send our grandkids to college. Heck, I might even buy me a new truck. The boy would like to see me with a new truck. Old Betsy has about seen her last," Mr. Wilhelm added.

The agent laughed and said, "Before this all ends, you will be able to buy a hundred trucks."

"Well, one would be enough, but like his mama said, I'd forgo all this if I could see him walking in the door."

Back to New York and Laura was off on book tours. After a launch party at the Plaza Hotel, the first stop would be Atlanta for visits to several bookstores and a reception at the *Journal*. She was also interviewed on television which the family was able to see because cable now enabled them to have reception from Atlanta.

Laura's wishes were honored, and the next stop was Waycross. The small town had no bookstore, and the only place large enough to hold the gathering of townsfolk, friends, and family was the high school auditorium. It was the most appropriate place to honor a hometown celebrity.

Laura spoke, signed books, and answered questions at each event. She was surprised that many questions were directed at her relationship with Ian. They seemed to want to know that he had experienced true love in his short life.

BJ and Wallace, along with their families, were at an Atlanta bookstore and special guests at the *Journal* reception. The rest of the family, including Myra, came to Waycross. Laura choked up when she saw her grandmother arrive. She looked so frail on the arm of Stephen. The loss of her daughter had taken an unforgiving toll on her. For the first time, Laura realized that her grandmother was elderly. Actually, she did not know her age.

Book tours were scheduled for three weeks in each geographic area. By the end of the year, she had visited most of the major cities from east to west and north to south. In each city, she was usually interviewed on television. She felt awkward about this, for Ian was the celebrity, not her.

When she returned to New York, she was a guest on several talk shows. This was embarrassing, for she was only tagging along and receiving the acclaim that should be for Ian.

The book was now in its third printing with a movie deal in the works. Protestors were reading from the novel at rallies. Ian would be pleased. Two years later, the book was still selling, and the movie was coming out. Laura continued to represent Ian, and the body count continued to go up in Vietnam.

Laura agreed to attend the movie premier but only if she was allowed to sit in audience and not be recognized for her contribution. She felt uncomfortable taking praise that was not for her but for Ian. His parents were invited also and would have received celebrity treatment. They refused. Seeing their son's death played out on the big screen would have been too painful.

All books reach a peak, and soon she would not need to devote all her time to representing Ian. Laura began to feel restless and wondered what she should do next. Should she return to the *Journal* and pick up her career as a reporter? That seemed a little lame after events of the past years. She also had to acknowledge that she was addicted to living in New York. The city never stopped being new and exciting, and there was much yet to explore. It was easy to fly home to see the family and to stay in close touch.

After the fanfare of the movie premier, she expected her usefulness to the publishing company to be over. Before she could give more thought to her future, she was offered a permanent position as an editorial assistant. She would read manuscripts and work with authors to edit their work. This seemed to be the path for her.

During the months she worked on the book and book tours, she lived primarily on an expense account. Her efficiency apartment was furnished by the publisher, and she received an adequate salary. This enabled her to live quite well, but all that would end when she was a permanent employee. The apartment would have to be available for use by another temporary. Her needs were simple, but finding a new place to live was a concern.

Her new salary was larger than she had ever expected to earn, but living expenses were much higher in New York than Atlanta. She spent an afternoon preparing a bare-bones budget and found there was a large surplus. *Heck,* she thought, *I am highly paid! I can splurge a little on a larger apartment, an occasional theater ticket, and of course, air fare to Georgia on special occasions and when I get homesick for Grandma.*

Finding an apartment was not an easy task, especially when she did not know the city like a native. On her many walks, she was most attracted to the Village. It fit all her primary needs— near one of the rivers, filled with quaint shops, small sidewalk cafes, and a haven for artists and writers. *Maybe I can find my muse and write the novel that Ian insisted was in me.*

Newspaper ads and checking with realtors brought only disappointment. When she expressed this to coworkers, she learned what all New Yorkers seemed to know. The best way to find an apartment was word of mouth.

She had gained the respect of her colleagues because of her humble Southern grace, even though she was somewhat a celebrity. They joined in the search. Soon, available apartments were being offered. Several seemed promising, but a visit ruled them out as too expensive or unsuitable. She was ready to lower her expectations and look in another area. The only nonnegotiable was to be near the subway line. Then a coworker told her of a sublet in a building where his parents lived. Her opinion had been that the Village was only inhabited by younger, more modish folks but learned that many of the brownstones were the home of older folks who had lived there for years. That appealed to her as a neighborhood.

A call to the owner sounded even more promising. He was leaving for a year in France and wanted to sublet for that time with an option to extend further if agreeable to both parties. Since her future was uncertain, she thought that was perfect. She left work and hurried to the Village. No one questioned her need to leave early because apartments had to be grabbed fast. It was a half-hour subway ride from work, but the stop was only a block from the building. The brownstone showed its age, but she liked the vintage look of it and especially the stoop and wide front steps. The apartment was on the third floor, which was the top. It did not have an elevator or doorman like the efficiency, but that was of no consequence to her. The lobby was small and only housed the mailboxes and staircase. She raced up the stairs and found apartment 304.

A middle-aged man ushered her in and gave the tour. Every room was filled with boxes ready for shipping. There was a wide living room with an operating fireplace, bookshelves across one wall, and area for dining table. The kitchen was small but serviceable. Small powder room was in the short hallway which led to a large bedroom with a closet built across one side and of course, a bathroom with claw-foot tub. When the man opened French doors behind the dining table to reveal a small balcony, Laura was sold. No matter what the sacrifice, she had to live in this apartment. When she heard the rent, she was dubious; but after some careful adjustments to her budget, she cut out most of the extras, except plane tickets to Georgia. She signed the lease and could move in the next weekend. Now another problem, she had no furniture.

She started prowling the second hand shops. This was the time to use some of the money from the sale of her mother's house. Instead of saving as she had planned, she would spend some of it to buy essentials. A must was a fold-out sofa because she expected visits from her aunts. Wallace had already informed her that she would be coming up in the fall to the Merchandise Mart to order clothes for her shop. Ruth chimed in that she would be coming with her. Now Laura could entertain her aunts and have room for them to stay with her. Life was good. Thinking of Ian and how much he would have loved the apartment and life in New York gave her pleasure instead of sorrow. She played an imaginary game of living with him there. *Since she was playing make-believe in her head, maybe it was time to put her fantasies on paper.*

Chapter XXXI

1973

Two years had passed since the death of her oldest daughter, but Myra's thoughts and night dreams were still filled with her. Sometimes she envisioned her first born as a child but most often the image was wearing the pink lace dress and lying lifeless in the casket.

At six years old, Idella contacted typhoid fever which almost took her life. One night as she twisted in fever and seemed to be getting weaker and weaker, James was determined that she would live and told Myra, "My baby girl will die some time, but it shore won't be tonight." She started improving shortly after that, and their daughter lived until middle age and gave them a beautiful granddaughter. *Maybe James was closer to the Lord than Myra thought.*

Lovely and peaceful were the comments made by all who viewed Idella in her casket. They didn't fool Myra. Her child looked like a corpse. The funeral home was filled with flowers, and a spray of pink roses covered the casket. The townsfolk had shown their love with the large number of wreaths and sprays that had been sent for her. To Myra, these were just dead flowers. A sickening sweet smell of carnations and roses had filled the air in the viewing room which left Myra with pangs of nausea. These vivid memories were impossible to wipe from her thoughts. Her only comfort was knowing that Idella and Laura Jean had made peace and enjoyed good times together in the months before the death of her daughter. The girl was a tribute to her mother.

Myra had looked forward to her granddaughter's return to Atlanta and seeing her often. Then Laura Jean was offered the big job in New York which seemed to make her happy. This was probably for the best; the girl had left a lot of sadness in Georgia.

It turned out the new job didn't keep her granddaughter from coming home. She flew to Atlanta often and drove her inherited car to visit Myra. That cost a lot of money, but the girl seemed to have plenty. What worried Myra most was the flying. Planes did crash, and that was sure a long way to fall. Stephen somewhat eased her mind by explaining that flying was much safer than driving.

Every night she prayed for each member of her family along with others who were sick or needed help and for peace to come. She also added a prayer for herself. *Dear Lord, I'm ashamed of the way I am carryin' on over Idella. I know I ain't the only one who is grievin' over a loss. Right now, I can't think of nothin' but my own achin' heart. Losing James was the same, but I did get where I could find comfort. I'm scared it won't be that way this time. It just ain't right for a daughter to die before her ma. Now I ain't sayin' you done wrong. I'm just sayin' it's hard for me to reconcile that with you lovin' us. Lord, forgive me and give me the strength to get over this unchristian feelin'. Show me where to turn. I can't go on like this. Amen, Myra.*

She didn't expect to receive a direct answer, but the answer would come as the Lord saw fit.

At the start of the New Year 1973, Myra was determined to get back to doing something other than grieving for her daughter. Little by little, she returned to the old Myra. Arthritis kept her from doing any sewing or walking very far, but that didn't keep folks from coming to her for help with their reading. When word spread that she was able to do this again, so many came that she had to start giving appointments. Working one to one was most successful. Soon, her afternoons were filled.

The librarian called with a new idea. She invited Myra to come one morning a week and read to the children. Arliss was all for that and offered to take her and bring her home. Myra was a storyteller but had never read stories even to her own grandchildren or her children because she did not learn to read until they were grown. She hesitated to say yes. One day, the librarian came by her house and brought a stack of children's books. She suggested that Myra read the books, and then she could tell the stories to the children. This appealed to Myra, and she had stories ready to tell by the next story hour.

The number of children attending to hear the stories of Miss Myra increased each week. She sat in a rocking chair, and the children sat on the floor in a semi-circle around her. Her presentation was very animated with all the animal sounds and voice changes to fit the character. She could growl like the Big Bad Wolf and then speak in the squeaky voice of Little Red Riding Hood. The stories were enhanced by her unique interpretations. Adults in the library often came over and stood behind the children to listen. An integrated head start class started attending. Her heart was filled with joy when she looked around the circle and saw little faces of different shades among the children and all enjoying her stories together. *If only grown folks could keep seein' through the eyes of children.*

Her heart would always have a tender spot for her daughter, just like for James. Sometimes, she felt the pain as intense as before, but it didn't happen as often when she was helping others. She knew she was blessed with a loving and caring family. Her peace came for knowing that she was *doing unto others* just as the Lord had asked.

The family was relieved to see their mama regaining concern for others and zest for life that had made her days meaningful. They called often, and one of the children visited her every Sunday. She was now willing to take trips to visit Laura James on the farm, Ruth in Jacksonville, Wallace in Macon and even rode the train to visit BJ in Atlanta. When Laura called and heard of her travels, she always asked, "When are you coming to see me?" Myra didn't have an answer for that and only chuckled.

Myra looked forward to seeing the little children in the library. She regretted that she had always been so busy when her own children were growing up that she did not get to enjoy their childhood days. She made up for that when her grandbabies came along. Now she was a great-grandmother. After Bonnie Ruth finished college and became a teacher, she married a nice young man who was also a teacher and a coach. Her twin girls were the delight of Stephen, Arliss, and Myra. Fortunately, they lived close enough to visit often.

Andy finished Emory University and would soon graduate from Emory Law School. He was determined to be governor as his grandpa had planned. Ruth's son, Jess, had started his first year at the University of Florida. BJ's oldest boy was at the University of Georgia, and his two girls were still in high school. Wallace's Little James was the youngest and still in grade school. They were a fine bunch and all getting the education that James wished for them. Because of the hard times, BJ was the only child to go to college, but the others made sure their children had this opportunity.

Later in the spring, an attractive black lady knocked at Myra's door. She was a stranger, but Myra was glad to invite her into the living room. The lady explained that she was part of an organization that encouraged black ladies to learn to read. (The most correct term for African-Americans had now become Black—Myra tried to remember this.) She had heard many good things about Myra and knew it would be an inspiration for the ladies to hear her speak at their meeting.

"Oh no, I ain't no speaker. I hardly went to school more than a few weeks. I wish them well, but I ain't qualified to help."

"That is exactly why we need you. You had the same difficult start in life as most of these ladies, and look what you have accomplished. You are a leading advocate for literacy, and there is standing room only at your library story hour. I read the big article about you that was in last week's paper to the ladies. They couldn't believe it when I told them of your hardships as a child and your age when you started learning to read. Please share this with us."

"I don't know what I can do, but I'll try. I'm still just an ignorant old country woman. I have to say 'What you see is what you'll get.' Now have a cup of coffee with me on this cold day."

"I could use a cup of coffee, thank you. We can talk more about the organization. We meet at Saint Matthews AME Church on Tuesday morning at nine o'clock. Could you come next Tuesday?"

"I don't drive, so I have to see if my daughter-in-law can take me."

"If you don't mind riding with me, I will be glad to take you and bring you home."

"If that doesn't put you out, I would be happy to take yore offer."

"Please pardon my bad manners. I was so excited to ask you about sharing your story with our ladies that I neglected to introduce myself. I am Helen Cole. Just call me Helen."

"I'm happy to meet you, Helen. I ain't Miz MacTavish. I'm just plain ole country Myra."

Helen smiled, but she never called her anything except Mrs. MacTavish.

She pondered telling Stephen about her new adventure. He had a kind heart and believed in helping everyone, but he was always hesitant when his mother started a new activity because he was afraid she might get into something that would not be good for her. They always went out to dinner after church on

Sunday. Myra had declined this treat at first and wanted to cook for them, but after trying it once, she enjoyed the tasty dinner and restful Sunday afternoon. This was a good time to tell Stephen.

"Mama, that is a fine thing to do. I know Helen Cole. She has been on several committees that have come to the county council meetings. (Stephen had been elected to the county council a few years back.) She is well educated, practical, and always has her ideas organized. Education is the most valuable thing we can give anyone. Look how much reading has meant to you."

"Thank you, son, I just hope I can do it. You know what a struggle I had tryin' to learn to read."

It was unusual for Arliss to speak up, but this time she did. "Mrs. Mac, you are the only one who could do this. This will be giving back for all the good that has come to you. You didn't think you could be the library storyteller, and now look how that is appreciated."

With that encouragement, Myra had no fear of failing. Tuesday morning she changed her dress several times. She wanted to look her best but not as if she was putting on airs. She settled on a navy shirtwaist dress with long sleeves and a short jacket for the chilly morning air.

Mrs. Cole was in front of her house a little before nine o'clock and found Myra waiting in the porch swing. She climbed into the car and was on her way to a new challenge.

"I didn't know if I should bring anything, but I have kept all of my notebooks from the very beginning. I thought the ladies might like to see how discouraging it was for me at first."

"That's very thoughtful. Showing is a lot better than telling. They will love you."

The meeting was held in a small building attached to the church. Myra stepped into the door and saw a packed room. There were ladies of all ages and means. She was led to a seat in front facing the audience. Mrs. Cole stood to introduce her, but she had already told Myra to remain seated in the chair. She had concern for Myra standing for such a long time, and also, sitting in the chair would create a more casual and friendly feeling.

"This lady needs no introduction. She is ' Miss Myra' to most of our town. You know of her work with the reading program and the hit she has made with our children at the library story hour. She has a story to tell that will touch your heart and that you will understand because many of you have lived the same life. She cherishes her ability to read, and it is a gift she wants to give to you." The audience stood and applauded.

Myra was ready to speak. "Y'all sit down 'cause I'm gonna be sittin'. I wore my ole knees and back out in the cotton patch and over the wash pot, and now I sit more than I stand. First of all, I'm gonna tell ya like I told Miz Cole, 'what you see is what you're gonna get.' I ain't nothin' but an ignorant ole country woman. I do know what some of you have been through. My mama was part Creek Indian, and I remember how she was put down. I worked from—Lord, I can't recall a time when I didn't work. My papa died when I was thirteen years old. It didn't seem like life could get any worse, but it shore did . . . ."

She was interrupted then with applause and comments of "I shore know what that's like," "Dem wuz hard times," and "Honey, I been there."

The audience relaxed and felt comfortable listening to the talk of this white woman. Myra talked *with* them not *to* them. She went through her struggles and emphasized how difficult it had been for her to take the first step to attend the classes. Hands went up for questions and comments. Myra's answers often brought a laugh to all. They loved hearing about her granddaughter helping her learn the alphabet by singing. Showing her first efforts at writing and the worksheets was a big hit.

The talk could have continued all morning, but Mrs. Cole took over to explain the plans for beginning the reading classes. Most were ready to sign up. Myra spoke up and said, "Don't you say 'I don't have time right now' 'cause that won't ever change. Make time." Again, there was a chorus of "That's the truth" and "If I wait till I have time, I'll be dead."

After the meeting, coffee and cinnamon rolls were served, and the ladies crowded around Myra to ask more questions. All were happily surprised when Mrs. Cole gave out notebooks and pencils to all.

I got to ask Bonnie Ruth where she got them pencil sharpeners. I'm gonna buy one for every one of these ladies. It shore looks better when you write with a sharp pencil.

What a day this had been. Myra could feel the happy laughs bubbling up inside. Mrs. Cole made her feel even better by thanking her for helping the program to get off to a good start.

"I'm happy to do it. What you said about reading was a gift I could give made me start thinkin'. I've had some hardships in my life and some heartaches, but the Lord has been good to ole Myra. I think it's fittin' that I give somethin' back. You let me know if I can help with the classes. Those are fine ladies, and they deserve a chance to better their lives, and there ain't no better gift than reading."

Stephen came over in the evening anxious to hear about her day. She told him how good the day had made her feel, and that she wanted to start giving back for all that she had received.

"Mama, you've done that all of your life. You shared with others when you were struggling to keep food on our table. There isn't a black family that you have ever known that didn't respect you and consider you a friend. I've tried my best to do the same all my life, and dear Mama, that has come from your example."

Myra didn't have to search for ways to give back. Her fame spread, and she was asked to give talks in churches, civic meetings, schools, and even the women's club. These audiences were not just made up of folks who needed to learn to read, but many in the audiences wanted to understand more about folks who had not been given a chance to learn until now. They wanted to get involved. Some helped by participating in the programs and others by giving money which was always needed.

Chapter XXXII

1973

Life had settled into a comfortable pattern for Laura. New York suited her. The work as an editing assistant was challenging. She was accomplished at reading the work of new authors and evaluating manuscripts. The manuscripts assigned to her were usually considered only as possible, but sometimes she found one of merit and would try to promote the publishing.

Manuscripts that been submitted by agents or requested by publisher after an appealing query letter and found lacking potential were relegated to a slush pile. After a second review, most were returned to the author. Laura disliked this part of her job, for she felt the pain of the hopeful writers when the returned manuscript arrived in their mailbox. She often fished through the slush pile and pulled out one that caught her eye and took it home to read thoroughly. So far, she had not found any that could be revitalized, but she kept hoping. Starting work on her own story crept into her thoughts. How could she say *my story* when she had no story? Sitting at the typewriter and waiting for words to come was futile.

The apartment was comfortably furnished to her taste. Most of her furnishings had been purchased from thrift or consignment shops. A comfortable nest egg was still in her bank account. She was determined that all future purchases and expenses must come from her income. *Is that my Scottish heritage or Myra speaking?*

The balcony was an added joy. Sitting outside and looking at the stars gave her a feeling of freedom after being confined inside all day. She had warm memories of her family spending so much time sitting on their porches. Again, her father crept into memory. The two of them often sat together on the front porch and listened to Saint Louis Cardinals baseball games from the radio that was propped in the open living room window. She learned later that they were Cardinals fans because that was the only game broadcast that their radio could receive.

Her promise to share the moon with Ian every evening was usually kept while she sat on the balcony. She never failed to look up at the sky when the hands reached nine o'clock. Even when walking on a busy New York street, she did not have to check her watch to know it was time to search for the moon.

The neighborhood was intriguing, and most of her weekends were spent exploring the small shops and ethnic restaurants. She had learned to feel comfortable eating alone if she took a book to read. It would be easy to meet a man if she were interested. Many approached her in restaurants or shops and tried to start a polite conversation, but she either returned to her book or became engrossed in an item in a shop. They quickly realized she was taken or just not interested. The prospect of a relationship with a man had been damaged beyond repair. This did not trouble her, for she was fulfilled with her memories. *No one could compare to Ian.*

The apartment had a window air conditioner which gave relief from the heat of the New York summer. Laura had never before complained about the hot summer sun. That was expected in South Georgia, but she hadn't expected it in New York—especially not in June. She remembered days in her childhood when the asphalt in the road melted, and shoes left an imprint if you dared to walk across the street, but you could always sit under a shade tree and catch a cool breeze. In New York, the sidewalks radiated the heat and the buildings and masses of people prevented any chance of a refreshing breeze.

The walk from the subway and climb up three flights of stairs had her panting until she hurried into the apartment and turned on the air conditioner to feel the rush of cool air. Summer in the city was avoided by many, but she had no choice. She had a week's vacation available but decided to keep it for a longer Christmas holiday.

She looked forward to changing from her tailored skirt, hose, and heels into shorts and T-shirt. Ian collected T-shirts from all his interests and travels, so she had a life supply of T-shirts. Tonight's shirt advertised *Rio Vista Catfish*, a favorite restaurant in Atlanta. Her days were hectic, but a short bit of relaxation and a cool gin and tonic released the stress—or the miseries as her grandmother called it.

Coming home to an empty apartment sometimes put her into a melancholy mood that she tried to avoid. The dread of opening a door devoid of any welcome was soon eliminated. Heading up the front steps juggling her bags of groceries, she almost tripped on something on the first step.

"Now where did you come from? Are you lost?" She put down a bag to pick up a little gray bundle of fur that looked up at her with baby blue eyes. She always had a cat and dog when her father was living. Her mother never wanted to replace a pet, so after the death of her little feist (a small dog of mixed ancestry popular in the South), PeeWee, there was never a pet in her mother's home again. This little kitty resembled her all-time favorite gray tabby cat, Mordecai. He had been given to her by a friend of her father who always gave his kittens Biblical names. Mordecai managed to escape the perils of cats who roamed outside, and he lived to a ripe old age.

No way could she leave the kitty on the steps. She would take it upstairs with her and put up notices to find the owner—if there should be an owner. The kitty was a female, but she would not consider a name until all effort to find the owner failed.

The kitten was young and had not learned to lap food, so Laura dipped her finger in cream and the kitten sucked it off. Tomorrow, she would buy a doll bottle. Probably the kitty had been abandoned by the mama cat before being weaned. Mama cats loved and cared for their offsprings, but the city was a perilous place for stray cats. When her little tummy was filled, the kitten curled up in Laura's lap to sleep. She was smitten and had to own this little soft, purring sleeping kitty. She would put up the notice but keep her fingers crossed for no response.

Besides, what kind of owner would leave a tiny kitten alone in the city?

Luckily, the next day was Saturday, and she could devote the day to operation kitty. After filling the little tummy again with milk sucked off her finger, she distributed the notices in the most likely places. Then she went to a pet store to learn about taking care of an infant kitten.

The clerk told her the kitten was probably placed on her steps by someone whose cat had a litter, and they did not want the trouble of taking the unwanted kittens to a shelter. It was not uncommon for kittens to turn up on door steps. For some reason, such people thought that leaving the kitten on a doorstep ensured finding a home. It did work this time.

Laura purchased a litter box and a can of dry formula that could be mixed with water to resemble the milk from the mama cat. She asked the clerk for a recommendation of a vet and planned to take the kitten Monday morning before going in late to work.

"If you're going to take her out, you need to buy a carrier. I can almost say for certain that no one will answer your notice. Give her a name and take her to the vet. She is lucky that you are the one who found her. So many of them get in the street and do not have a chance," the clerk advised her.

This made the little stray even more precious to Laura. She did wait a week before deciding on a name. By that time, the kitty was sleeping in her bed, following her every step and greeting her with meows and purrs.

Considerable thought went into the name. She didn't want to call her Fluffy, Muffy, Sox, Whiskers, or the usual kitty names.

This kitten was very refined and deserved a name to reflect this. Her grandmother Porter died when Laura was three, so she had no memories of her except stories she had been told. In her mind, she had always pictured her as loving, kind, and very dignified, exactly like this kitty. Elizabeth would be her name in honor of the grandmother she never knew. The name fit her well, and Elizabeth filled the apartment with devotion. The contentment that came from having another living being in her life caused Laura to think about reaching out for other companions.

Her grandmother often talked about her sister, Dolly, who lived in New York and suggested that Laura go to see her. In Myra's eyes, if both lived in New York, they were neighbors and should get together. Laura had the phone number and decided to give it a try.

On the third ring, a lady with a slight Southern accent answered, "Hello."

"This is Laura Porter, the granddaughter of Myra MacTavish. I hope I have reached the correct party. I would like to speak with Ms. Dolly Stuart."

"Yes, you have. This is Dolly, and I know you, Laura. We met long ago. Your grandmother, Myra, has told me about you living in the city. I have hoped to hear from you."

The Southern voice and hearing the name of her grandmother put Laura right at ease. She immediately knew she wanted to get to know this aunt better. They had a long chat about Laura's career and how she liked New York. To her surprise, Dolly knew all about Ian and had read his book. It was like the chance finding of a relative in a foreign land. Dolly lived in Queens and suggested meeting for lunch at a place near Laura's apartment. They set up a date for the next Saturday. She could find Laura easier than Laura could find her.

The meeting was a treat for both. They talked easily about all the relatives and missing Georgia while loving New York. Dolly had descriptive memories of growing up with Idella and introduced Laura to another side of her mother. Anthony, Dolly's only child, had completed medical school at Columbia and was now an intern. He did not live at home. They talked through a long lunch and for several hours on a park bench. Both had found a kindred spirit with the bond of Myra's influence on their lives.

The friendship grew, and they spent much time together. Both enjoyed the theater and often went to a Saturday matinee. Dolly introduced her great-niece to parts of New York that she would have missed. A big event was to ride the train to Long Island and spend Sunday with Great Uncle Arno. After his wife died, her uncle had moved into a retirement home on the Island. He had owned and operated a parking garage for many years, and Dolly had been his assistant. The sale of the garage provided a comfortable retirement for both.

Laura always called Myra to give an account of the visits, and she could tell this made her grandmother especially happy. Myra always ended the conversation with "It's good to have family close by. You never know when you'll need 'em. There's nothin' to take the place of family."

The relationship grew into the kind of open friendship that Laura had not been able to have with her mother until after the death of Ian. Both Laura and Dolly opened their hearts and shared some of their deepest feelings which filled a void in both lives. Dolly had not been near family in so many years, and she laughingly said, "Arno is just not someone who wants to hear about women's emotions."

Laura's career escalated after she rescued a manuscript about the friendship between a black maid and her employer from the slush pile. The author was Southern and knew her topic intimately. On her own time, Laura corresponded and made revisions with the author and pitched it to the editorial board. A senior editor became interested, and the book was published and quickly became a best seller. The name of Laura Porter now carried weight. She was promoted to associate editor with a substantial raise.

Her career was flourishing, and New York was always exciting. The apartment was all she could desire. Elizabeth welcomed her home every evening and showered her with love. Dolly was a companion for shows, dinners, and getaways to New Hampshire. Her income covered an extensive wardrobe and frequent trips to visit her grandmother. A cruise with Dolly, Ruth, and Wallace was being planned. Life was good. So why did she feel something was missing? Maybe what she needed was a dose of Grandma Myra.

Including the three days the publishing house would be closed for Christmas and seven vacation days, Laura could have a long holiday in Georgia. It was much easier to take time away from a publishing house than a newspaper. Publishing affairs could wait, but news didn't take a holiday. In the past, she had shied away from extended visits with family or friends; but this year, she would take a sentimental journey with stops in Atlanta and Swainsboro before spending the remaining days with her grandmother.

She flew into Atlanta on December 20. Her uncle had sold Idella's car for her after she made the decision to remain in New York. Both had agreed that it was unwise to keep the expense of the car. A rental took her from the airport to complete the rest of her journey.

The drive from the airport brought back her familiarity with Atlanta streets, and she drove immediately to the *Journal*. On her walk through the newsroom, she was greeted warmly by old and new staff members. Ian's name was well known, and Laura was readily recognized. Her former editor gave a tour and stopped in front of the office that had been Ian's. Outside the door was his picture (not as a soldier but standing on the sideline of a football game) and a framed write-up that had appeared in the *Journal* after his death.

Lunch was planned with some of her closest coworkers at the nearby grill where she and Ian had eaten many times. Conversation was a collection of war stories about her and Ian. These were stories of news reporting and not from Ian's time in Vietnam.

The banter turned serious when someone asked, "Laura, when can we expect a novel from you? I know that publisher will find no better writer."

"That's not going to happen. I seem to write well with facts and descriptions, but I do not have a story."

Her former editor spoke up. "Of course, you do. You just have to allow it to come out. You need some inspiration. Are you in a hurry this afternoon?"

"I'm going to dinner and spend the night with my uncle, but I have all afternoon."

"Drive out to Tenth Street and park if you can find a place. There's a home that used to be called the Crescent Apartments. It's in bad shape and about to be torn down, but it has to be saved. Get as close as you can to the house and think about the budding writer who sat in a small apartment and typed on a manual Underwood. She let her story take over, and she did quite well. That's what you must do."

She knew without being told the name of the author. Her daddy gave *Gone with the Wind* to her on her eleventh birthday. She had read it so many times that she could almost quote every word. This shot of memory caused her to realize that she had a better relationship with her daddy than she had thought. To give this book to an eleven-year-old showed that he knew his daughter well. It was his last gift to her. She still remembered the scene between her parents after she opened the gift.

"LeGrand, what were you thinking? She can't read that dirty book. It's got cuss words in it. Give it here, Laura Jean. You don't want to read that."

Laura Jean started to cry. She had heard so much about the book and was dying to read it. Eavesdropping had become her proficient skill, and she knew the exact word her mother was protecting her from—frankly, my dear I don't give a *damn*. Pretty tame dialogue in 1973—but shocking in 1955.

"Idella, if these are the worst words she'll ever read, I will be surprised. Give her back the book. I will not prevent my daughter from reading one of the greatest novels ever written. You heard me. I *said* give it back."

Her mother threw the book on the floor and stomped out of the room. Laura Jean grabbed the book and ran to hide it in a safe place.

After leaving the *Journal*, she turned onto Peachtree Street and took the editor's suggestion to turn down Tenth Street. Driving these familiar streets filled her with nostalgia and pride in this gracious city. A convenient parking spot became available just as she reached her destination. This was surely a good omen.

She spent an hour walking around and thinking of all the Margaret Mitchell stories she had heard and absorbing the environment of this old Atlanta neighborhood. Remembering that day of her eleventh birthday, she belatedly said, "Thank you, Daddy. I wish you were enjoying this walk with me."

The spot where Ian's rooming house once stood had given way to progress. The empty lot contained only a large sign, *"Commercial Property for Sale."* Last stop was in front of the theater where Margaret Mitchell had been hit by a car on a rainy night and died. She didn't stop but drove slowly past what she knew to be the exact spot. This might not inspire a story, but it did make her proud of the legacy of a fellow Georgian. She remembered Ian telling her that she came from the land of Margaret Mitchell. This had been a good way to spend the afternoon.

After an enjoyable evening with BJ and his family, she started the drive to South Georgia. She decided to make a detour through Milledgeville for a little dose of Flannery O'Connor, another famous Georgia author that she had read in college and held in esteem. She always thought that Flannery was lucky because her parents gave her such an appropriate author name. Georgia State College for Women (GSCW) was Flannery's alma mater and would have been Laura's except for the death of her father. It was a tradition for the girls in the Porter family to be *Jessies.* How he would have paid for it was questionable, but he would have managed. *How would her life have been if she had spent four years in Milledgeville instead of Atlanta?*

She reached Norristown in time for supper with Laura James and Carlton. They treated her like an adored daughter, and she was in need of a dose of that.

The next day was a long overdue visit to Swainsboro. She walked the court house square and stopped to greet anyone she knew. Two planned visits were with her church school teacher and her favorite high school teacher. Both had made an impact on her and each gave her an inspiration to remember. Her church school teacher told the class many times, "Unto those much is given, much is asked." The high school English teacher complimented her with "You have a way with words." It was time to say thank you.

A drive down Church Street took her by her home which was now occupied by a young couple. She was pleased to see several children playing in the yard under the ancient mulberry tree. When she had left after the death of her mother, her old home had the desolate appearance of an empty, deserted house. She made no other stops because visiting neighbors would have taken too much time away from her aunt and uncle. She knew Laura James would have supper waiting.

After a pleasant evening and catfish stew supper with Laura James and Carlton, Laura was on her way to Fitzgerald and Grandma.

Myra was excited to have her granddaughter all to herself for a full day. Laura spent the day in the kitchen with her and watched as each dish was prepared. Duplicating would be tricky since Myra used no recipes. The pound cake would require a recipe. Laura watched as Myra worked on the cake. She tried to write down each step and the ingredients. It was impossible to get an accurate measurement because of statements like: "Use a half dozen eggs if you have that many" and "A little over a half pound of butter, more or less." One thing was emphatic: "Be shore to beat the egg whites till they're stiff and *fold* in, don't stir."

With some creative figuring, Laura did come up with a recipe. (According to the author, the recipe is accurate, and the cake will be delicious. This is not a light pound cake. It is dense for today's taste—but so delicious.)

Myra's Pound Cake
1 ½ cups butter (the real kind from the cow)
1 box confectioner's sugar
6 eggs
Pinch of salt
1 tsp. baking powder
1 sugar box (from above) of plain flour
1 tsp. vanilla
Separate eggs. Beat whites until stiff.
Mix sugar and butter. Add half of egg yolks.
Add rest of egg yolks and 1 cup four.
Fold in 1/3 beaten egg whites
Add rest of flour and egg whites.
Add vanilla and beat.
Bake at 325' degrees for 1 hour.

Other hints from Myra were: "Use the good vanilla, the kind you get from the Watkins Man, and you just have to use your own judgment on when it's done. A broom straw is a good way to test."

Laura had a moment of tenderness realizing that her grandmother thought the Watkins Man called on households everywhere.

BJ and family would arrive on Christmas Eve and spend that night in a motel. Ruth, Woody, and Jess spent that evening with Woody's mother—his father had died during the time his son was overseas in the war—and would arrive on Christmas morning. Wallace, Grady, Little James, Laura James, and Carlton would also join them on Christmas morning. The family now numbered twenty-one, so there was no way for Myra to have sleeping accommodations. Stephen's home would be filled with Bonnie Ruth, her husband, two little girls and Andy. Times had changed and so had their usual Christmas celebration.

Stephen had arranged to use the social hall at his church for their dinner. Everyone could be seated at tables and chairs. The family would cook all the food and use the church kitchen to warm up if needed. Myra still served her specialties of dressing, candied sweet potatoes, raisin cake, and pound cake. A raisin cake was a must because it was BJ's favorite, and Christmas Day was his birthday. Arliss would bake two turkeys and make her traditional ambrosia. Laura James would bring a fresh pork ham, mustard greens, and a pot of dumplings. Ruth always brought oysters from Florida which were used in the dressing and eaten raw by some. Wallace took care of the rolls and cranberry salad. Charlotte always brought a tray of cookies and candies.

Myra protested at first, but then acknowledged the difficulty she had walking and standing on her feet, and they did need more room than either of the houses could provide.

When the plans were made, Myra sadly remarked, "I wish I could keep adoin' Christmas like me and yore papa always did, but to tell you the truth, I just plain ain't able."

Selecting a gift for her grandmother was always a great dilemma for Laura, but this year, she had the perfect gifts. It was hard to keep the secret, but no one knew except BJ who was included in the plan.

Myra would have supper ready and waiting for BJ and his family to arrive. They would eat with her before going to a motel to sleep. Laura had wanted to save her grandmother the work of preparing a big meal, so she begged to be allowed to cook supper. She had found a recipe for something she remembered from her childhood that all enjoyed and tested it several times before leaving New York.

Myra finally said yes, mainly because she wanted to encourage the girl in her cooking. After going to the store, Laura started preparing a huge pot of chili with beans and potatoes MacTavish style. She made cabbage slaw and Mexican cornbread to accompany the chili. She did allow Myra to make the sweet tea.

"Girl, you shore picked the right dish. We all love it. I remember the first time yore Aunt Ruth made it for all of us, and James thought it was the grandest thing he'd ever had. Do you remember?"

Laura laughed at how her grandmother thought she should remember everything. "I don't remember the first time, but I do remember eating chili a lot and how much Grandpa loved it."

BJ arrived in his car by himself. Charlotte and the children were coming behind. Myra thought that was a silly thing to do, but she didn't say anything as such.

As soon as he came in the door, he said, "Laura, do you want to get that package in from the car that you asked me to bring?"

Laura didn't say anything and walked out to the car. When she came back, she hesitated at the door and said, "Merry Christmas, Grandma. Here's a special delivery present for you."

In walked Dolly, her baby sister from New York whom she had not seen in years. Myra's mouth gaped open, and for once, she was speechless. Then she threw down her cane and hurried to her sister. After many hugs and happy tears, Dolly remembered that she had left a gift in the car and asked Laura to get it for her. Myra was curious and walked onto the porch. A stooped little man on a walker was helped out of the car. She couldn't imagine who in the world could have come with them.

BJ helped him onto the porch. He was old and bent, but he was a dapper man with a stock of snow white hair and black eyes that caught her attention. He said, "Myra, you don't know me?"

"I can't say that I do, but you're shore welcome to be here. Wait a minute. Wait a minute. Arno, is it really you?"

"Yes, yes, my dear sister. I never thought I would see you again, but your granddaughter and Dolly put this all together and convinced me to come. Our nephew, Anthony, offered to come for me on Long Island and take us to the airport. He stayed until we were comfortable on the plane. I could not pass up the chance to see you again."

"I haven't seen ya since Jesse's funeral. I shore am sorry that Ava (Arno's wife) died. I wish I could have been with ya then. I have thought of ya every day and prayed to live long enough to see my brother again." Myra's voice was hoarse and mixed with tears.

What a reunion for the two sisters and brother. They had gone through the hardest of times together and had memories of tears and laughter. Most of all, Arno and Dolly remembered that Myra was the one who kept the family together and somehow provided for them. Seeing the happiness of the three gave everyone a true Christmas blessing.

Christmas Day was hectic with a huge dinner and jolly times at the Christmas tree. Dolly and Arno were the stars of the day, and everyone wanted time with them. The party went on into the night and was far from *the hard candy Christmases* of their childhood.

By noon of the next day, all had returned home, except for Laura, Dolly, and Arno. They would stay another day and return to Atlanta and fly back to New York together.

The next day, Laura left the brother and sisters to enjoy their alone time. This provided an opportunity to visit Ian's family in Waycross. They had so much to share and wanted to hear all about Laura's book signing tours and the success of their son's book. They were also very proud to hear of Laura's interesting life in New York.

Mrs. Wilhelm made a point to encourage Laura to go on with her life. "Honey, you don't need to be alone for the rest of your life. Ian would never want that for you. Don't you spend your life working and grieving for him. That's exactly what he would say to you. It's hard, but we've all got to keep on going for his sake. That's how we keep him a part of us."

Laura gave a weak smile and only said, "I know he is proud of you and your strength." She wasn't ready to make this commitment.

"Ian's book has left us well fixed for life, but I'd give it up to have him beside us. We've paid off the mortgage, fixed up the place, bought our first new car, and have plenty to send all four grandchildren to college. What's left we've put in our will to evenly divide among our two girls and you," Mr. Wilhelm added.

"Please don't leave me anything. It should be for your family."

"Little Lady, I'll do as I please," he said with a laugh.

Laura knew that he would, but she also had plans for any money she received. A scholarship fund for a journalism student at Georgia State could be established in Ian's memory. From what she knew of the book sales and movie residuals, this would be well funded.

The next morning, Laura, Dolly, and Arno returned to Atlanta and caught a flight which would have them in New York by dinner time. When they landed, Laura settled each into a taxi to take them straight home.

Chapter XXXIII

1974

New York did not have a white Christmas, but New Year's Eve morning brought a beautiful cascade of snowflakes. The city was covered by evening. Snow did not slow down New Yorker's revelry—it only made taxis harder to hail.

Laura was still on her vacation days, and the office would be closed for New Year's Day, so she could stay snug and warm in her apartment.

She had worried about leaving Elizabeth for the long period she would be in Georgia until she learned from a coworker about pet sitters. New Yorkers seem to have a service for every need. She called a number recommended by the pet store (which she visited often and kept Elizabeth well fed, pampered, and supplied with toys). A young college girl took the job and would visit Elizabeth once a day to feed and play with her. Laura had emphasized that she wanted petting for her kitty. The sitter also watered the plants which Laura kept accumulating. Even with all that care, Elizabeth was overjoyed to have her mama home. Laura took this as a great compliment.

A neighborhood market delivered to her building, so she phoned in an order which included ingredients for chili and a pound cake. After ordering, she realized that a tube pan was needed for the pound cake. That baking would have to wait until she could go shopping.

Several bottles of wine and a big pot of chili kept her quite satisfied to stay home and look out her window at the winter wonderland. She had brought home three manuscripts from the slush pile, and combined with old classic movies on TV, the days were filled.

She did consider Ian's mother's words to her about not spending her life alone and decided that did not apply to her. Her life was filled, and she was never lonely.

Back to work on Monday, she returned the manuscripts to the slush pile. She always hoped to find a winner but had to be reasonable that all books are not accepted, even though the author had great hopes.

For the rest of the week, snow was still on the ground and slushy. The winter wonderland had turned into dingy piles on each side of the streets. Christmas was a happy memory and left nothing more to anticipate for a while. She thought of treating Dolly to a matinee but realized it would not be a good time for her elderly aunt to travel into the city. She had vowed to herself that her life was fulfilling and never lonely, but the walk home from the subway on the freezing, dismal evenings gave her a pensiveness that she fought to ward off.

The next Sunday morning was bright and sunny. The apartment walls were beginning to seem confining which even Elizabeth could not change. It was time to rejoin the world. She decided to walk over to a park and hoped to see children sledding. On the way, she picked up a gigantic cup of coffee and bagel with cream cheese and jam to eat on a park bench. She was turning into quite a New Yorker but couldn't develop a taste for lox with her bagel. The only salmon she had eaten was her grandmother's patties made with canned salmon and lots of onions which she smothered in catchup. The cream cheese with jam was more to her taste.

On her walk to the park, she passed a small church that must have been on that spot for ages. The bricks were weathered, and some of the people gathering to enter looked the same. It gave her heart a tug because from the cross and red door, she knew it was the same as Ian's church. She cherished the memory of seeing him kneel in prayer before sitting in the pew and going to the altar to receive communion. She thought of how his service had not been a funeral but a celebration of his life. As a child, attending church had been a regular part of her life; but after leaving home, this stopped. Ian's devotion to his faith was a wonderment to her.

The bell rang calling the people to worship. She wasn't dressed for church, and her hands were filled with coffee cup and bagel, but her feet didn't seem to know. After tossing her breakfast into a nearby trash container, she followed the latecomers into the church and sat on a back pew. Her knees seemed to have their own intentions, and she found herself kneeling. She was embarrassed before God for she didn't know a prayer to say, but that began to feel okay.

The music and processional started, and she watched the servers and priests follow the cross to the front of the church. Someone reached over her shoulder and handed her a prayer book opened to the right page. She followed the liturgies with her eyes but did not make a sound. The youngest of the priests gave a short sermon, but she was distracted by thoughts of how she could make an unnoticed exit before the Eucharist. Then she heard, *Let us humbly confess our sins unto Almighty God.* She found herself on her knees again. She did not have to locate the general confession, for the same arm reached over her shoulder and exchanged prayer books with her. She was on the right page again and read every word of the confession which seemed to include all her committed and omitted sins.

She was trapped. There were people on either side of her and all on their knees. There was no way to leave without stumbling over them. The service continued, and she heard the young priest tell her that God had promised forgiveness of all sins of those who repented and turned to him with true faith. *Could she do that?* As the Eucharistic service continued, she followed in the prayer book.

Then without a thought, she was in the line to the altar. From Ian, she had learned to cup her hands to receive the bread and to bring the cup to her lips, so she was not at loss. The young priest was giving the bread on her end of the altar. When he reached her, she looked into his eyes as he said, *The Body of Christ, the bread of heaven* and placed the wafer in her hand. For a moment, their eyes seemed locked together. Following him was a man serving the cup, and she felt the tingle of good red wine pulse through her body. She crossed herself and walked out the side door without disturbing anyone. This had been an experience, but it was not for her.

At the end of the week, she decided to take her walk on Saturday and avoid passing the church on Sunday with its doors open and bell ringing. She stopped for her usual coffee and bagel from a cart to enjoy with the fresh air and children playing in the park. There was no route to take without passing the church, but it should be closed and locked tight on a Saturday.

Wrong—there was a crowd gathering by the side of the church. One look identified them as some of New York's multitudes of homeless and street people. She always felt guilt when she passed them on the street and looked straight ahead but tried to made up for this by sending a monthly check to a homeless shelter that she often passed.

Suddenly, the group started moving toward a back door. Intrigued, she followed and saw them entering. The young priest from the past Sunday was standing at the door and greeting each person. The priest saw her standing on the sidewalk as the last of the crowd entered. She turned to leave, and he called out, "Wait."

Startled, she did wait. He hurried over and said, "I remember you were at the altar last Sunday. I am so happy to see you again. Perhaps you do not know about the mission we do here on Saturdays."

Laura was embarrassed to have been caught watching and could only say, "I just happened to be walking by and wondered if you had church on Saturday." She realized this was a silly answer.

The young man was in a pullover sweater with a clerical collar underneath but no robes or coat. His dark brown curly hair was blowing in the wind, and his soft brown eyes looked directly at her just as he had at the altar.

"This isn't a formal church service, but we are following the teachings of Christ to feed his sheep. We serve a hearty breakfast every Saturday morning to anyone in need of a meal. The soup kitchens in this area close on weekends, but folks are still hungry, so we try to meet that need."

Laura opened her purse ready to give a donation, but he raised his hand in protest and said, "No, no. We can always use money, but today, you can give something more. Come inside and help us serve."

If a tornado had swept down and swallowed her up, she would have been thankful. She was ashamed to say that less fortunate people were always on her conscience but at a distance. She did love Peter, Paul, and Mary who admonished with the words of the Bob Dylan song, *How many times must a man turn his head, pretending he just doesn't see.* She followed the priest into the parish hall which was filled with the arousing smells of breakfast.

"How about you pouring the juice? Just remember, no seconds until everyone has been served."

That surprised Laura, for she would have given everyone all they wanted but then realized the juice might be in short supply. A donation could help here.

Two hundred hands reached for a glass of juice from her that morning. All showed the ravage of life on the streets. Eyes were blank, hands rough and scarred, clothes definitely had not been washed in weeks. The distinct odor of people who survived without a home or shower identified them before they reached her offering of juice. Many said, "Thank you, miss," but others said nothing and kept their eyes lowered. She was shocked to see women in the line.

Juice was a favorite, and quickly seconds were being requested. She shared their desire for the fresh taste of orange juice and was disillusioned when the priest brought out a jar of orange juice powder to be mixed in the pitchers. *How sad that they could not even be served real orange juice.*

The serving time ended, and the priest came over with a cup of coffee for her. "Come sit down with me to catch our breath before we start to clean up." Laura thought her duty was completed. She hadn't thought about cleaning up but realized that must also be done. Fortunately, all paper products had been used so the cleanup would not be difficult.

The priest pulled out two chairs, and they sat at a table while other volunteers cleared and wiped the tables. "Thank you. I know you were roped in from the streets, but I was short-handed today and needed you," he said as a weak apology.

"I was glad to help. Actually, I enjoyed it."

"I am the associate rector of Saint James and in charge of this mission, so I have to conscript folks to help. By the way, my name is Paul Alcott. Father Paul here at church, but Paul to you. Now who are you, and what are you doing in the middle of Manhattan with that tantalizing Southern accent?"

Laura giggled, and the first thing she said was "Are you related to Louisa May?"

"Who?" he replied.

"*Little Women,* or don't boys who grow up to be priests read that?"

"Oh, you caught me off guard. Of course I've read *Little Women.*"

"Really, my favorite character was Meg. Everyone has a favorite in the March family. Who was your favorite?"

He was caught and blushed to his temples. He did not know what she meant by the March family. His head shake, and fake laugh revealed his guilt, but he quickly went on to say, "You haven't answered my questions."

"I'm Laura Porter, and I'm from Georgia."

"So what landed you in Manhattan, Laura Porter from Georgia? By the way, are you related to William Sydney Porter?" Paul thought he was paying her back, but he did not know he was dealing with a literary fanatic.

"Not related, except by admiration for the works of O'Henry. My favorite is *The Gift of the Magi.*"

"Let me guess. You are either an English teacher or work in publishing."

"Publishing, I worked for the *Atlanta Journal* before I came to New York to work on editing the book of my late fiancé." She was surprised at revealing this to a stranger for she never shared her background.

"Game over—you're Laura."

"How do you know that?"

"Ian Wilhelm's book led me on many marches during my seminary days. His book will be a poignant chronicle for this ungodly war. Your introduction made me feel as if I knew him well. I have my copy at home. If I bring it, will you sign it after church tomorrow? Also, you are much prettier than the actress who played you in the movie."

Laura blushed and said, "Thank you, but my character was only in one scene—telling him good-bye before boarding the plane."

Attending church again had not been in her plans, but how could she say no?

By the time their conversation ended, the tables had been cleaned and all dishwashing done.

He reached for her hand and said, "Thank you again, Laura. I will see you at the altar tomorrow. Wait for me after the recessional. I do want my book signed by the real Laura."

Her thoughts on the walk home were filled with images of people sitting and waiting for Paul's blessing before breaking their bread together. She found herself humming the reply to Bob Dylan's question, *The answer, my friend, is blowing in the wind. The answer is blowing in the wind.*

Father Paul did not preach the next day, and she did not kneel on the side of the altar where he was serving the bread. Using the prayer book and following the service was more comfortable for her. As the recessional passed her pew, he looked directly at her and smiled.

She waited near the door until the worshippers had finished shaking hands or hugging. He caught her eye and mouthed "wait." He went to the vesting room in back and returned with book in hand.

To Father Paul, Thank you for reading and living my book. Laura Porter for Ian Wilhelm was the inscription she always wrote.

Chapter XXXIV

1974

The next Saturday found Laura out of bed before eight o'clock and dressed in jeans and a Georgia State sweatshirt. She felt a rush of unexpected enthusiasm and hurried to the church to help with the cooking before the doors opened at nine o'clock. Father Paul greeted her with an embrace as did several others. This seemed to be a hugging church.

"How are you at scrambling eggs?" Father Paul asked.

"I should be good. That's one of my favorite suppers." This was true.

The first chore was cracking six dozen eggs and mixing with milk to pour into a huge frying pan. She turned the heat low like her grandmother's instruction and started stirring. This was going to be slow, and the doors would open in fifteen minutes with hungry folks expecting eggs.

A lady buttering toast saw Laura's skillet of still liquid eggs and said, "Honey, that is probably the best heat for eggs, but here we have to do things fast. Just turn up that heat and keep them stirring around."

The eggs were ready on time. As soon as the pan went to the serving line, another pan was set on the stove for her to stir. She went through three pans of eggs until diners had to be turned away for seconds because there were no more eggs.

As the last stragglers were finishing their plates, an ancient black man scuffled up to her. "Missus, I shore enjoy hearin' ya talkin'. I ain't heard that kinda takin' since I left home many a year ago. That's one of the things I get plain hongry fer—that and some grits to go along with these here good eggs."

"I want grits with my eggs too. My aunt in Georgia sends me packages with foods I can't get up here, like grits. I think some stores have them, but they're not the same."

"Youse from Georgia. I'm is too. Where you from? I wuz born in a little place called Cobbtown. You ever heard of it?"

"Of course, I know Cobbtown. It's not far from Swainsboro, my home."

"Sho nuf, that's right up the road and makes us near kin, if you don't mind me sayin' that. Ma'am, when I wuz in Georgia, they used to call me Ace 'cause that's what kinda baseball pitcher I wuz back then."

She looked at the desolate man and thought of the book Ian had intended to write about the traveling black baseball teams. He would have been one of those players who played the game before Jackie Robinson broke the color barrier. Ian would have found this a great interview for his book. She wouldn't embarrass Ace by asking more of his background.

"Glad to meet you, Ace. I'm Laura or Laura Jean back in Georgia." Laura knew she had a friend for life. She also knew that next week he would have grits with his eggs.

She mentioned grits to Father Paul. He thought it a grand idea after she explained that grits are very filling and would help the problem of running out of eggs. She also offered to furnish the grits. Luckily, she had just received a care package from Laura James which contained three pounds of grits and other Georgia delicacies.

Sunday morning she pulled one of her better dresses from the wardrobe, took time to arrange her hair and makeup. Since she had a long walk, she wore flat shoes and covered her head from the wind with a scarf. With her long wool coat, she looked dressed for church. She had noticed that most of the church goers did not dress up as much as she remembered from church goers in the South. Father Paul had explained to her that Saint James had once been a thriving parish of upper middle-class parishioners, but in time they had either died or moved away. Now the church struggled with a less affluent congregation who made up for their lack of resources with their willingness to serve and give their time. No one had extra money to spend on expensive clothes. That made her feel slightly guilty, but for this one Sunday, she wanted to look especially nice. *Who was she trying to impress?*

This time she felt quite comfortable in the service and listened intently to the sermon of Father Paul. After the recessional, she joined the line of folks waiting for a turn to speak to him.

When she greeted Paul at the door, he asked her to wait. After shaking the hand of the last man leaving the church and hugging the last lady, he found Laura sitting in a pew waiting.

"I was wondering, if you don't have anything planned for the afternoon, maybe we could have some lunch together. I get tired of eating alone."

"So do I, and I am free until this evening." She was being coy because all she had to do in the evening was call her grandmother.

"Okay, let me change, and we will get some food." He went into a side room to remove his vestments and came out wearing a turtleneck sweater, jeans, and a leather jacket."

"So what happened to the priest?" She laughed.

"He's off duty until Tuesday morning. Tomorrow is my day off. Do you want brunch or lunch?"

"Lunch, please. After scrambling two hundred eggs yesterday, I have lost my appetite for breakfast."

His response surprised her. He put his arm around her and drew her close. "You smell so good and are too beautiful for a priest to keep his eyes off when he is trying to preach a sermon."

Laura blushed and did not know how to reply, so she changed the subject to lunch. "What do you like to eat?"

"Everything except caviar."

"That narrows it down considerably. I love deli food."

"So do I, and I know just the place with the greatest corned beef," he replied.

After sitting over an extended lunch of corned beef sandwiches, several cups of coffee, and intense conversation, he walked her home, kissed her on the cheek, and said, "I'll see you Saturday with the grits."

Laura took a cab to the church the next Saturday. She couldn't make the long walk carrying three pounds of grits, two pounds of butter, a block of cheese, and box of black pepper. When Ace, her Georgia friend, arrived, a huge pot of grits filled with cheese, lots of butter and sprinkled with black pepper was bubbling on the serving line.

Ace's eyes lit up, and he broke into a smile when he saw her and the pot of grits. "Now this lady knows how to cook some grits. Look at all that black pepper on top."

The grits were a hit with all, and for the first time, every diner left with a full stomach because as Laura explained; grits are filling. Father Paul and many of the servers had a dish of grits and declared delicious. She had converted a few Yankees.

Word of the Grits Lady spread on the street, and new diners were added each week. They came from Georgia, South and North Carolina, Mississippi, Tennessee, and Alabama to get a taste of home. Father Paul suspected some were pseudo-Southerners. He suggested they take a dialect test before being served seconds. Laura laughed at this and relished in the popularity of her grits. She made a telephone plea to Laura James to send more grits. When she explained the need, her aunt was delighted to be a part of this service.

Her Saturday mornings were spent at the breakfast mission. Paul was strictly Father Paul during this time. After cleaning up, both went separate ways since the work was tiring. Laura did household chores and took a long nap with Elizabeth. Paul polished his sermons for the next week. She really did not know or care what else took his time. She learned he preached two Sundays a month, but he also did two weekday services.

Sunday became their day together. After removing vestments, he became Paul to her. First lunch, sometimes a movie, a long walk, and much conversation. She learned Paul was from a small town in New Hampshire. Both of his parents were killed in an auto accident while he was in college, leaving him with an older sister who lived in Italy. He went to college at William and Mary in Virginia. After college, he spent a year in Europe visiting his sister and traveling around the continent. Then he spent two years working in a drug rehab program and pondering his calling. How/why did he know he was called to the priesthood? It just slowly consumed him and accelerated after the death of his parents. His seminary days were spent in Pennsylvania.

Laura shared similar information about herself but avoided any talk of Ian. One day, she confessed to him that she was not really religious and sometimes questioned the existence of God. She amended that with "But I do know Jesus lived, and I believe in the things he said."

Paul was not perplexed at that, explained his understanding of the Trinity and ended with "If you only believe in one of the three, you chose well."

Many times she did not understand his statements. She also had difficulty separating Father Paul at the altar who gave her the body of Christ from the Paul in jeans and sweatshirts who gave her the wonderful kisses.

After a few weeks of wandering around the city to find places to be together, she invited him to her apartment. She had hesitated, but he readily accepted the invitation. This extended their time together, and he usually stayed until late in the evening. Sometimes they fixed a light supper to enjoy in front of the TV. Sometimes they sat on the balcony and quietly listened to music. Elizabeth became his pal and divided her time between their laps. Conversation was the main activity, and they bantered, argued, and agreed just as she had done with Ian. There she said it; he was like Ian. Was this why he was so appealing, and she had no inclination to stop his kisses? Her conscience told her to refrain from asking him to stay the night, but her lonely body told her otherwise. His sensibility kept him from asking.

New York is at its best in spring. It is a time for falling in love, and this was happening. They walked through the parks and streets holding hands or with arms linked and sometimes stopped to steal a kiss in a secluded spot. On one of those walks, he said it, "Laura Jean Porter, I am so much in love with you that I must tell you and the world." She said nothing. Her mind was a whirlwind of confusion. How could she love him and still feel so much love for Ian?

He knew he had spoken too soon, but he just couldn't hold back any longer. Showing indifference was unlike her. If a couple had come to him for counseling in such a situation, he would lead them to an open discussion of their true feelings and doubts. But did he really want to know her true feeling and doubts about being in love with him? He knew there was a strong attraction between them. Lord knows, he had almost weakened many times and asked to spend the night. He wanted her more than anything he had ever known, and he wanted to be her husband. Did her coolness come from him being a priest, or was he in an unfair competition with a dead man? He had to do some thinking.

Laura was having similar questions. Did she want to give him up and go through the rest of her life with only the memories of Ian to love? Could memories replace a warm body and kisses that made your heart race? She had some thinking to do also. Probably best if she did it alone, so she called the church to say that she would be away and could not serve on Saturday. The person answering the phone said, "We will miss you. Father Paul will be away also."

Both sought solitude for the weekend to go over every aspect of their relationship—why it wouldn't work—why it had to work because they were in love. Laura was already in her pajamas on Sunday evening when the call came from the lobby. "Laura, it's me. May I come up?" Her heart leaped with joy.

She threw on a robe and fell into his arms when the door opened. There was no question that this had to be resolved so they could be together. Paul told her his thoughts about laying all the cards on the table and talking about their true feelings.

"Do you love me?" He was taking a chance.

"I have to tell you that I do, but how can I love you when there is still so much love in my heart for Ian?"

"Oh, my darling, there is no limit on how much you can love. You have enough love in your heart that there is plenty for the memory of Ian and enough for me too. I would never want to take him away from you. I just want you to love me too. I won't compete with him for your love. He was your first love, and that will never change. He is a hero to you and to me. That will never change. I gladly share your love with his memory."

Laura was so moved that she could do nothing but snuggle in his arms and cry, but she did muffle out, "I do love you, Paul, and I want to keep Ian in my heart also. Will that work?"

"Of course, it will work. We both understand that. Now another question, do you fear being

the wife of a priest?"

"Oh no, I would be honored. My fear is that I am not worthy to be the wife of a priest. I am afraid I will be a handicap for you."

"That could never be. You will be a perfect wife for a priest. Just look at the impression you have made on the breakfast diners." He said this to make her laugh and it worked. "I fully expect you to continue your career. I promise that I won't pressure you to be president of the church women, sing in the choir, or iron the vestments." This again made her laugh.

"Another thing we must recognize is that I will never earn a lot of money. You will always have a much higher income. Does that bother you?"

"Does it bother you?" Laura had never had that thought.

"No, I didn't choose this vocation. It was chosen for me, and money was never discussed. However . . . I would not object if you used some of your exorbitant publishing money to purchase more and better cooking ware."

"You nut, shut up and kiss me." And he did, and he did, and he did.

"One other small detail, how do you feel about children?" This was necessary to Paul since he knew Laura would continue her career.

"If they're your children, I want a bunch. I was an only child and always wished for brothers and sisters. I hope we can have a large family."

"If we can't, we will get them from somewhere." Paul was delighted. "Now one more question. Will you marry me? And it better be soon?"

There were no more issues and only joy excelling. Paul took money from the investments he had inherited from his parents and bought a half-karat solitaire diamond. Laura insisted that she only wanted a gold band, but he wanted to show the whole world.

Word quickly spread through the parish that Father Paul was marrying the Grits Lady. The breakfast diners were as happy as if they were family. Ace congratulated Paul by saying, "Now you got them grits fer yore breakfast every day."

Neither wanted a large wedding. Paul had a fellow seminarian who was the priest of a small parish in Maine. He offered to have a quiet wedding for them and to loan them a cottage on the Canadian border for their honeymoon. That appealed to both.

The task ahead was to inform all of Laura's family. First, she took him to Queens to meet Aunt Dolly. She fell to Paul's charm at once, and was relieved that her niece would have someone to share her life. She knew too well the loneliness of being a single woman in old age. She asked them to go with her to introduce Paul to Arno. Laura took Monday off, and the three of them rode the train to Long Island. Arno was as happy as Dolly. In the short time he had known Laura, she had grown very dear to him.

First call was to Myra. It was a great surprise because Laura had not mentioned Paul to any of the family. Her grandmother's happiness was unbounded. *"Thank you, Lord, for answering my prayers that my girl would find happiness again. You doubly pleased me. He's a preacher to boot."* Laura promised to bring him down as soon as possible after the wedding.

The aunts were as excited and thankful as Myra. Laura had a hard time talking Ruth and Wallace out of coming up for the wedding. They were appeased when she promised to let them throw a big party in Fitzgerald in their honor.

To let her hometown friends know, she sent a small announcement to the *Forest Blade*. It only announced her engagement to the Reverend Paul Alcott and that the wedding would be in Maine.

That was not sufficient for the *Blade*. Laura James sent her the article that carried a head shot she had sent to her grandmother and aunts and practically gave a biography and genealogy of her. Paul was listed as a well-respected clergyman in New York City. They wanted to show off their successful hometown girl.

A package from Wallace contained a white filmy gown and negligee. Although she was no longer qualified for this, she would love wearing it for Paul. He would not question the eligibility—only admire the fragile beauty of the lingerie. She shopped until she found a simple lace sheath for her wedding dress. The rest of her honeymoon wardrobe would be warm and comfortable for Maine. It was still summer in the city, but Paul had warned her that the cottage would be chilly in mornings and evenings.

An early flight from LaGuardia got them to Bangor before noon. They changed to a small plane to reach an airport near the township where Henry, Paul's friend from seminary, was a rector. A rental car finished the journey. The wedding was scheduled for four o'clock in Henry's church. Laura immediately found lifelong friends in Henry and his wife Casey. After a bit of a rest for the bride and groom, they dressed for their wedding. Laura was surprised but pleased to see that Paul was wearing a black suit and his clerical collar.

The tiny church was picturesque New England. All dark wood and boxed pews. The stained glass window behind the altar let in light from the brilliant setting sun. The altar guild had placed the wedding linens and lit the candles. It was a surreal scene with only candlelight and a priest to perform the marriage service for a colleague. Casey was the only attendant.

When they walked into the church, Laura was surprised and confused to see a dozen or more people sitting in the pews. Later, Paul explained that weddings were a celebration for the church, and all were invited.

Laura had taken the time to learn every part of the marriage ceremony in the prayer book by heart. She and Paul looked deeply into each other's eyes the entire service and said their "*I do*" and enunciated each word, "*for better, for worse, for richer, for poorer, in sickness, and in health, to love and to cherish, until we are parted by death.*" This solemn vow was welded into their hearts. Rings were exchanged; they were pronounced man and wife. The Eucharist was celebrated, and the Reverend Paul Alcott and his new bride, Laura Porter, received their first communion as man and wife from his friend. After the service, Laura greeted and thanked the dear folks who had been a part of her most special day.

Laura would continue to use her maiden name professionally but agreed all children would be Alcotts.

After dinner with Henry and Casey at a local restaurant, they made the two hour drive to the cabin. Darkness had fallen before they arrived. Paul was navigating on handwritten instructions, and the roads were narrow with many turns. After missing a turn for the second time, Laura laughed and exclaimed, "Now I've heard a preacher cuss."

The cabin was all they could have hoped, a real log structure with a front porch nestled in a densely wooded area. One room served as bedroom, sitting room, and kitchen. There was running water, but the only light was from lanterns and heat from a fireplace. The refrigerator was a real ice box.

Their friends had stocked the pantry with breakfast items and left a note that additional groceries and ice could be bought at a store two miles away. Casey left a clam chowder recipe for their use and instructions for where to buy fresh clams, lobsters, and fish.

They were exhausted from the day and the excitement of being alone at last as husband and wife and immediately snuggled into bed under a warm down quilt to make love and unite their bodies and souls.

After a trek to the store and fish market, they spent the rest of the days walking in the woods, canoeing on the lake, watching wildlife and birds, sitting on the porch to await the fall of darkness, conversation that never ended, and most of all, in each other's arms.

This blissful time came to an end, and they would return to the new ecstasy of living together forever. After a stop off with Henry and Casey to return the key and give their thanks, the car was returned, and they were on flights back to New York.

Elizabeth was at the door to greet her returning parents. Paul's clothes were hanging in the closet, and his belongings piled together awaiting decision on where these would fit. Being home was good because it was now their home.

Happy days were filled with work, rushing home to embrace, cooking, enjoying a meal together, and majesty of sharing their bed.

Over Labor Day weekend, they made the trip to Georgia. The travel time was shortened by flying into Macon and driving directly to Fitzgerald. The family party was planned for Saturday at the church hall. The entire family would be there to meet their niece's new husband. They arrived Saturday morning and would leave on Monday. Laura and Paul would stay with Myra. Laura felt a little shy about sleeping with Paul in her grandmother's small extra bedroom, but this soon felt natural.

Paul fit right into the family and talked easily with everyone. He purposely spent as much time as possible beside Grandma Myra. They had serious talks, and Myra knew her precious Laura was in hands that were serving the Lord. That gave her peace.

The party was a typical MacTavish event—plentiful food, abundance of gifts, and much laughter and good natured teasing. Everyone felt awkward about addressing Paul until he assured them that he was "Paul" and no other title necessary, except when he was in church.

In the evening, Laura left Paul in the company of Myra and went up to Stephen's house to have a private talk with him. He was anticipating this discussion.

"Uncle Stephen, I can see Grandma has gone downhill even more since I last saw her at Christmas. What do her doctors say?"

"Honey, we have to prepare ourselves that Mama is getting old, and from the hard life she had when she was young, her body is just worn out. She's been to doctors, and Wallace even took her to a specialist in Macon. She has heart problems, but she is not in shape for any kind of heart surgery, and she wouldn't agree to it anyway. We're doing good to even get her to take medicine."

"I've never seen her just sit and not join in the group. I couldn't believe she hadn't cooked even one dish for the party. That's not like her."

"She can't hold out to do much, and she knows it. I think she didn't want to get far away from Paul. She shore took to him. In fact, we all did. I'd love to hear him preach a sermon."

'Tell me the truth, Uncle Stephen. Is she dying?"

"Baby girl, we're all dying. She just might go sooner."

Monday morning when they prepared to leave, Laura had trouble saying good-bye. She held onto Myra as long as she could. She didn't say, "Good-bye" but "We'll see you again soon."

When they drove away to catch their flight in Macon, Myra didn't feel the sorrow that she usually felt when her granddaughter left. All was well.

Thank you, precious Lord, for bringing my granddaughter to this place in her life. She has had sorrows and upsets, but you knew all would be well. I'm just thankful it happened while I'm still on earth, and I can go to my rest without a troubled heart. I guess I should have learned by now to stay out of your way and put my trust in you. Amen, Myra.

A Christmas celebration was held at Stephen's house. Most of the family came for a quiet holiday. Laura did not come until New Year's Day and only stayed a day and night. She had shared the Christmas church services with Paul. Myra enjoyed every minute of the visit.

As Laura bent to give her a final hug and kiss, Myra's eyes sparkled with happiness, and she said, "Baby girl, I can get a good night's sleep now and know that you are well and with a good man."

Chapter XXXV

1975

"Mrs. MacTavish, I know you want me to be honest with you, and I will. Your heart is getting weaker, and these spells you describe are coming more frequently."

"Most of my folks died from heart dropsy. They say it runs in families." Myra had always expected this diagnosis.

"I am not familiar with that term, but I imagine the word, *dropsy*, was used to label several heart conditions. We do know that heredity is a factor. There are ways to control this and better medications today than in your ancestor's day."

Arliss interrupted, "What can we do to help her, doctor?"

He understood Arliss's question but turned to look directly at Myra. "The spells you are having are called angina. A heart must have oxygen to function. Oxygen is in the blood. Your arteries carry blood to your heart. If the arteries are damaged, the heart does not get enough oxygen. That is the cause of the pain you feel."

"When the pain comes, I always have what I call shortness of breath and feel like a ton of bricks is on my chest. How can I get my breathing to do better?" Myra had always believed that she could fix anything if only she understood the cause.

The doctor waited a moment before speaking. "It's not that simple, Mrs. Mac. New techniques and surgeries—" She interrupted before the doctor could finish.

"Stop right there, doctor. I've lived a long life, and I know where I'm goin'. I want to just live out my days for as long as I have left without the awful pain,"

"I understand what you're saying, and I did not mean for you to think I was setting you up for surgery. Hard work, diet, and stress have contributed to your problem, but we can't change what happened in the past. I can prescribe some medicine that will help with the pain. You will put it under your tongue when you feel the symptoms coming on. It will lower the pain level, and that will improve your breathing. Will you promise to use the medication as prescribed?"

"I reckon I'm lucky there is a medicine now. My poor papa must have suffered awful."

"Mrs. Mac, you still have a lot of value to this world. I know of the good you have done with the story hours and literacy programs. We want you with us as long as possible. Place the tablet under your tongue when you feel the pain coming on and get as much rest as you need."

They went home with a prescription for nitroglycerin. Stephen was anxious to hear what the doctor had said, but he waited to hear it from Arliss. She gave the full report which was not encouraging except for the medicine to lessen the pain.

As the oldest boy, he had stood by his mama's side through many hardships, but he could not make her well. "Let's just keep this to ourselves, and let her be the one to tell the others."

There was no need to tell. The rest of the family knew their precious mother was awaiting her time.

The pills gave Myra some relief. Just knowing that slipping a pill under her tongue would ease the pain, gave her freedom to go on with her life.

Arliss was always thoughtful and took her to the places that she wanted to visit. Her stops at the reading programs and the library were welcomed with festivity. This lifted her spirits, but she only sat in the rocker at the library and listened to the story being read to the children by one of the librarians. At the reading class, she only complimented and encouraged the new readers.

The doctor insisted that she limit her company and get more rest. She didn't want her callers to think that they weren't welcome, so she devised a way to have her company and get her rest too. She made a sign to put on her door:

I appreciate you coming by, and wish I could see you.
Right now, I am resting like the doctor told me to do.
Please come back later, and we will sit and visit. Myra

This worked, and visitors soon learned to check for the sign. Arliss's phone rang constantly with inquiries about her mother-in-law. Of course, Arliss did not complain and always answered with a cheery "Hello." The family came often, but only one family visited at a time. This gave them one-on-one time with her and was not as tiring.

Stephen arranged for a lady to sit with her every day, but Myra did not like this and said, "I'm supposed to be gettin' rest, and now I gotta entertain someone I don't even know."

This was solved by her friends from the Projects taking turns to sit quietly with her. Her refrigerator was kept stocked with prepared food by the church women's group. Stephen or Arliss sat with her each evening until she was asleep in bed. The buzzer beside her bed that connected to Stephen's bedside could bring him to her side in a moment. They preferred for her to have a caretaker around the clock, but they had to respect her wishes.

Myra spent her time thinking over memories that were so clear she felt as if she had had a visit from the person. Her thoughts went into the past. The sweet teacher who taught her to crochet popped in along with Miz Sara who taught her to can and her friend Annie's mother who taught her to sew. She couldn't have made out in life nearly as well as she did without these skills. *Oh my dear Lord, I don't say thank you enough for putting these kind folks into my life. I know you see 'em a lot. Tell 'em how thankful I am for their help. Amen, Myra.*

This happened almost every time she took a rest, and she never knew who might turn up. Sometimes there would be someone that she didn't recognize, and then her mind would flash back to the time when this person was a part of her life. She began to look forward to these dream visits.

Through January and February, each day found her less active. She stayed in bed longer and usually got no further than her recliner. Her Christmas presents had included a lot of books. She looked through each one but couldn't stick with it after a few pages. One of the children had given her a tape player several Christmases ago and taped music to play. When Laura visited on New Year's Day, her gift was two tapes. One was the *Harlem Gospel Choir* who sang the old hymns Myra remembered and loved. She could tell the singers were black because nobody could sing Gospel as good as black singers. They sang from their heart and soul. The second tape Laura had recorded specially for her grandmother. It was the sermon Paul delivered on Christmas Eve. She had to put the recorder under the pulpit so it would not be seen and hoped it wouldn't make any sound or be noticed. This worked fine, and Laura could enable her grandmother to hear the preaching of her grandson-in- law. Myra listened to both tapes every day.

March came in like a lamb, and Myra enjoyed the pleasant sunny days that were warm enough for her to sit on the porch. This seemed to revive her, and all hoped she would be able to enjoy spring.

One night near the middle of March, the chest pain hit her after she had been sleeping for a few hours. Breathing was a struggle, and she felt like an elephant was sitting on her chest. Her pills were in the living room, but she didn't have energy to get them or to push the bedside button to summon Stephen. As the pain eased up a bit, she dragged herself to the front door. *If I can just get out to the porch and take in some fresh air, I think I can breathe better.* Her thoughts did not include the pills or calling Stephen. Her goal was the rocking chair, and she made it there.

She sank into the chair, put her head back on the cushion, and dozed off. The dreams started. First, a young lady holding the hand of a little girl came up the steps. When she looked carefully, she recognized Idella in the dress that she had made for her high school graduation. But who was this little girl? Suddenly, she knew. "Come to me, honey. You shore are making a pretty girl and look a lot like yore big sister." Her angel baby had died at six weeks, but her heart told her she was seeing baby Mary Alice at an older age. They left as quickly as they had come.

Following them came a soldier boy in his uniform. He didn't say anything but just sat on the step. A man in overalls and straw hat joined the soldier on the steps and took out a corncob pipe to light. His blue eyes were twinkling, and he looked rested and not tired from working in the field. Not a word was spoken. Myra sat rocking and enjoying the familiar smell of rabbit tobacco. She was thankful to see her papa and brother Jesse looking well and peaceful. When she opened her eyes they were gone. The dream must have ended.

All pain was gone. Myra was breathing like a young girl. The fresh air had been better than a pill.

She wanted the dreams to come back, so she leaned onto the cushion and closed her eyes. It seemed like that was the end of her dreams, so she just continued to rest in the cool of the dark night.

Then she saw the headlights of a car. When it pulled up in front of the house, it wasn't a new model like folks drove today. It looked like the first car James had ever owned. A young man got out and started walking toward the porch. He had a full head of dark hair and a smirk of a smile. She was a little afraid until she got the scent of Old Spice aftershave, and he spoke. "Miss Myra, you are as pretty as the day I met you. I've been waiting for you." He extended his hand. Myra took it and followed him to the car.

"Momma, Momma, why are you out here in the dark? Momma, are you awake?"

Myra lifted her eyes to look at her son. She smiled and closed her eyes again.

Arliss followed Stephen after he left their bed and said he needed to see about his mother. Something had disturbed his sleep, and he ran through the backyards to reach her.

"Call the doctor, Arliss, and tell him we need him right now. I think she might be in a coma. She seems to be breathing, but I can't wake her up."

He continued to call, "Mama, Mama, wake up. Don't you leave me now. Mama, do you hear me?"

The doctor drove up and ran to the porch. He checked her heart and pulse and put his mouth over her mouth to try to get her to breathe. "Stephen, she is still breathing faintly, but that won't last long. Do you want to take her to the hospital?"

Stephen didn't have to consider the answer. "No, let her go in peace in a place she loves. Look Mama, the sun is coming up. You always said there was joy in the morning. Arliss,

when I found her, she opened her eyes and smiled at me."

"The doctor put his tools away and said, "She's gone." Myra was eighty years old.

Now Stephen had the sad task of telling the others. Word spread quickly through the town that a much loved lady had left them. The family gathered quickly, and arrangements were made.

The funeral was held in the church she had attended with Stephen and Arliss. The crowd spilled out of the large church into the hallways and basement. Her friends crossed all lines of color, social, and economic. Tears shed for Miz Mac were in thanksgiving for the blessing she had been in their lives. Paul read the twenty-third Psalm and noted that when they met for the first time, she told him that she had said this Psalm every night for most of her life. The Lord was her Shepherd.

Cars lined up behind the hearse for the trip to Glencoe. It was a silent two-hour drive for the family. Generations of MacTavish and Stuarts, along with friends, were gathered around the funeral tent when the procession arrived.

As the casket was lowered, Rosa and her daughters sang "Amazing Grace." Myra was sleeping beside her beloved James and back home in Glencoe.

Chapter XXXVI

1975

Laura stared out the window of the plane for most of the flight to New York. Life would never be the same without Grandma. No matter what turmoil had touched her life, Grandma was always there with a tea cake or new dress to soothe away the hurt. She had accepted that all lives must end but had never included her grandmother in this reasoning. *Why does it have to hurt so much?*

"Babe, what are you seeing out that window?" Paul broke into her solitude.

"Georgia fading away." She could think of no other answer.

"Come closer. I need a hug and so do you." She snuggled over, and the tears finally came.

She cried for most of the trip, and Paul only held her. They were oblivious to the other passengers.

When they arrived at the apartment and changed from their traveling clothes, Paul led her to the balcony with a bottle of wine.

Laura's tears started anew. This time Paul reached for her hand and softly said, "You know God invented crying. Tears are a healthy and necessary part of life. I give thanks for tears. Grief would be unbearable without tears."

She looked at his sad eyes and thought of the young college boy receiving news that both of his parents had perished in an automobile accident. He did not have the support of a large, caring family or a life partner to help him.

"Paul, I am so sorry."

"Don't be. Tears are a gift of God."

"I didn't mean sorry for crying so much. I mean sorry that I didn't think of the loss you suffered alone."

"I was never alone, darling, and neither will you ever be alone."

For the first time, she shared a bond of faith with her husband.

She could return to her life with the memory of her grandmother and know that even without family or husband, she would never be alone.

The next day was Saturday, and breakfast had to be served. Unknown to Laura, during the time in Georgia, Paul had picked up ten pounds of grits that he knew she would need as soon as they arrived home.

When Paul gave his blessing before the meal, he added, "Dear Lord, we ask for the repose of the soul of Myra MacTavish, Laura's dear grandmother, who was laid to rest this week."

This recognized the need of the breakfast diners to offer their condolences and share the sadness of their friend. There was no stronger bond of love and friendship than was shown to Laura that day.

Sunday was not Paul's turn in the rotation to preach. He asked the rector if he could be excused of duties at the altar so that he could sit in the pew with his wife. They had never had this opportunity before and held hands throughout the service.

At noon, Aunt Dolly met them at the station, and they rode the train to Long Island to be with Uncle Arno. The visit was healing for Laura and her great-aunt and great-uncle. Laura went through every detail of the funeral. The rest of the afternoon was spent on grandma stories from Laura and childhood memories related by her great-aunt and great-uncle.

They returned to the city, and after a light deli supper, Dolly insisted on taking the subway to Queens. She was a tough New York woman and did not need to be escorted home.

Exhaustion took over when they reached the apartment. Monday was Paul's day off, and Laura decided to take a day of leave also. They needed time to talk.

Paul tiptoed around the apartment for most of the next morning and allowed Laura to sleep as long as she needed. When he heard her stirring, he brought in a tray of bagels with cream cheese and jam, fruit, and a pot of coffee. Her smile and "Good morning, Love" answered his hopes and prayers. They cuddled in the bed and devoured the food. The coffee lasted through the morning while Laura began her talk.

"When I was looking out the plane window and watching my home being left behind, I could see Grandma sitting and pedaling the sewing machine and telling me her wonderful stories. I must somehow preserve those stories."

Paul nodded and did not interrupt to hear more.

"I enjoy my work in publishing, but it is not what I want to do with the rest of my life."

Again, Paul did not comment and only listened intently.

"My grandmother was not educated, but she was so wise. She knew she had been given gifts and these should be shared. Like my church school teacher told me, 'To those whom much is given, much is asked.'"

Paul had no idea where this was heading, but he did not question.

"I know I have a gift of writing, but I do not have a story. I think I can use that talent to teach others who do have a story just as I have helped writers improve their manuscripts. I want to change directions in my career and become a teacher."

Now Paul was ready to speak. "Of course, you should. Leaving your job will give you time to return to school. What about Columbia? You could get a MFA and even a doctorate in creative writing. Let's go for it, babe. Don't worry about the details. I can work it out."

"I was afraid you would think it was foolish to give up a promising career and large income, but I should have known better. I do have some savings but not enough to support us for long."

"Do you think I married you for your money? We can economize on the luxuries, and there are lots of teaching fellowships and scholarships to investigate. I am so proud that you recognize your talent and that you do have so much to give."

Laura was ready to talk on a lighter topic, so she added, "You didn't marry me for my income. You married me for my Southern cooking. Now that you have developed a taste for grits, I can cut our grocery bill in half and keep you filled."

Everything seemed to be in Laura's favor. She made an appointment to talk with an advisor at Columbia to discuss acceptance into the graduate school. After recognizing her background, wheels started turning in the Fine Arts Department. She completed entrance requirements and excelled on the acceptance exam. Her experience in publishing and newspaper journalism brought her a teaching assistant fellowship that would cover her tuition and offer a small stipend.

The publishing job did not end. When she turned in her resignation, the editor did not want to lose her expertise in working with fledgling writers and knew her university training would only increase her abilities. She was asked to continue as a contract assistant to work as much or as little as her university work allowed.

One other topic had to be discussed. Paul had never mentioned her church affiliation. She had been baptized in the church as an infant and attended all through her childhood, but that stopped when she left home. Until dropping in at Paul's church, her only attendance had been the time with Ian and his family, once in Atlanta and Ian's funeral. She did know that communion was open to all baptized Christians, which made her feel a part of the church. She was ready in her heart to take the next step.

"Paul, do I need to actually join the Episcopal Church? I haven't figured out how you do it."

He snickered at the last remark. "You don't *have* to be confirmed as a member unless that is your desire. You can continue to participate and take communion, but you can't serve on the vestry, vote at annual meetings, or be a convention delegate."

"You know that's not what I have in mind. What do I have to do? I feel peace when I enter the church, and I want to be confirmed."

Paul pulled her close and said tenderly said, "I thought you'd never ask. You know I'm not pushing this on you."

"You also know that no one can push me into anything that I do not choose for myself."

"Father Allen will have adult confirmation classes starting in September, and the bishop will be here for confirmation in early November.

"Laura, I am so happy, thankful, and just plain proud to be able to share God's love with you."

Laura kneeled with a heart filled with love as the bishop placed his hands on her head and said, *Defend, O Lord, this thy child, Laura, with thy heavenly grace that she may continue thine forever and daily increase in thy Holy Spirit more and more until she come into thy everlasting kingdom. Amen.* (Rite of Confirmation from 1928 Book of Common Prayer of the Protestant Episcopal Church)

The depth of Laura's faith continued to grow. However, she was never president of the church women, sang in the choir, or ironed vestments. She found her own path to use the gifts that she had received.

Life was good. Juggling their budget was not as difficult as first thought. They could still afford the apartment and basic necessities. Items eliminated were fewer theater tickets and expensive dinners. She had enough clothes to last several years, and Paul's work clothes were not a consideration. Jeans and sweatshirts were their chosen attire when not working. They gave up little and gained so much.

Chapter XXXVII

1985–FUTURE

Happy, productive years pass unnoticed. After completing a doctorate at Columbia, Laura Porter, PhD was now a full professor in their Fine Arts Department. Word of her talent quickly spread, and graduate students lined up to be on the class roll of *the Laura Porter* of movie and book fame. They were never disappointed.

The contract work in publishing continued as her time permitted. Discovering and assisting a talented novice writer was an achievement that she continued to enjoy. Each time she helped develop a student writer, she felt much pride and . . . a little envy.

Paul was called to be the priest of a parish on Staten Island. He accepted after visiting and finding mainly middle-class parishioners who were devoted to their church and dedicated to outreach. Not that he welcomed seeing a multitude of the poor, but he was eager to continue this service ministry. Laura also liked the neighborhoods of small homes. It was time for them to have a house with a yard. They found a Cape Cod bungalow in their price range and were able to make the down payment from savings and the mortgage payments from Paul's housing allowance. The house had a living room, dining room, large eat-in kitchen, half bath downstairs, and four bedrooms, two baths upstairs. There was a full basement which was partially finished. Paul had plans for a playroom and possible additional bedroom when their family grew as both hoped. The house was thirty years old and perfect for their taste.

Myra MacTavish Alcott came first. She was a female copy of Paul with her brown curls and soft brown eyes. Both parents were overjoyed to have a daughter. Laura took six months maternity leave from Columbia but continued her work with authors from home. Her contract work, salary from Columbia, and the increased income Paul received in the new parish were adequate to hire a well-referenced nannie for little Myra.

After several interviews, they settled on a middle-aged lady who had been born and raised in—you guessed it—Georgia. Before selecting her, they checked all references and found she lived on Staten Island and had worked with a family for twelve years until their four children were beyond needing a nannie.

Laura rode the ferry and then the subway to work. This was not a tiring long commute but a respite time to transition from home to work. She felt comfortable leaving the baby with Ruby and knowing that Paul was close. In a short time, Ruby became invaluable and adored little Myra.

Cooking was not part of Ruby's duties, but without being asked, she started having dinner ready when they arrived home. What a pleasure to come home to the aroma of fried chicken, meat loaf, pot roast, or Ruby's other specialties. She kidded Paul that she was making a Southern boy out of him. He chuckled and kept on eating.

Laura continued to hold a strong tie to her Georgia family. Little Myra went down to meet them when she was six months old and smiling big toothless grins. Everyone fell in love with her and vowed that she looked just like Idella, which was far from the truth, but they liked to think that. Ruth and Wallace came to visit once a year. Both had become enchanted with the city along with seeing their niece. BJ came on business occasionally and always allowed enough time to visit them on Staten Island. They were so comfortable in their new home that they seldom went into the city.

Laura James never made the New York trip with her sisters. She was hesitant to be in the big city. After the death of Myra, she went through a period of depression. The loss of her sister and then her mother had been more than she could face. Carlton realized that his wife was troubled from more than the deaths. They had worked together and built a prosperous farm and profitable pulpwood and timber business which provided a beautiful home and anything they needed or desired. The inability to have children was a disappointment for both of them.

Carlton recognized that his dear Laura James had always longed to be a mother. He decided to find a way to do this and talked with Mrs. Scarboro, the head of the county welfare department. She told him of the many children who needed homes but were considered unadoptable for various reasons. Would they consider giving a home to a foster child?

After hearing all the explanations and responsibilities of being a foster parent, Carlton was excited. Mrs. Scarboro showed him a picture of a little ten-year-old boy who had recently been placed in the children's home. Carlton looked at the forlorn face of the little fellow, and his heart melted.

When he told Laura James about his thoughts, she surprised him by saying, "Go get him." She wanted to cook that little boy a good meal, take him to town to buy new clothes, and look out the back door and see him playing on the swing that Carlton would make for him.

"Honey, it's not that easy. We have to fill out a lot of forms, have a medical examination, and let them inspect our house and other stuff. There's no reason why we wouldn't pass, but it will take time. The welfare lady said it should be about a month. Also, we might not get that same little boy. It might even be a girl."

"I don't care. I want whatever they can give us. I'm tired of seeing the school bus pass and never stop at our house. Let's get started."

The procedure moved quickly, and in a month, they drove to the children's home and picked up a little redheaded, freckle-faced eight-year-old boy named Benny. He found a good home with loving foster parents, and they found their home filled with more noise, muddy footprints, and joy than they had ever imagined. Benny stayed for four years until a sister was able to care for him. Their heart broke when he left, but they were satisfied that their care had given him help when it was most needed, and now he could return to a family member who would continue that care and love. Benny was quickly replaced by a little girl named Susie. This continued, and Laura James and Carlton were foster parents to many children.

Staten Island was a community and a good place to raise their family. Paul's parish grew under his leadership and pastoral care. It was a busy and fulfilling life. Soon, their home was filled with the family they had planned. After Myra came David Ian, Paul Langston (called Pauley to distinguish him from his father), Stuart Porter, and Marie Claire (named for Paul's mother), Ruby continued to be their indispensable helper. The basement rooms were finished and well used.

Laura had it all—a loving husband and family, wonderful home, and fulfilling career. But she did not have a story. She could help other writers, but she could not help herself.

One evening after the children were sleeping and Paul was working on his sermon, she pulled out the old Underwood portable typewriter that she had owned since high school and focused on typing the dedication that was sealed on her heart.

Written with loving memory and thanksgiving
For the life
of
Myra Stuart MacTavish
You provided both anchor and sail for me.

She read it aloud several times, and it did sound right. Maybe this was all that she could write, but after this dedication, there had to be more. Suddenly, the words started coming faster than her fingers could move. She didn't have to compose. The words just came . . .

Hard packed red clay pounded Myra's bare feet, and dry red dust scattered in her wake as she raced away from the schoolhouse door . . .

She had a story.

And to whom ever much is given, much will be demanded.
Luke 12:48

Epilogue

Neither the author nor readers were ready to give up Myra, but forever is not a word used with a lifetime. From the little girl in the cotton patch to the esteemed lady she became, readers related to Myra and valued her faith, love, acceptance of all people, and eternal optimism. Her spirit remains to encourage her family and all that she touched.

Laura inherited much of her grandmother's qualities and extended these to fulfill her life by giving back the gifts she had received. She told Myra's story through three novels. These did not become best sellers, but her reward was sharing Grandma Myra's incredible life. The novels were well loved and popular throughout the South, and she gave readings and signing at many bookstores, book clubs, and libraries. Writing fulfilled her need to preserve her grandmother's stories, but the prestige she achieved came from her status in teaching and developing writers. She proudly returned to her alma mater, Georgia State University, each year to present the *Ian Wilhelm Scholarship* to a sophomore journalism student. Nine o'clock in the evening remained a time of reverence. *Even though they are gone, we can still feel their presence tucked away in our heart.*

Paul's service to his church on Staten Island continued throughout his life. The parish flourished and grew to require more space and staff for the growing congregations and the varied missions. Under the direction of Paul and Laura, the breakfast program spread to other areas of need, and grits were always on the menu. During his tenure as a priest, he was offered the opportunity of higher positions in the diocese and more prominent churches. He did not consider these opportunities for he was fulfilling his calling. The family's home remained Staten Island.

Myra's family remained close and devoted to their memories. One annual gathering was held throughout their lives. The older family members continued to prosper in later years, and their lives were a tribute to their mother. Future generations of the family honored their heritage by living up to it.

Grandpa James's ambition for one of his offsprings to become governor of Georgia was not fulfilled by Andy. After starting a law practice, he was offered a judgeship and knew that this was his calling. He would rise to the Supreme Court of Georgia.

However, young James Findley at age twenty-five ran successfully for a seat on the city council of Macon and became a rising politician to watch. Later, he was elected to the Georgia Senate. *Could he be the one?*

Discussion Questions
for Book Groups

In the first chapters, Myra's focus is mainly on the loss of her husband. When/why/how does this start to change.

After seeing Rosa Parks on TV, Myra is concerned for her throughout the rest of the book. What led her to identify so closely with Rosa Parks? The civil rights movement continued to be a perplexity for Myra. Why?

Did she have a latent desire to learn to read? Why was she hesitant? What led her to the classes? How was she able to succeed so quickly? Was this a life changing event?

Why was her daughter, Idella, always a concern? Could Myra have improved their relationship? How?

Her granddaughter, Laura Jean, becomes prevalent early in the book. Can you see a pattern unfolding to indicate her later prominence in the story? Why does Myra give this grandchild more regard? Why do the other family members accept and understand this?

What factors cause Laura Jean's life to change from her high school graduation forward?

Did the untimely death of Idella seem inevitable?

As tragedies and deaths continued in her life, how did Myra's strength prevail?

Did her prayers reveal her faith and relationship with God?

Granddaughter, Laura, had the fulfillment of her dreams with Ian. What were the things that prevented his death from destroying these dreams?

Was she in the right place at the right time to meet Paul? Was this a coincidence? Did Ian continue to have a place in her heart? Did Laura fulfill her destiny?

Were you prepared for the death of Myra? Did you find comfort?

Other than Myra, who do you chose as the strongest character? Who was your favorite? Why?

In what genre would you place this book?

What message does the author's choice of title convey?

The Family

Brian James MacTavish and Myra Stuart MacTavish

Children	Spouse	Grandchildren
Idella	LeGrand Porter	Laura Jean (Laura)
Laura James	Carlton Larson	Many foster children
Stephen	Arliss Harmon	Bonnie Ruth Andrew (Andy)
Ruth	Woodrow Rayborn (Woody)	Jess
Wallace	Grady Findley	James
Brian James Jr. (BJ)		Hannah, Catherine, Brian

CPSIA information can be obtained at www.ICGtesting.com
Printed in the USA
LVOW07s2301181215

466936LV00001B/17/P